THE LADY AND THE MOUNTAIN CALL

THE MOUNTAIN SERIES ~ BOOK 5

MISTY M. BELLER

Misty M. Beller
BOOKS

ISBN-13 Trade Paperback: 978-0-9982087-6-3

ISBN-13 Large Print Paperback: 978-1-954810-24-2

ISBN-13 Casebound Hardback: 978-1-954810-20-4

To my sweet Laney Grace,
our special gift from God.
I love you more than you could ever imagine.

Forgetting those things which are behind, and reaching forth unto those things which are before,
I press toward the mark for the prize of the high calling of God in Christ Jesus.

Phillipians 3:13b-14 (KJV)

PROLOGUE

FEBRUARY 4TH, 1879
MOUNTAINS NEAR BUTTE, MONTANA TERRITORY

She was going to lose both her feet. And maybe her life, too, if he didn't do something quick.

Bryan Donaghue nudged his horse faster to close the distance as the tiny shrew of a woman tromped through six inches of snow on the far side of the clearing wearing no shoes and only short sleeves. She was by the edge of the woods, a basket in one hand, the other clutching a rooster tight to her side. From this distance, it looked like the bird pecked steadily at her arm, but he couldn't make out what she prattled on to the animal as she walked. She didn't seem bothered by the blood oozing down her wrinkled hand.

"Mrs. Scott?" He called across the thirty or so feet separating them. She paused to look up. "Yep?"

As he reined his horse to a stop, a movement above her head grabbed his attention. In the tree. The branches shifted. Not the branches—an animal, long and lean. The perfect mottled brown to hide among the leafless limbs.

A mountain lion.

Heart pounding, he reached for his rifle and pulled it from the scabbard on the saddle, not taking his focus from the predator. Just like the animal never took its beady eyes from its prey.

Mrs. Scott.

He didn't dare cry out to the woman. Any movement could make the cat strike. Instead, he cocked the Winchester and raised it to his shoulder, sighting down the barrel.

"What ya need?" Mrs. Scott turned and started toward him.

The cougar raised onto its all fours, tensing to leap.

He pulled the trigger, sending a prayer heavenward that his aim would hold true against the gun's recoil.

A blast rent the air, then a terrific scream.

The animal soared from the tree. It didn't quite land on the woman, but only a few feet separated them.

Bryan pumped the rifle's lever and aimed again. The cat writhed on the ground, then seemed to regain its footing, again setting its sights on the woman.

Bryan squeezed the trigger a second time. The explosion ricocheted through the clearing.

The mountain lion slumped to the ground, motionless, as an eerie silence took over the area.

Bryan vaulted from his horse and lunged through the snow to meet the older woman. "Are you hurt, ma'am?" A glance at the cat showed a bloody patch where the second shot had done its job.

She turned to him, squinting against the sunlight's reflection on ice. "What?" The rooster in her arms wiggled and pecked furiously at her restraining hand.

"Can I help you with that bird? What are you doing in this snow without shoes and a coat? We have to get you inside."

She tilted her head, eyeing him as though he'd told her to stand on her head and recite the alphabet. "Why'd I wanna do that?"

Bryan reached for the bird. The poor woman's arm was almost mutilated by its steady pecks. At her age, she stood a strong risk of infection from the open wound growing wider by the second.

Mrs. Scott pulled back, clutching the rooster tighter to her side. It responded with a squawk and pecked even faster.

"Ma'am, I'll carry that rooster wherever you want me to take him. Just let me help." And as soon as he wrested the bird from her, he had to get the old lady out of this snow. What little he could see of the skin on her feet shone a waxy pink. It'd be a miracle akin to raising Lazarus if she came out of this with all her toes intact.

With her wrinkled lips pinched so hard they disappeared, she finally extended the rooster to him. "I was on my way to the chopping block with this one. Gonna surprise your pa with a good stew tonight. Would you knock his head off for me, son?"

Bryan clutched the wriggling creature in both hands. "Yes, ma'am." He turned away and took long strides toward the chicken shed.

The bird craned its neck to peck him.

"No you don't." Just like he'd done a hundred times with his mother's chickens, Bryan gripped both legs and hung the animal upside down.

As he settled the rooster into the pen and secured the door behind it, his mind played through Mrs. Scott's words. It sure sounded like she thought he was her son, not the doctor from the town five hours north. And didn't she remember her husband had passed away two months before? He'd been worried about her mental state then. She'd seemed confused and forgetful. But nothing like this.

He turned to face Mrs. Scott. Somehow he'd have to explain why he'd shoved the rooster back in the shed instead of *knocking its head off* like she'd asked. But his first priority was to get her inside so he could tend her frostbite and bleeding hand.

But the yard was empty.

"Mrs. Scott?" He scanned the snowy expanse between the cabin and outbuildings.

Too many footprints marred the ground to tell which ones were most recently hers. And they were footprints—made by bare feet—not sturdy, warm boots. Not even moccasins sewn from the furs her mountain man son supplied them with. Bryan hadn't met the man, but the Scotts said he stopped by a couple times a year. Did he have any idea yet about his father's death or his mother's mental state?

Scuffling sounds drifted from the house, so Bryan headed that way at a jog.

After a quick detour to grab his saddle pack from where Cloud stood quietly, he vaulted onto the porch. He tapped the snow from his boots, then knocked on the door and pushed it open with his knuckles.

Mrs. Scott stood by the stove, stirring something in a big pot. "I've got water boiling for supper. You think you could go clean me that ol' rooster?"

"Um, maybe." Bryan stepped inside the dark room. The scant bit of sunlight filtering through the single dirty window was the only thing that lit the place. No fire in the hearth, but on the opposite side of the room, a few red embers showed around the edge of the cook stove's door. "Mrs. Scott, can I take a look at that hand? You're still bleeding a good bit."

She frowned down at her hand clutching the spoon. Blood oozed down its wooden handle into whatever she was stirring. He swallowed against the bile churning in his stomach. No matter what she offered him to eat, there was no chance he'd accept.

Her gaze lifted to his, and the creases in her brow furrowed even deeper. Was she trying to remember who he was? Or how she'd been injured?

He stepped closer. "I'm Doc Bryan, ma'am. From Butte. I just stopped by to check on you. Can you sit in this chair and let me tend your wounds?" He slipped a hand around her arm, and she allowed him to lead her to one of the ladder-back chairs around the table. He had to breathe through his mouth to fight against the human stench that emanated from her.

The bleeding at her hand didn't seem eager to slow, probably due to her age and the thinness of her papery skin. Cayenne powder did the trick though, and he soon had it cleaned and wrapped tight.

Next her feet. He dropped to his knees and studied the pale, waxy skin. He tentatively touched the right foot. His own fingers were cool, which made it even easier to feel the warmth radiating from her feet. Not good. That warmth was probably the tissues breaking down after being frozen.

He glanced up at the stove. *Lord, let that really be water she was heating.* He found a bowl on the counter that looked mostly clean, and poured liquid from the pot. Only a slight reddish tinge colored it. This would do to rewarm her. The temperature felt about right, too.

When he dipped her left foot into the bowl, she tried to pull it back out. "Ain't no need to fuss about me, son. My feet are jest fine. Let me up an' I'll pour ya a cup of yer Mum's good coffee."

Bryan pressed a hand to her forearm to hold her still. "Please, Mrs. Scott. We need to rewarm your feet to stop any more damage from the cold."

It took all the patience he possessed, and most of his charm, but he finally convinced the woman to relax and let him work on her feet. About five minutes into the rewarming process, the older woman took up moaning and rocking in her chair. The pain had to be intense. She didn't voice a complaint though, despite the mottling of blue and purple as her skin came to life.

By the time he had her feet wrapped in bandages and a blanket settled around the rest of her body, tears coursed down Mrs. Scott's lined face.

"I'm sorry, ma'am. Those feet are going to be hurting for a few days." The pain was actually a good sign, meant maybe not all the tissue would die. He settled into the chair beside her, leaned forward to rest his elbows on his knees, and gave his most earnest doctor expression. "You need to wear boots and a coat any time you're outside in the winter. Can you do that for me?"

The woman's eyes drifted to half-mast, as though she didn't have the strength to hold them open. Or maybe she just didn't want to listen—or couldn't.

"Mrs. Scott. Did you hear me? I'm hoping I won't have to amputate this time, but if you walk barefoot in the snow again, you might lose both your feet. It's very dangerous to go out in the snow without shoes."

A soft snore drifted from her.

Bryan sank back into his chair. What was he going to do with this woman? He sure couldn't leave her here to fend for herself. Dementia was obviously taking a quick hold on her mind. Where was her son in all this?

O'Hennessy, the closest neighbor, had said he would come by to check her when he could. But the man lived over an hour away, and he was already caring for the herd of cattle Mr. Scott's death had left behind.

Nope, there was no choice but to take her down the mountain and back to town. They could stop by O'Hennessey's on the way and ask the man to come gather the chickens and any other animals left here. And he could leave a note for Mrs. Scott's son. Maybe someone in town would know how to reach the man.

~

*T*he woman screamed just like a mountain lion.

Bryan clamped his jaw tight and tried not to squeeze Mrs. Scott's frail arms as he did his best to lead her to the wagon. "We're just going to make a little visit to town."

"Nooooooooooo..." The howl would have scared off a bear if it weren't the dead of winter. Might have even woken a few from hibernation. "You're not going to take me." She writhed in his arms, twisting and scratching like a wild cat.

He pulled her closer, trying to instill a sense of protection with his touch. "It's all right, Mrs. Sc— Ow!" Sharp teeth pierced the skin of his unprotected hands. He jerked back.

She tore from his grip and ran like a jackrabbit toward the house.

As he took off after her, one boot slipped on an icy porch step, and he scrambled to catch his balance. It was just the lead the woman needed, because by the time he reached the door, she'd slammed it shut.

"Mrs. Scott?" He pounded on the door. The construction was solid, maybe a double thickness of wood. And it felt like she braced it with a metal rod. It'd not be easy to break through. "I just want to take you to the doctor's clinic for a few days until your wounds heal."

"You'll not be stealin' me away from my Quinn. He'll find you and hurt you somethin' fierce if you even try."

Bryan let out a long breath. What was he to do now? Break down the door or shatter the window? The woman obviously thought she was being kidnapped. And even if he did find a way to get her out of the cabin, he'd have to use chloroform on the trip to town. That really would be a kidnapping, even if it were for her own good.

He turned and scanned the yard. The Scotts' farm horses stood patiently hitched to the wagon where he'd left them, Cloud tied to the back of the conveyance.

Maybe he could find someone in town who knew the woman. Someone who'd be willing to stay up here for a week or two to nurse her until her son could be located.

Surely the neighbor would be willing to come check her tomorrow. By the next day, Bryan could have a nurse sent up.

As it was, he couldn't stay any longer himself. Claire had been expecting him back two days before and was probably pacing the floor from worry by now. And the baby. How much had little Amanda grown in these five days he'd been gone? She'd just started holding her head up in the last week. And that smile she'd gifted him with the last time he held her…

Yep, it was time to go home.

CHAPTER 1

FEBRUARY 5TH, 1879
BUTTE, MONTANA TERRITORY

"*I*'m sure he'll be back today, Claire." Cathleen Donaghue watched her sister-in-law pace to the window again and peer out at the dreary, snow-covered town. Claire and Bryan's home had been built on the outskirts of Butte, making it feel slightly removed from the business of the city. "Bryan's probably just delayed with a patient, but he'll come as soon as he can."

Claire turned troubled eyes to Cathleen. "He's never been two days late from a trip to the mountains, though."

The infant propped on Cathleen's shoulder let out a squawk and started rooting toward her neck. She bobbed with her little niece and rubbed her back. "Go feed this girl before dinner's ready. I need to help with the food."

As Cathleen handed little Amanda to her worried mother, she sent up another prayer for Bryan's safety. Her brother was stubborn at times, but he usually had the good sense required to stay safe on the icy mountain trails. If only he weren't always so focused on the needs

9

of his patients. He was going to give his poor wife an apoplexy one of these days.

A quarter hour later, Cathleen stepped back out of the kitchen, leading her boisterous one-year-old nephew, William. Her sisters-in-law seemed to have the food preparations well under control. "I guess we'll occupy ourselves out here, huh, mister?" She eyed the neat stack of toys in the corner. "Let's see if we can find the animals?"

The stomp of boots on the porch jerked her attention to the door. Was that her other brother and the minister, coming in from the church? They'd all planned to meet here for lunch. Bryan was supposed to have been a part of the lunch gathering, but he'd have to make it home first.

The door pushed open, and in stepped the weary traveler, her eldest brother Bryan. He was bundled in his winter coat and pushed the fur-lined hood off as he stepped into the room.

"It's about time you showed up." Cathleen offered a smile to soften the sassy words. "Claire was about to go looking for you."

He eased out a long sigh as he unfastened the button closures on his coat. "Got held up at the Scott ranch. Poor Mrs. Scott's dementia is getting bad. Had to treat her for frostbite and severe chicken pecking before I could leave. Got too late to make it down the mountain last night, so I had to wait until today."

"Bryan?" Claire appeared in the bedroom doorway, relief flooding her voice. A blanket was wrapped around her front and draped across her shoulders.

His hands dropped from his buttons with two still to go as his gaze found his wife's. In three steps he crossed the room and took her in his arms.

"You're home." Claire snuggled into his embrace as a muffled complaint drifted from under the blanket in her arms.

Cathleen turned away from the tender scene, as much to squelch the yearning in her chest as to give them privacy. Both her brothers had found such happiness here. It was good to see. Good to have helped these past three months as their families grew. But the baby was older and maybe now "Aunt Cathy" wasn't needed so much anymore. Maybe it was time to move on.

Would she ever have a family of her own? According to Dad and her two big brothers, no suitor had ever been acceptable. Not that she'd pushed hard for any particular man. She'd never thought herself picky, but shouldn't a girl feel...something...for a prospective husband? Shouldn't there be some kind of spark?

Pushing those thoughts aside, she carried William to the toys and settled cross-legged on the floor. She tried to snuggle him in her lap as she pulled out the carved animal collection, but the restless toddler would have none of it. So she let him loose and exclaimed over each animal he showed her.

But between the cows and horses and ducks, she couldn't stop her mind from wandering. Should she go back home to Boston? It was only February, so there weren't likely to be ships traveling the Missouri River yet. The water could even be frozen for all she knew. She'd have to talk through it with her brothers to see if there was another way back across the country.

Mum and Dad might be ready for some help again. Her brothers and their capable wives certainly had things under control here.

More footsteps sounded on the porch, and in tromped Alex, her other brother, and Marcus, the preacher. The family was all here. Time to enjoy them while she could.

～

"The chicken was doing what?" Cathleen studied Bryan's face, as a surge of concern swept through her. A glance at their middle sibling, Alex, showed that his face mirrored her own emotions. Why was an elderly woman living alone up in those rough mountains?

After a pleasant lunch, mothers and babes had all settled in for a nap, so Cathleen had a rare moment to enjoy just her two brothers. But the story Bryan shared was anything but enjoyable.

Bryan's mouth pinched. "It pecked quite a hole in her hand. The skin was too thin for stitches. Bled like a head wound, though. That certainly wasn't the worst of it. No telling how long she'd been out in the snow without shoes or a coat, nothing more than a thin cotton calico, as far as I could tell." He scrubbed a hand through his hair, leaving it standing in spikes.

"So what'd you do?"

"Shot the mountain lion first, then got her inside and doctored as best I could." As Bryan told the tale of how he tried to convince the woman to come down the mountain with him, he put enough of a humorous spin to his efforts to bring on a chuckle from Alex. But Cathleen couldn't push away the images her mind conjured of a frail old woman—like great-aunt Arlene had been—half frozen to death and bleeding, alone in a remote mountain cabin.

She gripped the arms of her chair and scooted to the edge. The urge to do something to help swelled inside her. "She doesn't have any family left?"

Bryan's mouth sobered, and worry lines took their usual place at the corners of his eyes. "We buried her husband two months ago. They have a son, but he's some kind of wild, mountain man. O'Hennessy is the nearest neighbor, about an hour's ride east, but he doesn't know how to find the son. I'm hoping someone here in town does."

An image of a wild-eyed man formed in her mind, full beard matching the fur hanging from his clothing. Maybe missing a tooth or two. Poor Mrs. Scott. Even if her son showed up, how could a man like that do anything to help her condition?

Bryan leaned forward, resting his elbows on his knees as he studied Alex. "Think there's a nurse we can send up there in the next couple days?"

Alex frowned. "The nurses we've used before are all married women. Most with children. There's no way they could leave town to go half a day's ride into the mountains." He squinted. "Maybe Mrs. Walker if she took her twins with her."

Bryan shook his head. "I'd hate to see what those twins would do to this woman's nerves. She didn't know who I was most of the time.

Thought I was her son, I think. And she didn't seem to remember her husband had passed either."

As Cathleen watched the volley between her brothers, an idea took shape in her mind. Leaving the poor woman up there alone even another day was unacceptable. She cleared her throat to get their attention. "I can care for her."

Alex frowned. "You can't stay alone in the mountains."

She fought down a flare of frustration. "Of course, I can. And I wouldn't be alone, I'd be helping Mrs. Scott. You were just talking about sending a woman up there with a pair of five-year-old twins. You think I'd be worse off than her?"

"Cathy, I don't think you understand what the conditions are like in those mountain homesteads." Alex set his coffee on the side table. "It's primitive in the worst way. There's danger from all kinds of wild animals. No stores to shop at like you're accustomed to. You have to make do with the food and supplies on hand, or else make your own. And the creeks are probably frozen over, so who knows where she's getting water from. Some of the mountain trails are impassible when it snows. What if you were stranded up there and needed help? It's nothing like the life you were used to back home. Not even half as civilized as it is here in Butte."

She wrinkled her nose at him. Alex had been smelling too much chloroform if he thought the words *civilized* and *Butte* should be used in the same sentence.

But she'd done just fine adjusting to life here in this rough, western mining town, where they didn't have decent baking supplies and not enough of a fabric selection to clothe a pauper. And she'd do just as well in the mountains. She'd read books about primitive life. What she didn't know, Mrs. Scott could probably remember. How hard could it be to clean a rooster for supper?

She turned to Bryan and gave him one of those looks he should remember well. The one that said she'd made up her mind but would give him a little bit of time to get used to the idea. "Think about it, Bryan. The woman's obviously in a bad way. And your wife doesn't need me so much around here anymore. I can ride up first thing tomorrow. Whenever her son can be found, he can take over. But until then, I'm needed. There's no one else for the job."

Bryan let out a longsuffering sigh. "Cathy, don't be pigheaded about this."

She leaned back in her chair. She was pretty sure she'd made her point, but if Bryan didn't come around by dinnertime, he'd find out what pigheaded looked like. Somewhere, even now, a woman wandered around in the mountains—hurt, confused, and maybe even dying. That simply wouldn't do.

Cathleen Donaghue didn't turn her back on someone in need.

~

"So I'll leave in the morning to go care for Mrs. Scott?" Cathleen set a plate of dried apple pie on the table in front of Bryan that evening, then another before Claire. They'd just finished dinner, and the darkness outside made Claire's kitchen feel like a cozy haven. She loved the round dark wood table in the center of the room, large enough for several families to gather around.

But now it was just the three of them—four, if you counted little Amanda whom Claire nursed while they talked.

"What do you mean?" Claire looked up, her fork hovering over the pie crust.

Cathleen started to answer, but Bryan spoke first.

"Cathy, I really don't think that's a good idea." Bryan looked like he might be considering whether physical restraint would be necessary. He'd obviously read her earlier determination. Perhaps he thought he might ship her back home to Boston, no matter if the river was frozen or not.

She plopped into her chair at the table and leaned forward. "You know this is the only way, Bryan. And besides, it actually makes *sense*. I'm not needed here anymore." She motioned toward Claire and the baby. "Claire has everything under control. But Mrs. Scott is injured and alone. I'll only stay there until her son comes to take over, then I'll be right back here, safe and sound where you won't have to worry about me."

"I do still need you, Cathleen." Claire's voice held a hint of a motherly tone. "I don't know what we would have done these past few months without you. There's some days it seems Amanda thinks you're her mother and I'm the auntie."

Cathleen couldn't help a smile at her sweet sister-in-law and the baby. Claire had such a charitable personality and had become a dear friend through these past months. Surely she could understand why she had to help Mrs. Scott.

She turned back to her over-protective brother. "Just let me try it, Bryan. If things don't work out, I'll come back to Butte straightaway."

As he looked at her, his brown eyes turned liquid. Pleading. "Cathy, if I let you go up there and something happens, Dad would have me brought before the Inquisition. You know he sent you here into my care. They can't handle losing another daughter."

A stab of familiar pain tightened her chest. None of their family had been the same after her big sister, Britt, died at the tender age of eight. The last thing she wanted to do was bring that kind of grief on her parents. But this was entirely different. Britt had a lung condition from birth, and it had only been a matter of time until she succumbed. Cathleen was strong and capable, and a feeble old lady needed her somewhere in those mountains.

She gave Bryan her most earnest expression. "I'll be careful. If there's any hint of danger, I'll come right back. Maybe I can even get Mrs. Scott to come with me."

Releasing a long breath, he scrubbed a hand through his hair. "All right. But let the record state that I *do not* agree that this is a good idea."

The relief that flowed through her left behind a solid sense of rightness as she squeezed her brother's big, calloused hand. She was fulfilling her calling.

Lord, help me help Mrs. Scott.

CHAPTER 2

*A*s they rode into the little mountain clearing, Cathleen took in the sight of the log cabin with smoke drifting up through a stovepipe in the roof. A porch spanned the front of the building, and an outhouse peeked out from behind. A low lean-to on the side of the house held a thin layer of firewood, but the covering hadn't done much to protect the wood from the snow. Only the logs on one end had the white powder brushed from their surface.

Bryan reined his horse to a stop in front of the house, and her own mount followed suit. He dismounted, and Cathleen scanned the cabin again while she waited for his assistance. She'd only ridden side-saddle during all her years in Boston, but a few trips into the country-side around Butte had taught her how to ride astride. And the five hours they'd been on the trail this morning had certainly finished the job. Between the cold and the length of time in the same position, she couldn't feel her feet. There was a good chance they might not support her weight once she asked it of them.

Bryan gripped her waist and lowered her to the ground, and she clutched the saddle as needles stabbed her ankles. A flicker in the window to the left of the door caught her attention, offering a welcome distraction from the prickles. The panes were covered with some kind of solid fabric, but a corner of the material had definitely moved.

"Let's get inside." She turned a smile on her brother as she loosened one hand from its death-grip on the saddle.

He tied both horses to the rail on the front porch. "We'll see what we're up against first. Then I'll come back out and settle these two and get the supplies unloaded."

They ascended the steps, and Bryan slid his coat hood from his head, then knocked on the door. Cathleen glanced behind her at the view from the porch. She caught her breath. Through a break in the trees, a distant mountain peak rose high above them, majestic with its snowy cap and regal bearing. "Look, Bryan."

But before he could obey, the cabin door opened, letting out a rush of warm, stale air. Cathleen turned toward the opening and shared her brightest smile with the gray-haired woman who peered out.

"Mrs. Scott. It's Doc Bryan from town. How are you today, ma'am?"

She squinted at them, still half-hiding behind the door frame. Only one hand showed, and from the lack of a scar, it must not be the injured one. "Oh. Just fine." The hesitation in her voice sounded like she couldn't quite place him, even though he'd just said his name and had visited only a couple days before.

"I'm glad to hear it. I'd like to introduce you to my sister, Miss Cathleen Donaghue." Bryan touched her elbow, and Cathleen stepped forward.

"It's nice to meet you, Mrs. Scott."

The woman turned confused eyes on Cathleen but didn't say anything.

Bryan cleared his throat. "Would you mind if we come in for a minute?"

Mrs. Scott turned her attention back to him slowly, as if she struggled to keep up with what was happening. "I suppose." Shuffling backward, she pulled the door wide and hobbled toward the stove. "I'll put some coffee on to warm you. Quinn should be back anytime now."

Cathleen glanced at Bryan and mouthed *the husband*? Bryan had only referred to the man as Mr. Scott when he'd shared his knowledge of the family on their long ride up.

He nodded, mouth pinched. Looking up at the older woman, he raised his voice a bit louder than usual. "No need for coffee, ma'am. But I'd like to check your injuries from the other day. Can we sit here at the table?"

Cathleen reached to unfasten the buttons on her coat. Bryan had said not to trust anything the woman cooked, so that must be his way of skirting the topic. Hot coffee would be perfect right now, though.

She scanned the dark room around them. What she'd thought was a cloth curtain over the window now looked like some kind of animal skin. An elaborate beadwork design spanned the edges, and fringe hung from the bottom. Other skins lined the walls, some with the fur intact, others more like buckskin. A large fur hung over the fireplace, a striking brown and tan spotted pattern marking the hair. She'd seen the men in Butte wear buckskins on occasion, but never furs like these. And she'd never seen so many hides in one place.

Noises from the stove snagged her attention, and she glanced over as Mrs. Scott shifted pots around on its surface. There didn't seem to be a reason behind her actions though. She just slid a pan here, then another where the first had been, finally sliding the first pot to a new burner.

A wash of sympathy slid through Cathleen, and she stopped unfastening her coat to step forward. "Here, Mrs. Scott. How about if I make coffee while you let the doctor check your bandage." She slipped a hand around the woman's thin shoulders. There was even less substance there than her brown wool dress made it appear.

The woman allowed Cathleen to guide her to a chair at the table, and Bryan settled into the one beside it. She raised the bandaged arm to the table's surface. The cloth that had surely been white when Bryan put it on two days ago was now a speckled brown with splashes of darker colors that could have been blood—or some other substance Cathleen didn't want to consider. The smells of human odors tinged the air around the older woman.

She turned to the stove as Bryan started his ministrations. Now for coffee. One of the pots did hold what looked to be water. The other two were empty. Should she trust the water here? She scanned the work counter, then peered into the dry sink. A bucket on the floor looked like it also held water, although the liquid there had bits of food particles floating in it. It was possible they were food, but she wasn't about to chance it.

With a glance back at the pair, she picked up the bucket handle and squared her shoulders. "I'm going to get fresh water."

Bryan peered so intently under Mrs. Scott's bandage, he only murmured "All right" when she passed.

Cathleen pulled her coat tighter around herself as she stepped out the door into the whipping wind. She should have grabbed her gloves on the way out. Next time, she'd remember.

She scanned the yard for a well. A barn stood about thirty feet to the left, and beside it a shed of some kind. Maybe a chicken house, judging by the noises emanating from the wooden plank siding. She stepped down the porch stairs and patted their horses as she made her way around them. Another small building behind the house must be the outhouse. So where was the well?

Something Bryan had said flickered through her mind. Sometimes these mountain farms used streams instead of digging wells. It made sense if the ground underneath was mostly rock. She scanned the area again. No sign of a stream in the clearing. But there was a trail of footprints in the snow leading toward the trees on one side. She headed that direction.

∾

*I*t was over an hour later by the time Cathleen had located an icy stream, steeped the coffee, and fixed a simple meal of boiled potatoes and some kind of jerked meat she found in the root cellar. She hadn't taken time to unpack the supplies she and Bryan brought, but there was no doubt they'd come in handy later.

As they ate at the kitchen table, she and Bryan tried to draw Mrs.

Scott into conversation. The woman downed the food like she hadn't had a decent meal in weeks.

Which she probably hadn't.

A fresh bandage wrapped her left hand, although the smell of human odor still clung to her. As soon as Bryan left, they'd be looking for a bath tub.

"The bandages weren't on her feet anymore." Bryan spoke in a low, conversational tone. Cathleen still wasn't sure whether Mrs. Scott had trouble hearing or just struggled to focus on the conversation. A glance at the woman showed her intent on gathering a soft potato onto her spoon.

She looked back at her brother as he continued. "But the right sole had blistered, so I rewrapped it. They seem to be giving her a bit of pain still. I hope that lessens in the next few days, but we'll see."

"What should I do to help?"

"Keep her warm. I wouldn't make her walk too much, especially until that blister goes away. Propping her feet should help, and maybe soak them in warm water." He shrugged. "That's about all you can do. I'll leave a stronger medicine to use if the pain gets bad, but I'd save it for a last resort. Willow bark would be easier on her system. You have a full kit of herbals in the supplies we brought."

Cathleen nodded. In his apothecary shop, Dad had taught them all to use herbs whenever possible instead of the medical tonics. Too many questionable ingredients in the man-made stuff, and often the most plentiful was a substantial dose of alcohol.

Bryan turned to the older woman and raised his voice a bit. "Mrs. Scott, would it be all right if my sister stays with you for a while? She can help around the farm until you're feeling better."

The older woman looked up at Bryan, her eyes sharpening more than they had yet. Then she glanced at Cathleen and her expression softened. "I feel fine, but if she needs a place to stay, she's welcome. Quinn and me always have a shelter ready for one o' God's lambs."

Cathleen returned her smile. If she had to pretend to be a charity case for the woman to accept her, she could do that. "Thank you, ma'am."

~

"*I*'m not sure I should leave you here, Cathy."

Cathleen stroked the wooly neck of her brother's horse with one hand while shading her eyes with the other so she could look up at him. "Don't worry. Mrs. Scott and I will get along just fine."

He scanned the cabin again, then met her gaze. "I don't think she realizes you'll be staying more than a few days."

She offered a sad smile. "I have a feeling one day is the same as the next to her. I don't know how she's managed on her own this long." She tapped his knee. "It'll be good, the two of us here together. She needs me, and I need a new project."

With a sigh, his shoulders slumped. "The horse I rented from the livery is in the barn. If anything happens or you're worried in the least, come back home."

Poor Bryan. He couldn't help but worry. It was how he showed his love. She patted his knee again. "I will, big brother. Now get home before your wife starts pacing the parlor again."

His face twisted into a silly half-smile. The kind only a love-struck man could produce. Then he sobered. "Take care, Cathy. Please."

As he rode away, Cathleen stepped onto the porch and watched until he disappeared around a stand of trees. Then she turned toward the front door. Her heart was lighter than it had been in months as she stepped inside to begin her work.

It may not be easy to live this far away from town, but there was a need to fill here. And she was the right person for the job.

~

*R*euben Scott ran a hand over his mare's bulging side. She should still have another couple months to go, but this foal was growing quickly. He stroked his way up her shoulder and neck to rub the favorite spot behind her ears. "How're you feelin', girl?"

21

The mare turned to nuzzle his free hand, and Reuben deepened the scratching. She was a good horse, had been a good companion through the winter. And with the weather colder and the snow deeper than he could ever remember it, companions had been scarce. The elements had driven much of the game to lower mountains, which meant Akecheta and his small band of Crow Indians had followed. Taking away Reuben's primary source of human interaction.

With a final pat, he turned away from the mare. "I have work to do, girl. Can't stand around all day."

Reuben stepped into his little cabin and whistled. "You ready to work, North?"

The huge mound of white fur lying in front of the cook stove moved. A black nose appeared, then a pink tongue lolling underneath.

"Come on, lazy. Let's go check the traps."

Grabbing his pack and a handful of jerked venison, Reuben checked his knife in the pouch at his waist, then whistled again as he slipped out the door.

North fell into step beside him as they followed the creek branch south. The dog enjoyed his naps but loved a good jaunt through the woods, too. He was a good trapper's dog, with the sense to know when to lay low and when to strike and the discipline to follow orders. He'd saved his owner's life more than once. And that mass of white hair tended to help them both stay warm at night, snuggled under buffalo hides on the cabin's dirt floor.

How were his parents faring with this bitter weather? Or maybe it wasn't as cold on their mountain, where the elevations weren't so high. That's why he didn't spend his winters near them. The pelts from these colder regions tended to be higher quality.

That was mostly the reason anyway.

That and the fact that they simply didn't need him. Pa could build and run a homestead better than any man alive in the Montana Territory. And Mum? She had more energy and savvy to live off the land than five women her age. He'd tried his best to follow in their shoes, but it always seemed better if he just got out of the way.

So, that's what he'd done.

Going back to the homestead a couple times a year seemed like the perfect mix. He could check on them, Mum could spend a few weeks fulfilling her nurturing needs, and he could tan his hides and restock his parents' supplies in Butte. Then he was off. Just him, North, the two horses, and the untamed wildness of the Rocky Mountains. Perfect.

Mostly.

The first three traps were empty, the fourth sprung, but only holding a clump of what looked like beaver fur. Surprising. He'd only seen a handful of beaver this year. Nothing like the yarns the old timers spun of seeing a dozen beaver every time you looked out at a river. It was a good thing this fellow got away and lived to produce more little ones.

The entire three-mile trot line yielded only a single marten, and as he padded beside North on the trek back to the cabin, Reuben couldn't stop his mind from drifting to his parents again. Maybe he should head back early this year. With his fur count down and Tashunka looking like she might foal early, it would be wise to make the move now. And maybe there would be something he could help with around the homestead.

Maybe.

CHAPTER 3

The cabin was mercilessly hot, between the fire in the hearth and the blaze Cathleen had going in the cook stove to boil the stench out of the underclothes. Over the past four days, she'd taken to keeping both fires going. Necessity required the heat to keep the older woman warm enough, but at the rate they were using firewood, she'd need to split more in a couple weeks.

Despite the mugginess, Cathleen stood with her face over the steam emanating from the big pot on the stove, inhaling the scent of lye to purge the other rancid odors from her senses. Perhaps she should crack the door, but it was so icy cold outside with this fresh bout of snow, she hated to expose Mrs. Scott's freshly bathed person to the elements. Too bad the window wasn't closer to the kitchen area. Of course, it wasn't a sliding window, so that wouldn't make much difference.

When the steam became overbearing, she used a wooden rod to pull the cloths from the water, then dropped them in a bucket of icy water to cool so she could wring them out to dry. Since the garments were small, she'd opted not to drag out the big washtub.

That done, she forced a pleasant smile as she turned to face Mrs. Scott, nestled in a wing-backed chair by the hearth.

She didn't have to force the smile for long, though. The dear lady was watching her, a soft expression on her lined face. "Come and visit with me, dearie, while I stitch this quilt top." Not that she was doing any sewing. The quilt covering her was the finished product, and well-worn from the look of it.

After scooting the boiling pot to the back of the stove, Cathleen crossed the room to sit in the rocker beside Mrs. Scott's chair. She took one of the older woman's hands in hers and stroked its sun-darkened surface. "Would you like to do some needlework? I imagine you might enjoy it."

The older lady's blue eyes clouded as she sank deeper in the seat and gazed toward the window on the far wall. "Oh, yes. I love to sew. I've made my share of quilts, mind you." She dipped her chin as she eyed Cathleen, then turned back to the window, which still held the buckskin covering. "But what I really love is beadwork."

"Beadwork?" Cathleen squinted at the piece covering the glass. "Did you make that?"

"Oh, no. Those curtains were one of the first designs my Reuben sewed. Back when he'd just learned to tan hides." Her voice drifted into long-ago memories. "He took to the beadwork like a baby to milk. Made me so proud."

Cathleen didn't try to fill the silence that drifted over them, just stroked her thumb over the work-worn hand and watched Mrs. Scott treasure her recollections.

Reuben must be her son. What sort of man had he grown to be? It was hard to reconcile a mountain man trapper who would leave his aging parents for months at a time with the tender way his mother described him. Possibly her distant memories were warping just like her recent ones? How hard must it be to slowly lose track of not only the skills she'd spent her life honing, but also the ability to think and remember.

After several minutes, Mrs. Scott's eyes drifted shut, and her mouth fell open. A soft snoring drifted from her lips. Cathleen settled the wrinkled hand under the quilt and tucked the blanket around the woman's shoulders, then eased up from the rocking chair.

She hung the damp underclothes from a rope strung along a wall, then scanned the room. She'd done a lot of cleaning these last few days, but it seemed like half of it had involved putting things back to rights after Mrs. Scott's accidents. In her spare time, Cathleen had scrubbed a layer of grime off the work counters and shelves in the kitchen and washed all the dishes with hot soapy water. But there was still much to be done.

Other than the blankets Mrs. Scott slept with at night, Cathleen had not laundered any bedding, not even what she herself had slept on in the smaller bedroom. And she'd gathered a pile of non-urgent clothes that needed to be washed when she found time.

Maybe now was the time.

Cathleen pulled the washtub from under the work counter and removed the sacks of flour and cornmeal stored inside. As she dragged the oversize basin closer to the cook stove, a noise drifted in from outside. She paused to listen.

All seemed quiet except for the steady snores from the chair by the fire. Mrs. Scott was certainly a good sleeper during the day. If only she were so consistent at night. Instead, she often got up and shuffled around at all hours.

Cathleen poured the icy water from the bucket into an empty pot on the stove, then picked up the second empty bucket from the floor and headed toward the door. She'd need several more if she was going to launder everything.

As she looped both bucket straps over one arm and reached for her coat, a muffled thumping sounded on the porch. Was a person out there? Or a wild animal? Before she could drop the buckets and reach for the rifle mounted on the wall, the door swung open.

Amidst a flurry of cold air and snow, a bear walked into the cabin, then reached back and pushed the door shut behind it.

She lurched back and opened her mouth to scream, but the creature shook its head, and she caught a glimpse of skin around the eyes. Human skin, bright red from the fierce cold outside. With a furry paw, it reached up and lowered the layer of hair covering its nose and mouth.

A man. Huge, with piercing blue eyes and a mountain-man beard.

"Who are you?" She clutched the buckets in front of her like a shield. Was this the missing son? Or a stranger she should defend against?

He turned those eyes on her, scanning her up and down as he pushed the fur hood from his head. "That's a better question for you." His gaze searched the cabin, finally landing on Mrs. Scott's snoring form.

Cathleen moistened her chapped lips, a surge of protection rising up in her. "State your name, sir."

He swung his immense form back to her, those blue eyes narrowing into slits so they almost disappeared between the thick brown of his hair, eyebrows, and beard. "Reuben Scott, ma'am."

Relief nearly wilted the strength in her legs. The son. But she didn't lower her bucket defense quite yet. Something about the hint of sarcasm that tinged his voice didn't sit right.

She straightened her backbone. "Please state your business, sir." It was only Mum's endless training on proper address that kept her tone civilized.

"My business?" A dark brow rose as he pulled off first one fur mitten then another. His gaze trailed back to Mrs. Scott. "I'm here to check on my parents."

He stepped toward the older woman still snoring in her chair by the fire, effectively turning his back on Cathleen. A few long strides brought him to the overstuffed chair, and Cathleen scurried to position herself behind the older woman. This man likely *was* her son as he'd said, although the blue eyes were the only resemblance between the petite elderly woman and this massive fur-covered giant. But Mrs. Scott's nerves were still delicate. If he hurt—or even frightened—the sweet lady, she'd see him tossed out on his ear before he knew what hit him.

The man lowered himself to a crouch in front of Mrs. Scott, and Cathleen gripped the tall upholstered back of the chair. His weather-roughened voice dropped to a gentle timbre. "Mum?"

The snores didn't cease, so he reached for her hand. "Mum?"

Cathleen moved around the chair to push between them. "Maybe I'd better wake her so she's not afraid."

The man's solid presence didn't budge as she crowded him. But before she could insist, Mrs. Scott snorted, and her eyelids fluttered open. She stared into the man's face, bewilderment clouding her features.

Cathleen touched her shoulder. "Mrs. Scott, you have a visitor."

The woman didn't take her eyes off the mountain man, and it was only a moment before they widened, and a smile lit her face. The sheer joy there made her look years younger. "My Reuben." She reached her quivering hand to his, patting the top. "Where ya been, boy. We was startin' to worry about you."

He leaned forward and planted a kiss on the woman's weathered cheek. "Too cold for much trapping this year, so I thought I'd come be a nuisance around this old place."

The tenderness between them was obvious, and Cathleen stepped back to allow them a bit more space. She'd expected Mrs. Scott's son to be a mountain man, but somehow hadn't envisioned him actually here inside this cabin. With a presence that almost overpowered.

She kept an eye on him while she set the buckets by the door, then retreated to the kitchen area. It was hard to tell with that fur coat covering halfway down to his knees, but his mass seemed to be a combination of height and the breadth of his shoulders. Or maybe it was just the wildness he seemed to carry into the room with him.

He straightened and sniffed the air, the movement pulling her attention. "Smells like the cabin could use a good airing, huh?"

He'd directed the words toward his mother, but Cathleen took her own deep inhale of the room. It wasn't as rank as a half hour ago, but leftover smells from Mrs. Scott's accident still lingered.

She turned to the shelves above the work counter. It was too cold to air the cabin, but maybe she could boil a cinnamon stick. She'd brought a substantial supply with the other provisions. A pity to use the treat for this reason, but the stench in the air needed to be rectified. Especially with this stranger in the room.

She kept her ear tuned to the conversation as she added another couple logs to the fire box, then dropped the spice into the pot of clean water on the stove.

"Did you bring me some pretty pelts this time?" Mrs. Scott's voice shook as she spoke, as if it was dragging across stones.

"Got a pretty wolf-skin I think you'll like. If you want, we can bead and fringe around the edges. If you don't want to keep it, I might do that anyway. I think it'll bring a decent price for trading."

She patted his face. "Don't trade away my pretties."

He sat back on his haunches and looked toward Cathleen, lowering his voice a register. "I didn't realize you'd be hiring help. Didn't think I'd ever see the day."

His voice carried even with the quieter tone, and Cathleen stiffened. Hired help? That she was not. She spun to set him straight, but he'd already moved onto another topic.

"Where's Pa? I have a couple things I wanted to run by him."

The words pinched in her chest, clearing out the anger from his last comment. He didn't know his father was dead. Of course he didn't, but that meant she would have to be the one to tell him.

Mrs. Scott's brow furrowed into a mass of wrinkles. "I think he must be out with the cattle. It's been awful cold lately."

A sick feeling tightened in Cathleen's stomach. She cleared her throat. "Mr. Scott, would you mind accompanying me out to the porch for a moment?"

He glanced at her, then back at his mother. Leaning forward to plant another peck on her cheek, he rose to his feet. "I reckon."

As he stepped across the small cabin to the door, his height closed in on her. He towered at least a foot over her, even though she'd always been considered tall for a woman.

She turned her back while she slipped into her wool coat, inhaling fortifying breaths. Surely the man wasn't dangerous, right? God had brought her to this place, He'd keep her safe with this mountain man. Her mind gripped onto the image of the man cradling his mother's hand. No, he couldn't be dangerous.

Cold air blasted when she opened the door, and Cathleen pulled her coat tighter to ward against the wind. She'd not stopped for gloves

MISTY M. BELLER

or hat, but this conversation shouldn't take long. Something furry touched her hand, and she jerked away from the unexpected touch, biting back a squeal.

A huge white animal stared up at her, his black eyes and muzzle the only contrast to the mass of white. And then a pink tongue slipped out and lolled to one side.

"Sit, North."

She almost jumped again at the man's words barked from behind her. Jerking her gaze to him, then back to the dog, she watched as the mountain man stepped forward and ran a hand over the animal's shaggy head. It obeyed the command and sat gazing into its owner's face.

"That's your dog?" A dumb question, because the mutt obviously adored and obeyed him. The surprises of the last few minutes must be fogging her mind.

He nodded, then straightened as his gaze roamed the clearing around them. Silence took over for a moment before he spoke. "This old homestead's not in as good a shape as usual. I suppose my parents are getting up in years." His focus tracked to her. "Reckon' that's why they hired you."

She stiffened. "Mr. Scott, I'm not a hired maid. I've been staying here this last week because your mother needed a nurse."

A line formed across his brow. "Mum's hurt? Why didn't you say something?" And then his mouth pinched and wariness formed between his eyes. "But Pa would want to tend her himself. He's real big on doin' for Mum when she needs help. They wouldn't bring in an outsider."

Cathleen gathered every ounce of her courage and met the man's gaze. "Your father died, Mr. Scott. About two months ago. Your mother has senile dementia, which seems to have progressed quickly since your father's death." Her voice sounded just like Bryan's did when he was giving a hard diagnosis to a patient. She hadn't meant the words to sound so clinical.

The man's face didn't change as she spoke. Not even a flicker.

30

When she finished, he turned to stare off into the distance, toward the break in the trees and the mountain beyond.

"I'm sorry." Cathleen's heartbeat pulsed in her throat while she waited for him to absorb the full impact of the news.

It was several long moments before he spoke. "Why did Mum say Pa's out with the cattle if he died?"

And that was the heartbreaking part. "The dementia's gotten pretty bad, and I think most times, she doesn't remember Mr. Scott's not with us any longer."

His Adam's apple bobbed. "How did it happen?"

"Your father? A fever. Your mother nursed him for days but nothing seemed to help. By the time my brother arrived, your father only lived a few more hours."

Still no wince or any sign that the words penetrated. This man was made of iron.

Finally, he flicked a glance at her. "And who are you?"

Not an irrational question. She straightened and gave him her most professional smile. "My brothers are both doctors in Butte. My father owns an apothecary shop in Boston, and I've helped him there for several years. When my brother told me about your mother's condition, I knew I had to help."

He nodded, and his gaze trailed down to the dog, still sitting by his feet. But his thoughts seemed far away. "So Mum just can't keep her facts straight?"

Cathleen swallowed. "Well, yes, but..." How much should she tell him about his mother's trouble with basic bodily functions? Her wandering at night? The numerous times she'd burned herself at the stove, or the unexplained bruises that appeared daily? He needed to know, especially if he would be assuming her care.

She straightened her backbone, fortifying her resolve. "There's more."

CHAPTER 4

*A*s Reuben listened to the words of this strange woman, his mind ached with all the new information. The shock of it. A haze formed around his thoughts, blocking out the deeper meaning of most of her words. He should chip through the barrier like he did a bucket of ice. He needed to absorb everything she was prattling on about and focus on what this meant for Mum. For him.

But just now, that protective haze was the only thing that kept him standing.

Pa was dead. How could that be? Reuben had just been here in the fall. Pa'd been doing his normal work, preparing the animals and the homestead for winter. Shoring up the buildings and working to split enough firewood to last two winters. Mum had just finished putting up food from the garden and was in her usual flurry to preserve everything possible from the hog he and Pa prepared for her. How could so much have changed in a few short months?

A cold snout touched the back of his hand, and he slipped his fingers into North's fur. The animal always knew when he needed a friend.

Silence finally permeated his awareness, and he glanced at the woman. She wasn't what he'd expected to find when he walked in the old cabin. Not in the least. A pretty thing with that thick auburn hair and skin like porcelain. Not the type to hang around in the mountain country. More like some fancy parlor back east. Sipping tea from china cups and discussing frivolous nonsense.

She wasn't talking now though. She looked at him like it was his turn to speak. But what was there to say? He needed time to process this. Needed to see Mum again. Maybe all the gibberish this woman had been spewing was nonsense.

He spun back to the door. "Thanks for the help, Miss—" He paused mid-sentence. Had she said her name? She was related to the docs in Butte, but he didn't have an inkling of their surname.

"Miss Donaghue," she supplied, her voice tight behind him.

He turned to eye her. She didn't look like she trusted him any more than he did her. At least they could agree on that. Although she had nothing to worry about from him. He had no desire to keep her here any longer than absolutely necessary. If he could get a handle on Mum's condition—and surely it wasn't anything they needed a stranger to help with—he'd send this little lady back to the fancy Eastern drawing rooms where she belonged.

Grabbing the door handle, he pushed it open. "Stay, North."

The dog obeyed, of course, and the woman didn't follow him in either, except to gather the water cans she'd stashed by the doorway. Then she disappeared back outside, leaving the cabin quiet except for Mum's snores.

One thing was certain. He'd never seen his mother sleep so much during the day. Usually she burned the candle at both ends, staying up late doing needlework and rising earlier than Pa to make breakfast. Maybe sleep would cure whatever ailed her—whatever had caused the doc's sister to come all the way up here to act as nurse.

He crouched in front of Mum and took a moment to catalogue the changes to her face. She'd lost a lot of weight in these few months. Although mourning Pa could account for that.

A fresh press of grief slammed into his chest, working its way up his throat. Reuben swallowed, trying to force it down. He had to focus on Mum right now.

She'd certainly added more lines to her face, and the skin sagged in layers across her cheeks and below her jaw. Most of the pepper had disappeared from her hair too, leaving behind only coarse white, tied back in her usual knot at the base of her head.

He took her hand, stroking his thumb over the back of her hand. The rough texture near her wrist caught his attention, and he held it up to see better in the dim light from the fire.

A thick crust of scab covered the skin, and red bruises spread from a spot that would obviously scar. Was this the cause for the nurse to come all the way up here and stay with Mum? It was a nasty sore, but nothing his mother hadn't treated herself for longer than he could remember.

He eyed the rest of her, but she was wrapped up tight in a blanket. No skin showed except her hands and face.

Her eyelids drifted open, and she peered at him with milky confusion. Was that only sleep clouding them?

"Quinn? Is that you?"

Something sharp pierced his heart. "No, Mum. It's me, Reuben. Pa's not here now."

Her brow knit in fierce lines. "Reuben? Why aren't you out helping your Pa with the hay? Is he hurt?" She gripped his hand tighter.

He gentled his voice as much as he could, forcing his words through the ache in his chest. "I just came back from my winter camp, Mum. Pa's...not with us anymore. He died a couple months ago from a fever. Do you remember?" It took every ounce of his self-control to get out those last sentences without his voice cracking.

Her confusion turned to pain as her milky eyes washed with moisture. "Died? Not Quinn. My Quinn wouldn't leave me." Her voice rose to a higher pitch as she jerked her hand from his and wrapped her arms around herself. She rocked in the chair as her eyes rimmed red and a big tear trailed down her cheek.

Suddenly, Miss Donaghue was there, kneeling beside the chair and wrapping both arms around Mum. When had she come in? She practically pushed him aside as she held his mother, murmuring consoling words and stroking her hair.

Reuben rose to his feet, but couldn't take his eyes from the pair. Should he have kept the truth to himself? Surely his mother had been told her husband was dead. So why did this grief look as fresh as the first shock? Could she really be losing her mind as much as Miss Donaghue made it seem? He should have forced himself to listen to her words when she was telling him about Mum's condition. He needed to know. Had to keep from hurting her in the future.

After a couple moments, Mum's tears settled into a few sniffles, and she sank her head back against the chair, turning red-rimmed eyes to Miss Donaghue. "Thank ye, dear. Don't know what came over me, but you're an angel to help."

Miss Donaghue patted Mum's hand, then rose to her feet. "I'll warm some tea, and we'll all feel better."

She shot him a look as she turned toward the kitchen, but he struggled to decipher it. Warning? Yes. And maybe a bit of pity.

Well, she could keep her pity. And if she thought he'd intentionally hurt Mum, she'd better get things straight. Now he just had to figure out where the traps were hidden, so he didn't trip one again.

❧

*T*he silence of the barn was a blessed relief, and Rueben stayed there with his thoughts the rest of the afternoon, settling his horses and storing the pelts and meat stock he'd brought.

North trotted at his side as he checked the animals around the place. It looked like they'd been fed and watered regularly. And Maggie, the milk cow, didn't look too miserable, so she must have been milked that morning. In the chicken shed, no eggs hid in the straw, although the birds probably weren't laying much with the deep cold. But evidence of food scraps littered the ground, and a bit of corn was left in the feeder. Someone was caring for the stock, whether it be Mum or the stranger who'd taken her place in the house.

"Mr. Scott?" Speaking of the lady, her voice called across the clearing as he stepped out of the chicken shed.

He latched the door, then turned to face her.

35

"Supper's ready. I wasn't sure if you planned to join us?"

Yes, he supposed he had to. And the pain gnawing at his insides needed to be satisfied. He headed that direction, North bounding ahead as if he smelled the food already.

A warm, spicy aroma greeted him as he stepped into the cabin this time. Nothing like the rank odor from before. He let North follow him in out of the cold, and as he unbuttoned his coat, his eyes drifted to the table. Three plates sat out, filled with what looked like ham steak, potatoes, and carrots. The savory scent wafting from the plates nearly made his eyes drift closed from sheer pleasure. It'd been an awful long time since he'd had any garden vegetables. Not since the Crow camp left for better hunting.

"Come to the table, Mrs. Scott. Do you smell the ham sizzling?"

He glanced across the room to Miss Donaghue, who was helping Mum out of her chair. She had one arm around Mum's waist and the other holding her hand. Could his mother really not walk to the table by herself?

North padded over to them, but Reuben let out a short whistle to call him back. The last thing he needed was Mum tripping over the animal. Best keep things simple until he figured out the truth of her condition. The dog eyed him with obvious disapproval but sat at Reuben's feet like he'd been trained.

Miss Donaghue glanced up to meet Reuben's gaze. "I don't mind, as long as he doesn't bother your mother."

He eyed Mum, who seemed oblivious to the animal's presence as she shuffled toward the table. Mum had always liked North, but that was before. Who could say now?

Her progress across the small cabin was slow, and his eyes roamed down to her feet. An old pair of worn moccasins peeked out from beneath her dress. Nothing that should slow her down or make her unsteady

"She's still recovering from the frostbite."

He jerked his focus up to Miss Donaghue. "Frostbite?"

She offered a sad smile, then turned toward Mum and spoke a little louder. "Your feet are feeling better today, aren't they?"

Mum turned a delighted smile on the younger woman. "Oh, yes, dear. My feet feel just fine. What shall we make for dinner, do you think?"

Miss Donaghue leaned in closer. "I made you a surprise this time. Irish ham and cabbage. Except I didn't have cabbage, so it's just potatoes. But I toasted sourdough bread, and we have fresh butter."

His feet seemed rooted to the floor as he watched the woman guide his mother into a chair, chattering as they progressed. And the smiles Mum bestowed on her? A flicker of envy lit in his gut, but he squashed it down. The last time she'd looked at him with so much pride was when he'd given her the bobcat fur over the mantle. Was it really a daughter she'd wanted all these years? Maybe that was why he never quite seemed to measure up. If only Nora had survived to be what Mum needed.

Once his mother was settled in her chair, fork in hand, Miss Donaghue glanced at him. A flush of pink stained the otherwise flawless skin on her cheeks. "It's not much of a meal. But it should be warm and nourishing. I'm still learning how to make do with the few provisions I've found here."

Few provisions? Mum and Pa normally had enough stored for winter to last till fall of the next year. What was this woman used to? Five different fully stocked larders and servants to cook it all?

And then the picture formed in his mind. She probably was accustomed to that. She dressed and spoke and looked like she'd come straight from an eastern mansion. So why was she all the way up here, trying to do something she had no business attempting? Montana winters were harsh under the best conditions, with no mercy shown to the weak or ignorant.

"I'm afraid I don't know which is your chair, Mr. Scott."

She stood behind an empty seat, the one closest to the stove. The one they'd always kept as an extra in case a guest stopped by.

He stepped around to the opposite side of the table to take his own place. North followed him, of course, and took up his usual spot at Reuben's feet. As Reuben settled himself and pulled a steaming plate close, the empty end of the table where Pa always sat loomed at the edge of his vision.

A burn took hold in his throat, but he tried not to look that direction. Taking up his fork, he plunged it into the ham steak.

"Do you mind if we say a blessing over the food?"

Miss Donaghue's voice brought him up short, and he eyed her, then lowered his gaze to where her hand clasped Mum's.

His fork made a little clatter as he dropped it back on the plate. "That's fine." Of course she'd want to say grace. Mum always did, too. But it was an easy habit to lose when he was on his own for months at a time. Not that the Almighty had ever paid attention to his requests. At mealtime or otherwise.

Cathleen prayed a few simple sentences, her voice rolling with intensity. She seemed to really mean the words she spoke.

He fell into the lilting cadence of it. Her voice was almost as smooth as the porcelain of her face, easing over him like clear water on a warm summer day. He could listen to that voice for hours.

When she said, "Amen," he had to force himself not to look up and watch her. He may have been raised in the mountains, but even he knew staring wasn't polite. It didn't stop him from wanting to look his fill, though.

～

Cathleen couldn't help staring at the man across the table from her. He truly was a mountain man, with overgrown hair and beard. The skin on his face and hands looked like it'd seen plenty of long days in the harsh wind and cold. But those eyes. Every time he turned them on her, she sank into the blue of them.

He didn't eat like a barbarian, exactly. Used a fork and a serviette like most people. And he didn't hunch over his food, although he did seem to relish it. He wasn't much of a talker, though. Hadn't said more than three words since she'd called him in for supper. But his silence made sense, because he spent most of his time alone in the wilds.

There was something about him that stirred her soul. Invigorated

38

her senses—and not just her curiosity. Something in the aura that surrounded him. She couldn't quite put her finger on it, but it was hard to take her eyes off him.

Now that he was here, she should make plans to return to town. That had been the plan, after all. She slipped a glance toward Mrs. Scott. The woman was still so fragile and confused. Could this oversized mountain man give her the care she needed? It didn't seem possible.

The least she could do was stay on a few more days until she could feel more comfortable with leaving her patient in the man's care.

Her gaze slid back to Mr. Scott, just as he looked up and caught her watching. Heat surged to her face, but she didn't look away. She had nothing to be ashamed of.

"Food's good." He raised a fork full of ham and potatoes. "Tastes like when Mum makes it."

A warmth filled her chest that had nothing to do with embarrassment. "Thank you. I thought with the name Scott, you might like recipes from the Old Country." She let a bit of her parents' brogue slip into those last two words.

He stopped chewing and raised a brow. "You're from Ireland?"

"My parents were. Mum was proud of the recipes she brought over, but I have to say we settled into the American ways pretty quickly."

He cocked his head and studied her for a moment, then ducked back to his food. What was he thinking under that head of thick brown hair? Did he think her a chatterling? A nuisance? Maybe she didn't want to know.

But really she *did*. His silence was driving her batty. If only she could peel back the layers of his mask and see what kind of man Reuben Scott really was.

CHAPTER 5

*R*euben wrapped the bear skin tighter around him as he
sank into the soft bedding. It was awfully cold this morning. With North's body heat adding to his own, his toes shouldn't be
so frigid.

He reached down to stroke the dog, but his fingers met only the
coarse hair from the bear skin. His eyelids slid open, and he glanced
around. Every muscle jumped to alert as he took in the unfamiliar
surroundings. Not his tiny winter cabin. Not even the little room he
used at his parents' house. This was a massive structure with a high
pitched-ceiling and cold air flowing through the space.

A barn. Memories flooded back as his racing heart began to slow.
There was a new woman in the house with Mum—sleeping in his
room, no less—so he'd stayed in the barn.

A rustle sounded in one of the stalls, grabbing his attention. Was
North bothering the milk cow? Indeed, the dog padded from the stall
opening, with another figure close on its heels.

Miss Donaghue.

Reuben bolted upright, tossing the bearskin aside and lurching to
his feet. If he'd not been awake before, the sight of her had the blood
flowing strong through his veins.

She glanced his way with a soft smile. Kind of like an angel, with the light from the lantern hanging on the stall post. "Good morning. I'm sorry if I woke you."

"No." His tongue stuck to the roof of his mouth, making it hard to force out even that gravely word. A cough caught in his throat.

What did he look like after tossing most of the night? He scrubbed a hand through his hair, but that probably didn't help much. He was long overdue for a shave and a haircut, the latter he'd been hoping Mum would do. He'd have to come up with an alternate plan now, though.

Miss Donaghue still eyed him with that gentle smile. She probably expected him to say something else.

"Uh, good morning." His gaze found the bucket in her hand. "Is there something you need?"

She followed his look. "I like to get the outside chores done before your mother wakes up. The milking's done, I just need to break the ice and let the animals out, then I'll be out of your hair."

Hair. Heat crawled up his face. Was that an off-handed comment about the burly mass on his head? He did his best to push it aside, but the sooner he got her out of the barn, the better. "I'll do that." He grabbed his coat from where he'd tossed it beside his sleeping furs, then started toward her. "You don't need to worry about the animals now that I'm here."

Her shoulders seemed to sag a bit, and something flashed across her face. Relief? He really was bad at reading people. Animals, he could anticipate every move before they'd made up their mind to take it. But people? Too many emotional games.

"That would be nice. Thank you." She held up the pail, full of white, frothy liquid. "I can still do the milking and gather eggs, if you'd like."

He shrugged, his hands searching his coat pocket for his gloves. "You don't have to. I imagine you have plenty of work in the cabin." Especially with Mum's challenges, from what he'd seen last night.

"Thank you." With the simple words, she turned away.

A memory sprang to Reuben's mind, the mental list of questions that had kept him from sleep for so many hours last night. "Miss Donaghue?"

She turned back, the shadows darkening her face, so he couldn't see the light in her eyes. "Yes?"

"Do you know where my father is…buried?" It was still so hard to fathom Pa could be gone. With the dawning of this new day, maybe she would tell him it had all been a dream. A nightmare.

"I'm not positive, but I think I saw a marker at the corner of the clearing. That way." She pointed toward the northeast and the corner of the land that bordered the creek. "Everything's covered with snow, so it's hard to tell for sure."

He nodded his thanks. "And do you know where the cattle are? I imagine half dead if they've had to fend for themselves these last months."

She shook her head before he could even finish that last sentence. "My brother said a neighbor's taking care of them. O'Hennessey, I think?"

Another slam to his gut. Reuben should have been here to take over when things got bad. Instead, Mum had had to rely on neighbors and the doctors' sister from town. But how could he have known his parents would suddenly need him, after thirty years of his presence being mostly a nuisance? Of course they'd never said that, but they'd always been so capable with the homestead. If only they could have passed some of that ability on to him.

Miss Donaghue was still staring at him. How many times had he lost himself in his thoughts while she'd watched? She probably thought he was a flaky half-wit by now.

He tried to form a normal expression as he met her gaze. "Thanks for the answers. I'll see to the animals now."

As she turned and left the barn, Reuben's hand slipped down to scratch North's head.

The animals, he could care for. This woman and the new reality of the family that had always been his rock—he'd rather confront a grizzly empty-handed.

≈

*F*acing his father's grave was as hard as Reuben had expected. While he stood before the simple wooden cross and mound of raised snow, so many memories surged. Pa trying to teach him farming and carpentry. He'd picked up quickly on the needle-work and beading that Mum taught, so he'd have thought carpentry would have come second nature, too. But there was no art in building square frames and perfectly measured beams and notches. No creativity required, like the ornate detail he'd learned from his Crow friends. Oh, he'd worked alongside Pa enough to be able to build a simple shed, but nothing like the impressive structures his father had produced here on the homestead and around their various pastures.

Had Pa been disappointed in him? Probably. That assumption was part of what drove him away for months at a time when he started trapping at eighteen. Maybe Pa had always wished the other baby had lived instead of him. His twin, girl though she was. The daughter his parents had always craved.

North slipped his muzzle into Reuben's hand, and he obliged by scratching through the thick fur behind the animal's ears. The dog panted his thanks as he stared up into Reuben's face. His constant companion. North never found fault with any of his shortcomings. Always stood nearby until he was needed.

"What say, boy? Think we need to head inside now?"

The dog snapped his mouth shut and rose to all fours, eagerness showing in his raised ears and the long bushy tail curled over his back.

Reuben's mouth pulled in the hint of a smile. "You like her cookin', too, huh?"

≈

*T*hwak!

The resounding sound of the log splitting under his ax-head echoed through the morning air two days later. He raised the ax

43

again, settled another log on the stump, then let the momentum flow through his upper body as he brought down another blow.

A cough gripped his chest, and he leaned against the ax handle until the spasms subsided. This irritating burn in his chest had plagued him for days now. He didn't have time for it to slow him down. Too much work to do around the place.

Most of the wood Pa had split was gone, and the little bit left was pine. That stuff didn't burn hot enough in the cook stove, although this territory sure provided plenty of it. So he'd spent most of the afternoon yesterday bringing down a maple and hauling it back to the house. And now it had to be chopped into pieces not even as thick as his hand so the oven would cook right. This was not one of his favorite parts of homesteading, but at least he was capable. And it sure gave him a chance to use up some energy and break a good sweat. Possibly even work off the cough.

And maybe he could work hard enough to clear his mind of the two women inside the cabin. Seeing Mum like that, just a shadow of the woman she used to be, was harder than he'd ever thought possible. And most of the times he'd sat down to visit with her in the cabin, she didn't even recognize him. Or thought he was his father. So he'd kept away from the cabin more than he should. There was certainly enough work for him to do outside.

He propped another log on the stump and raised the ax over his shoulder. *Thwak.*

Mum always seemed to know Miss Donaghue, though. Maybe not the lady's name, but certainly seemed to remember her unrelenting kindness. That was hard to watch sometimes, too. A stranger caring for his mother. And other times it seemed like she fit perfectly in their little cabin. Like when she smiled at him across the table. Or handed him a cup of coffee in the mornings.

He settled an extra-large log on the stump and drew back the ax.

"I brought coffee to warm you, but looks like you might be too warm already."

The aim of his swing jerked sideways at the unexpected voice, and the ax-head sank into the old stump. He straightened and turned to face the distraction.

Miss Donaghue eyed him with a smile, tin mugs in each hand, thick steam rising from both. She offered one to him. "I can bring water instead, if you prefer."

He reached for the cup. "Coffee's fine." But it was better than fine. Even through his rawhide gloves, the warmth of the cup seeped into his hands. And the savory scent of the brew opened up his senses. Another cough wracked his upper body, and he held the mug out to keep from spilling the precious stuff while he tried to rein in his body's reactions.

When he finally gathered his breath, Miss Donaghue stared at him, twin lines pinching her brow. "You're not well, Mr. Scott. I can make a tea that will help."

"I'm fine." He cleared the thick remnants from his throat, then took a deep sip of the coffee. The moment it touched his tongue, the flavors spread like rich cream, soothing the raw ache that had settled in his chest.

When he looked up, she was still watching him. Probably waiting for him to speak. He said the first thing that jumped into his mind. "You do good not to burn the coffee, cooking with that pine." He nodded toward the split wood that had thrown itself into two piles as he chopped. "This maple should make it easier."

She raised both delicate brows, and something like a curious smile touched her mouth. "I didn't realize the wood cooked differently. I suppose it makes sense, though. Thank you."

He couldn't help eyeing her. "You didn't cook before you came here?"

A flush brightened her face, more than just red circles from the cold. "Of course I cooked. But we had the wood delivered, so I never had to worry what kind it was."

Hmm… he still had no clear picture of her life before coming to this mountain. But wasn't sure he knew how to ask about it. Wouldn't direct questions seem like prying?

He took another swig of coffee, then glanced into the brew and used his most nonchalant voice. "You lived in Butte for a while?"

"Just since the fall. I came out to help with my new niece and nephew, and wherever else I'm needed." Her voice settled into that rolling cadence that was so soothing. The sound that made him crave more.

"You came from back east then?" He caught her nod out of the corner of his eye as he watched the steam rise from his drink.

"Boston." She said the name as casual as if she meant the next town over. Which out here was still a sizeable distance.

"That's awfully far east."

A hint of a smile touched her mouth. "Yes, it is. All the way to the ocean. Our home wasn't near the harbor, but Mum loved to spend the day by the water any chance we had."

"Your parents were rich, then?"

She tilted her head, studying him. "Not by Boston standards. Dad was an apothecary, so we weren't on the same level as the wealthy set."

He couldn't stop his gaze from sweeping over her. That coat she wore certainly had more style than function, what with no hood and too many ruffles that did almost nothing to keep her warm. And the way she carried herself—culture rolled off her in waves. "You just look..." He clamped down on the words before more crept out.

He took a long swig of his drink. Maybe she'd just ignore that last comment.

But when he lowered the cup, she was eyeing him, that soft smile still pulling at her lips. "I just look like what?"

See, this was why he didn't talk to women. Not that he'd had much opportunity. But there were just too many pitfalls.

A gentle laugh drifted from her, like the gentle melody of a stream around rocks. "I'm sorry, Mr. Scott. I don't know what to make of you sometimes."

He braved a glance at her. Was she mocking him? But no, the sweet expression on her face seemed to be pleasure, no derision there.

A twinkle lit her eyes. "My father was an apothecary, but my mother did come from a somewhat elite family in Ireland. She made sure I learned to comport myself like a lady." She glanced down at the frippery on her coat and the skirt peeking from beneath. "And I suppose she taught me to have…more refined taste in clothing."

Then, with a simple lift of her shoulders, she seemed to let her wealthy past slide off of her. "It doesn't make me a different person though. I'm still as capable as anyone." A hint of uncertainty flashed through her eyes. "There are some things I'm still learning about life up here, but I'm getting better."

And something about that pure honesty made her twice as pretty, despite her lace-trimmed skirt and layers of flounces. But she still didn't belong up here. The mountains would swallow her whole if she stayed too long.

CHAPTER 6

$\mathcal{A}$ few hours later, Cathleen had two pots on the stove and a slightly burnt aroma drifting from the oven when boot thumps sounded on the porch. She would have groaned at the man's timing, if she'd had a spare second to do it.

After giving the beans a final stir, she pushed the pot to a cooler part of the range, then grabbed a leather pad and jerked open the oven door. Smoke billowed out, but not as much as there could have been. She pulled the biscuit pan out of the heat and surveyed it. She should have stuck to stove-top cornbread, but they had more flour than cornmeal, so the biscuits had made sense. At the time.

The cabin door opened, letting in a blast of cold air and Mr. Scott, who carried a load of firewood tall enough to cover half his face. He dumped the stack in the wood box beside the cook stove and straightened to his full, massive height.

Cathleen swallowed. "Thank you."

She returned her focus to the pan in her hands but could still see his form at the edge of her vision. How tall was he exactly? Maybe it wasn't so much his height but the breadth of him that sucked the air from her lungs when he came near. His stature made her feel both insecure and protected. How convoluted was that? She supposed as long as he was on their side and his size didn't make him too rough with Mrs. Scott, his height would prove a good thing around the farm.

He turned away to remove his coat, and she forced herself to breathe. And focus on the biscuits. They were dark brown on top, not the golden color she'd been hoping for. She loosened the edge of one. Yep, black on the bottom. At least they'd be eating the things hot, before the lumps cooled into hard bricks.

A whistle from the kettle pulled her attention from the biscuits, and Cathleen inhaled quickly. The ginger tea that she'd been steeping for Mr. Scott was ready. She'd planned to hand him a mug the moment he walked in the door, but she hadn't quite accomplished that.

Grabbing the cup she'd already prepared with honey, she filled it to the brim with the tea and dropped in a peppermint stick. The taste might be unusual, but it should certainly do the trick for his cough.

Stirring the mixture, she turned to carry it to him with a smile. Everything went down better with a smile.

But she froze mid-step when she found him watching her. He'd shucked his coat, hat, and gloves, but still stood by the door. His hands rested at his waist, and her gaze traveled upward from there to those impossibly wide shoulders. Up further to his intense blue eyes. Even in the dim light of the cabin, she could still see their glow as he scrutinized her.

It was an effort, but she fought down the heat that surged to her neck. Offering a cheery smile, she extended the mug like a gift. "I made some tea to help your cough. It should be just ready to drink."

His gaze flicked. He didn't seem to like being fussed over, but he'd have to get used to it. She was here as a nurse, so where there was sickness, fussing was officially her job.

She added a little more honey to her smile. "Please, Mr. Scott. At least it'll warm you."

"Reuben."

She paused. "Beg pardon?"

"Name's Reuben. Mr. Scott was my Pa."

She swallowed down the lump that suddenly thickened her throat.

Naturally, anything that reminded him of his father would be painful. "Of course. I'm sorry." The least she could do was call him by his Christian name, if that helped even a particle.

His gaze shone wary, but he finally stepped forward and took the mug. "Thanks."

Well. Another word that hadn't been absolutely necessary. Maybe he was feeling more comfortable with her presence here. "I'll keep more tea here on the back of the stove, so you can get it any time. It'll be best if you add a spoon of honey to your cup."

He still stood there, staring at her, and Cathleen tried her best to focus on the final dinner preparations. This would not be her best meal, but she'd had her hands full with Mrs. Scott all afternoon. The woman kept trying to slip out the door—without a coat, of course. Cathleen had finally bundled the lady in her warmest wraps, and they'd taken a walk. The sweet woman had probably spent much of her life outside, which made it hard to stay confined in the cabin much of the day. But their outing had resulted in burned biscuits.

"Where's Mum?"

Her gaze pulled up to the man who stood like an enigma in the middle of the room. Didn't he know staring was rude? "She's in her room. We were busy this afternoon, so she finally lay down for a nap while I worked on dinner."

She turned back to the shelves and pulled down plates and cups for them all. Silence was the only response from behind her.

And then a hacking cough. An awful sound, radiating from deep in his chest. She spun to face him. "I don't think it's healthy for you to continue sleeping in the barn, Mr. Scott. It's too cold out there without a fire."

He tried to look at her, but the shudders wracking his body bent him over. The mug in his hands shook with each cough, and she reached out in case she needed to grab it. He'd drunk enough that nothing sloshed over the brim.

When he finally straightened, his eyes were rimmed red and his breath came in ragged gasps. "I'm fine in the barn. No need to put anyone out."

She pinched her lips. He was stubborn, no doubt about it. Stubborn and stoic and almost impossible to connect with. "Mr. Scott."

"Reuben."

A pang slid through her. How could she have forgotten his request so quickly? "Reuben, I'm sorry." She planted a fist on her hip to resurrect her former vehemence. "But you're not sleeping in the barn again. You put a pallet by that fire." She pointed toward the hearth. "Or I can move into your mother's chamber, and you can have the room I've been using. Take your choice, but you're not sleeping out in that cold."

She met his glare and arched her brows. If he thought she'd back down on this, he'd be sadly disappointed.

He didn't say a word, though. Didn't move a muscle, not even the flick of his gaze. The man was a rock.

A burning smell drifted through her senses, and Cathleen whirled. *The beans.* Great land of Jehoshaphat. If there were any part of this meal not burned by the time she got it on the table, it would truly be a miracle.

While she scurried around the kitchen, carrying food to the table and setting out plates, utensils, and jam for the biscuits, the big white dog padded up beside her and sat with a whine.

"Hey, boy. I can't pet you now, but I'll make you a plate. You hungry?"

He gazed up at her with sweet, sad eyes until a short whistle sounded from behind them.

The dog jumped to his feet and trotted toward the sitting area, his nails clicking on the floor with each step.

She refrained from looking at the man, because for some reason, the loss of the animal stung. Maybe she missed her mum's little Annie who'd always been underfoot. "I don't mind him here with me. What's his name?"

"North."

She bit back a smile. With his wooly white coat, it did seem like a fitting title. Eyeing the table laid out with dishes and the salvaged food, she wiped her hands on her apron. "I'll just get your mother up, and we'll be ready to eat."

*R*euben scratched the soft fur under North's jaw as he waited for Miss Donaghue and Mum to come from the bed chamber. He'd felt like an idiot standing around watching her these last few minutes, but he'd had no idea what else to do. She scurried around the kitchen from one task to the next like a woman on a mission. Like Mum used to do. It left him feeling like an oversized mule in a mercantile, clumsy and in the way.

If he didn't feel so out of place, it would be a pleasure to simply watch her. This woman was so...different...from any person he'd met, white or Indian. Part of it was her beauty, certainly. And maybe the kindness that flashed in her ready smiles.

Although she'd proved she could get riled if he crossed her. His mouth twitched as he pictured the fire in her eyes when she'd given him his choice of sleeping arrangements. He stroked his beard. It probably was time he cleaned himself up and got a little more presentable. A full bath was out of the question in this weather, but maybe he could fit in a shave and haircut after supper.

Mum's chamber door opened, and the voices that had been muffled came clear. "Your son, Reuben's, here, so we're all ready to eat." Miss Donaghue's voice carried clear and sweet in the tone she reserved for Mum. She really did have a gift with his mother and seemed to hold genuine affection for her. Mum, of course, adored the woman.

Reuben settled into his chair while Mum did the same, but Miss Donaghue placed a plate of scraps in the corner for North before she claimed her own seat. This time, he remembered not to eat until after they'd bowed their heads to say grace. Like the other times, Miss Donaghue's voice rang with earnestness as she spoke the simple words.

With the final "Amen," she raised her head and glanced at the pot of beans in the center of the table, then at him with a sheepish look. "I'm sorry if the meal is a bit overcooked."

He ladled a spoonful into his plate and tried not to stare at the black specks floating in the gooey brown sauce. "I'm sure it's fine."

Miss Donaghue helped his mother with her plate, then silence descended over the table as they worked at the meal. The beans were thick, and the biscuits charred on the bottom, but he'd eaten worse at his own hand in his winter camp. Besides, what could one expect from a woman raised in the city?

"How long have you had North?"

Her words caught him off guard, and he looked up from sopping his biscuit in the bean broth. "Since he was a pup. About five years."

She was watching the dog as it licked the plate clean in the corner. "He seems well behaved."

He nodded then went back to his food. Small talk had never been easy for him.

After the meal, Reuben slipped into his parents' room and found Pa's shaving kit, then pulled on his coat and gloves and headed to the barn. There'd be more privacy out there. He'd never kept a razor of his own. Whenever the urge to shave came on him in his trapping camp, he just sharpened his hunting knife. But the job was easier with the proper tools.

He checked Tashunka when he first entered the barn, but the mare dozed quietly in her stall. Her sides had narrowed over the last day or so, like the baby had dropped into the foaling position, but no other changes signaled the birth would be imminent. And Tash usually showed all the signs when she was ready for a foaling.

That was one thing he liked about this mare. She didn't hold back her thoughts for him to guess. Made things nice and clear so he knew what was going on and how to react. Not like most women.

He mixed the shaving soap using a bit of water from one of the icy buckets. Maybe not the most comfortable temperature, but it'd get the job done. After settling into his old bed in the hay, he reached for the shaving supplies.

It wasn't easy shaving with only Pa's tiny handheld mirror, but he finished with just a few nicks at his throat and a long one on his right cheek. He barely recognized himself in the small sliver of looking glass. But the freshly exposed skin made his bushy mass of hair stand out even more. He had to do something about that, too.

Would Mum be up to trimming it? Could she even be trusted with sharp tools? He didn't really know. Holding out a fistful of hair, he pressed the sharp side of the razor against the locks. After sawing for a moment, it cut through.

He was able to reach most of the top and sides, but the back proved a challenge. He did the best he could, then glanced into the two-inch-wide strip of mirror and studied himself. A bit ragged, but hopefully better than when he'd started. Hopefully.

~

Cathleen slipped from Mrs. Scott's room and pulled the door closed behind her. The older woman had gone to bed well enough, but there was no telling how long she'd actually stay there. Whether it be at midnight or long after the moon had disappeared from the black sky, Mrs. Scott almost always awoke and started shuffling through the cabin in the darkness.

A yawn forced its way through her jaw, but Cathleen was too tired to fight it. She'd not had time for her evening walk before Mrs. Scott's bedtime, and she wasn't sure she had the energy now. But she needed the clarity of mind that always came from talking to God under the stars. And she had a special question for the Almighty tonight. A particular topic she needed to sort through. Or, more honestly, a man she couldn't quite decipher.

As she buttoned her coat, boots thumped on the front porch. She grabbed the latch and pulled the door wide as Mr. Scott—Reuben— stepped in with an armload of wood. It didn't look like he'd brought his bedroll yet, though. Would she have to enforce her earlier directive?

He headed toward the hearth and dropped the logs in the wood box there. But when he straightened and turned to face her, Cathleen could scarcely draw a breath.

He was...different.

She squinted to make sure this man really was Reuben Scott. Same blue eyes. Same tall frame and broad shoulders. Same fur coat.

But no mountain-man beard. He actually had a face underneath all that hair. And what a face. Strong chiseled jaw, square chin. She still couldn't seem to draw a steady breath.

He slipped off the hood and glanced her direction. She should turn away, but her body refused to do it. His hair was cut shorter too, although it was a bit...choppy...in places. Almost as if that ornery rooster in the chicken shed had given it a good pecking.

He cleared his throat, jerking her from her thoughts. "Is there anything else you need for the night?"

She turned to the door, mostly to hide the heat flaring into her face. "No. Thank you. I was just, uh, going for a quick walk." And she slipped outside before she made an even bigger fool of herself.

The blast of frigid air on her face was a welcome relief.

CHAPTER 7

*A*ll night, Cathleen couldn't shake the image of the man out of her mind. He'd lost the unkempt trapper look but still held that strong aura of wildness. If anything, it was even more pronounced now than before. And getting rid of that beard had shed years off his face. She couldn't have said exactly how old he'd looked before, but now that his features were clear, it was obvious he couldn't be more than thirty. Not as old as she'd expected for the son of a widow with hair as white as Mrs. Scott's. It seemed like there might be more to that story. Maybe one day, Mrs. Scott would remember enough to share with her.

She peeked glances at him over the breakfast table while he ate, absorbing the differences in the dim light filtering in through the window.

"Son, after breakfast, I'll trim up yer hair a bit. Yer lookin' a bit scraggly."

Cathleen glanced over at Mrs. Scott. The older woman seemed clearer than normal this morning, without the confusion or lack of interest that seemed to cloud her eyes many days. But clear enough to use a pair of scissors? That was probably too much chance to take.

They shouldn't risk more gashes in the woman's already sensitive skin. Not to mention Reuben's neck.

She darted a look at him and saw the uncertainty plastered there as he studied his mother. For once, she didn't have to guess what he was thinking.

"We'll see, Mum." He nodded toward Mrs. Scott's boiled oats. "Eat up. You need your strength."

She sent him an adoring smile and took another bite of her gruel. Cathleen had mixed berry preserves in the pot after they'd cooked, and it came out pretty tasty, if she did say so herself. Almost as good as the cinnamon and sugar her mum used to serve with them at home.

As Cathleen took another bite from her own bowl, she worked the situation through in her mind. There was no way she'd let Mrs. Scott try to cut Reuben's hair. Not with her shaky hands and a sharp blade. It appeared he'd done the best he could on his own, but it certainly needed a woman's touch.

So…she was the only other option. But would he be offended if she offered? She could probably work through his objections. She'd gotten good at coercing patients into doing what was best for them, especially these last few weeks with Mrs. Scott.

It just took the right words and a smile.

$\sim$

"*R*euben, if you'll come back in after you finish with the animals, I can give you the haircut your mother mentioned."

Reuben froze with his hand on the door latch. Surely he'd heard her wrong. He eased back around to face her. Maybe the expression on her face could tell him what she'd really said.

She carried a load of used breakfast dishes but stopped to flash him one of her cheery smiles. "Unless you'd rather risk your jugular vein." She shot a glance toward his mother, who still sat at the table, folding a cloth into a tiny off-kilter square. Mum seemed oblivious to the conversation.

He looked back at Miss Donaghue. "I..."

She stepped forward to drop the dishes in a pan of water on the stove. "I have a good pair of scissors in my sewing kit, so we'll be done in minutes. Come back after you've fed the animals, and I'll be ready for you."

She turned her back to him and scraped a bit of soap into the pot, which gave him the fairly strong impression she'd dismissed him...in her cheery little way.

Opening the door, he slipped outside. Out into a world where he could at least feel like he had a bit of control.

Three quarters of an hour later, he dragged himself back into the cabin with a bucket of milk and four eggs. He'd made the barn chores last as long as he could, but then he'd pictured Miss Donaghue sitting forlornly at the table with her scissors, waiting for him. The guilt had been stronger than he was willing to push aside.

But it turned out that wasn't quite the picture that greeted him when he stepped into the room. Instead, Miss Donaghue looked up from a corner of the kitchen, broom in hand and one of those smiles lighting her face.

"Oh, good. You're just in time." She leaned the broom in the corner and crossed to the stove. "Have a seat at the table, and we'll get started."

He glanced around the room as he stripped off his coat. "Where's Mum?"

"She's tinkering in her room, preparing for the day." Miss Donaghue's smile changed to something a bit conspiratorial. "I'll go in there in a bit and make sure she hasn't stripped the blankets from the bed or soaked all her clean underclothes in the full wash basin."

He cocked his head. "She's done those things?"

"And then some." Miss Donaghue set a mug of steaming liquid by his place at the table and motioned to his chair. "Sit."

Then she turned her back to him, fiddling with something at the counter. The woman was always doing something.

He eyed the mug, inhaling the spicy aroma as he settled in his chair. Smelled like more of that tea concoction she'd put together for his cough. The stuff seemed to help, and it sure did please his tasters. Even though her cooking had proved spotty—like the burnt beans and biscuits from last night—most of the things she produced in the kitchen were just short of heavenly.

She turned back to face him with scissors in one hand, a comb in the other, and a cloth draped over her arm. He raised the mug to his lips as she approached, doing his best not to show how much her nearness put him on edge.

After setting the tools on the table, she stepped behind him and draped the cloth over his shoulders, the scent of cinnamon floating up. Other than his first evening home last week, he'd not smelled that wonderful, spicy aroma in years. What was it that made the scent cling to her now?

When her fingers slipped through his hair, he froze. Every bit of breath stalled in his chest. His lungs wouldn't work.

Then he felt the bite of the comb against his head, and his muscles eased. A little anyway. He forced himself to focus on breathing—in and out—but his mind wouldn't cooperate very well.

When was the last time a woman had touched him? Other than Mum or some of the gray-haired Crow women when he ate in their camp...never.

What was running through Miss Donaghue's mind as she worked the comb and scissors through his hair? That he'd made an awful mess with the razor? Probably, since the damage had been obvious enough for Mum to notice, even in her confused state.

Had she ever trimmed a man's hair before? She said she had two brothers, so surely she had. What must she think of him?

But this line of questioning wasn't helping his heart rate slow any. He forced his mind onto his Crow friends. Had Akecheta and the others found better hunting in their new winter camp? Maybe he should have gone with them.

He gave himself a mental slap. If he'd gone with them, he wouldn't have come home early and still wouldn't know about Pa and Mum. He wouldn't be here to help. Not that he was all that helpful anyway. He wanted to be, but Miss Donaghue seemed to have everything under control.

At least he could handle things with the animals. As soon as this little session was over, he'd ride over to O'Hennessey's and see about the cattle. The man had been a good neighbor. Quiet enough, but pleasant the few times he'd come over for a visit. Now that Reuben was home, though, they didn't need the man's charity any longer.

A soft, cool hand touched his cheek, and he sucked in a breath. The distractions just weren't working. Her cinnamon scent surrounded him, soaking into his pores in an intoxicating aroma. How much longer until she was done? At least she hadn't been chattering the whole time. Trying to make conversation with her so near, touching him...that would have pushed him to the edge of control.

~

*C*athleen forced another breath into her lungs as she trimmed the hair behind Reuben's right ear. Trying to think of him as a patient simply wasn't working. Even the man's ears were perfect, neatly set and just the right size.

And the feel of his thick locks. Everything about him was masculine and wild, yet his hair was soft as silk. But she refused to allow herself to stop and enjoy the touch of it.

As she shifted over to trim his right sideburn, her little finger grazed his cheek. She froze. Did he just flinch under her touch? Did he feel the same tingle that ran up her hand when their skin met?

She glanced at the spot and frowned. A red line marred the skin, a cut that had recently scabbed over. From shaving most likely. Her eyes ran over the rest of his cheek, as far as she could see from her position behind him. She moved around to his side, noting the muscle play in his jaw as he swallowed, and the way his Adam's apple bobbed in his throat.

As her eyes tracked down his neck, more cuts spoiled the smooth skin, some red and inflamed.

She turned away and moved to the shelf where she'd stored her medicines. The first salve her hand found was the one she was looking for. The same one she used on his mother's many abrasions.

Spinning back to Reuben, she made a point of not meeting his gaze, even though she could feel it tracking her progress as she made her way to him. "I'm just going to put this salve on your cuts."

"No need to bother."

Was it just her, or did his voice sound more hoarse than its usual rich fullness? Of course, she didn't hear it often enough to be sure. "It's no bother. This will keep them from getting infected."

He didn't speak again, and she stood as far back as possible while she dabbed the cream onto the angry marks. That done, she eased out a breath and forced all her focus back onto his hair.

When she'd finally trimmed all the way around his head, Cathleen eyed her work from behind, then from either side. A few more snips to make the left side even with the right. It'd been a while since she'd trimmed a man's hair, not since Mum was sick a couple years back, but she'd done a decent job this time. Honestly, with the way Reuben's face was so perfectly proportioned in strong features, she could have hacked a few chunks out and called it done, and he still would have stolen her breath every time she looked at him.

She ran her fingers through the thickest part in the back one final time, relishing the luxury of it. Then she stepped away. "All right. Go look in the mirror and see if you like it." She pulled the cloth from his shirt and carried her tools to the work counter. After standing so close for so long, a bit of distance was a good thing.

"It's fine. Much obliged, ma'am." He walked out the door.

~

*C*athleen pulled the fur cap tighter on her head as she slipped into the barn later that afternoon. Reuben had gone to the neighbor's to check the cows, but he'd mentioned a mare in the barn whose foaling could be imminent. Something about the way he'd said it pressed concern into her chest. And since Mrs. Scott seemed to be deeply entrenched in a nap in her chair by the fire—Reuben's dog nestled by her feet—a quick check on the mare couldn't hurt.

She slipped down the row of stalls, peering into each one. All the animals looked to be in the corral, as they should be. The stalls were cleaned, the hay stacked in a corner of each for the night's feeding. Reuben did keep the place neat, that was for certain. Much more than she had before his arrival.

The mare was the only horse in the barn and stood dozing in a back corner of her stall. "Hey, girl. I hear you're going to have a baby." As she watched, the horse shifted from one back foot to the other, like she couldn't quite get comfortable under the weight of her hefty abdomen. But her head stayed in that sleepy, lowered position.

Cathleen wanted to slip into the stall and pet the mare, but would the animal object? From the look of things, she was docile enough. She raised the bar holding the door closed and slipped inside.

The horse's thick wool-like hair was softer than Cathleen had expected as she ran her hand down the reddish-brown neck. "What's your name, girl?" The mare answered by bringing her head around to nuzzle Cathleen's elbow. She'd not spent much time around horses in the past. Mostly buggy rides back in Boston and the few times she'd ridden since she came to Butte. And of course that five hour ride up the mountain to this homestead. This horse seemed different than the others she'd ridden, though. She had a mellowness that was relaxing, yet the keen look in her eyes bespoke intelligence.

Cathleen ran her hand down the horse's abdomen, taking a step back to eye the whole of her. A flash of white pulled her eye, down in the shadows of the mare's hind legs. She leaned closer, but not so close she was in danger of being kicked by those powerful limbs. Drips of white liquid fell from the mare's udder and splashed on the dark hair below. The horse was leaking milk? Was that normal? She'd never been close to a female horse right before birth. If the mare kept this up, would she have enough milk to feed the foal when it arrived?

Stepping back, Cathleen gave the horse a final pat on the shoulder, then slipped from the stall. Who knew when Reuben would return, but maybe Mrs. Scott would know what to do. Surely the woman had seen enough foals born to have the process deeply engrained in the recesses of her memory.

In her more lucid moments, Mrs. Scott had shared some sweet—and sometimes humorous—memories from the early days of their time in these mountains. Some even included Reuben's adventures. Like the time he'd sneaked away early one morning, riding atop one of the plow horses. He'd been five at the time, and Mrs. Scott had thought him merely sleeping late. It wasn't until Mr. Scott missed the plow horse that they discovered their son gone also.

It took two hours to find him that morning, and even after he was returned home safe and sound—although a little sore on his rump—that first taste of freedom had stuck with him. Of course, he didn't ever leave again without telling them goodbye. Mrs. Scott's face had held a mixture of pride and sadness with those last words.

Cathleen's chest squeezed as she thought about the mother's love that was so obviously strong in Mrs. Scott, even in her confusion.

After stomping her boots on the front porch to clear the snow, she lifted the latch string and pushed open the cabin door. It took a second for her eyes to adjust to the dim light inside, especially after the brightness of sunlight on snow outside. As Cathleen peeled off her wool gloves, her gaze searched out Mrs. Scott's chair.

Empty. She scanned the room, but no movement stirred.

"Mrs. Scott?" Cathleen surged forward to check the woman's room. She'd been sound asleep just minutes before, but maybe she'd awoken and wandered into the bed chamber to retrieve something.

The cool room was utterly still. No Mrs. Scott in sight. Cathleen bobbed around the wall into her own chamber.

"Mrs. Scott?" The concern planted only moments before now flamed into panic. "Mrs. Scott, can you hear me?"

Slipping her gloves back on, Cathleen charged toward the cabin door and pushed outside. On the porch, she stalled, scanning the yard around her. The snow was still six or eight inches deep in most places, but footprints marred the surface everywhere she looked. Where would the woman go?

The outhouse. She leapt off the porch, skipping the steps

completely so their slippery surface didn't slow her down. She'd become adept at maneuvering through the snow and made it to the outhouse door in seconds.

She was panting, though, and had to swallow hard to get enough moisture in her mouth to speak. "Mrs. Scott?" She banged on the door. "Are you in there, ma'am?"

No answer. No sound at all.

She gripped the handle and pulled. Empty.

"Oh, God, where is she?" Panic clawed in her chest like a wild animal, fighting for release.

She started for the chicken shed. Maybe the older woman had gone to collect eggs or kill a chicken for supper like that first day Bryan found her. But if she wasn't there, where else could Cathleen look?

"Mrs. Scott!" She yelled as loudly as she could while running.

Then a horrific sound filled the air. Barks or the cries of wild animals or something. Cathleen's heart stopped as she veered that direction, a prayer rising to her lips. "Oh, God. No!"

CHAPTER 8

*T*he sounds didn't stop, and echoes filled the woods on the back side of the cabin. Cathleen plunged into the trees, praying with every frantic beat of her heart. Visions swam through her mind of Mrs. Scott lying in a pool of blood, North bravely defending her to his death. How had she let this happen?

Movement filtered into view through the trees ahead. The wild growls, barks, and yelps sounded like they came from dogs...several dogs. Wolves? She could only see a flurry of gray and white through the brush. And then a taller brown figure, looming over them.

Mrs. Scott.

Cathleen's fear gave way to a scream as she plunged through the last of the saplings hiding the group.

Mrs. Scott held a stick in both hands, slamming it down onto two animals writhing on the ground. The ferocious noises coming from the dogs had risen to a deafening scale, and the woman was close enough to be knocked over and dragged into the mix.

One of the creatures was, indeed, North. The other was a flurry of gray hair, half the size of North, but quick and wiry. She caught a flash of white teeth from the beast, just before Mrs. Scott landed a hard blow on its head.

It yelped, and Cathleen grabbed the stick from the woman and took over the attack. She screamed and yelled, but she couldn't even hear her own voice amidst the din.

The creature had a solid hold on North's flank with its powerful jaw, and she swung blow after blow at its head. One of her harder efforts connected with the side of the creature's muzzle, and it yelped, then it released the dog and leapt backward.

She honed in on the victory with something akin to a battle cry, slashing at the creature with all her might. It slunk backward, just out of reach, but baring its teeth in a growl that seized her chest.

But she didn't relent. Another blow swiped within a few inches of the animal's head. It yelped again, then spun in a low crouch and sprinted away.

When it disappeared through the trees, an eerie silence took over the area. She was shaking, and she had to lock her knees to keep from collapsing. But the worst was probably yet to come. She turned back to face the damage behind her.

Mrs. Scott leaned over the furry form of North, the white dog almost blending into the snow except for bright patches of crimson. The woman murmured shaky words to him as her fingers prodded the bloody fur.

Cathleen dropped to her knees beside him. "What's wrong, boy?"

He raised his head, and those trusting eyes had a sheen of sadness over them. A whine drifted from him, even as his tail thumped the slightest bit in the snow. At least he was breathing and aware.

She glanced up at Mrs. Scott to make sure the woman hadn't been injured in the fight. A swipe of blood marred her hand, but that could be North's blood. Otherwise, she appeared to be whole.

Forcing her hands to stop trembling, Cathleen slipped them into North's fur and began to investigate the bloody areas. He had a patch of missing skin on his nose, probably from claws. A bit of blood at the throat, but that wound didn't look as deep as she feared. It'd not hit a vein, at least. The worst of it seemed to be his rump, where several missing chunks of hair revealed deeper layers of inner flesh, and maybe even muscle. Blood oozed out of him in steady succession, but at least dogs didn't have major arteries in that area. Did they? She had to get him back to the house.

She eyed their surroundings to get her bearings, then glanced at Mrs. Scott. The woman had at least remembered to grab her coat and shoes, although no gloves or hat. This frigid air couldn't be good for her feet, nor any other part of her.

Her gaze tracked back down to North. The dog had to be more than half her weight, and came almost to her waist when he stood on all fours. No matter how she carried him, she wouldn't be able to stop it from being painful. But she'd have to do her best.

Slipping off her coat, she draped it over the animal, wrapping it under him as she positioned her arms at his chest and hindquarters, then lifted. His soft whimper was almost lost in her grunts as she struggled to stand upright with the load. More than half her weight? The dog stood a better chance of carrying her than she did him.

But she gritted her teeth and started walking. "Let's get him back to the house, Mrs. Scott. Can you walk with me?"

The woman followed, but their progress was slow with her unsteady steps through the deep, virgin snow. Cathleen watched for tracks that might show the trail Mrs. Scott and the dog had taken to get to this place, but saw only her own frantic strides. How long had they been out that they'd wandered this far? And what would have happened if she'd arrived even minutes later?

The muscles in her arms had turned to mush by the time they stepped into the clearing. Cathleen glanced at the woman beside her. "I'm going to take the dog inside the house. Will you come help me tend him?" She couldn't keep up this slow pace much longer, and maybe Mrs. Scott would follow her inside if she felt an urgent need to help.

The woman waved her forward. "Go on, dearie. I'll be right there."

Relief washed through her, and she trudged forward as fast as her tired legs would carry her. After stumbling up the steps and through the cabin door, Cathleen aimed for the open area in front of the fire. North seemed to be shivering, although she couldn't be sure if that was from cold or pain.

After easing him down, she peeled back the coat she'd wrapped around him. The cloth came away bloody where it had touched his haunches. She parted the thick white hair to get a better look at the wound, but the dim light of the cabin made it difficult.

She stroked a hand over his head. "Stay here, boy, while I get a lantern." After lighting a lamp and gathering her medicine kit, Cathleen glanced at the door. She'd better go make sure Mrs. Scott made it inside before she tended the dog.

But a soft tread on the porch saved her the trouble. Cathleen opened the door and helped the woman inside. "Will you sit and talk to the dog while I warm some water to clean his wounds?"

"You do what you need to. North and I will be just fine." At least Mrs. Scott remembered the dog's name. Cathleen helped her into the chair near North's head and moved to the stove. She still wasn't sure whether the injuries were life-threatening, but she'd need clean water no matter what.

With a light to see by and supplies gathered close, Cathleen cleaned the dog's wounds. The rump was definitely the worst part. The skin had been ripped away to reveal a goodly portion of muscle and deep flesh tissue. Her stomach churned at the sight, but she pressed the feeling down. She had to think like a doctor here. Clinical. A whine from North nearly sidetracked her intentions, but she forced her focus back on the injury.

After cleansing and sprinkling powdered cayenne pepper in the wound, she covered it as well as she could. Dad and both her brothers said the pepper worked wonders to stop bleeding and start the healing process. *Lord, please let it work this time, too.*

North lay with his head on her coat throughout her ministrations. His quivers gradually subsided to panting, which tugged at her heart even more. She stroked his head and neck. "I'm sorry, boy. You were so brave." His eyes, dark and soulful, met hers, but he still didn't raise his head. She stroked his favorite spot behind his ear, careful not to get close to the wounds at his neck.

What a special animal this was. Loyal to the bitter end. He'd stopped panting now but lay with his mouth slightly ajar and his eyes at half-mast, like it was a struggle just to be awake.

A knot formed in her throat, burning its way up to sting her eyes. "You can't die on me, boy. I know it hurts, but you have to pull through."

He didn't raise his head, but his tail stroked the floor in a half-wag. Which only brought the tears closer to the edge of her control. What could she do to ease his suffering? Maybe a bit of stewed beef from supper last night would be a welcome treat.

She rose to get it, and when she returned, Mrs. Scott had taken up a steady humming. The woman swayed to the rhythm as she sat in her overstuffed chair and picked at the blanket on her lap. The tune was familiar, one they'd sung so many times at her church in Boston. "Rock of Ages, Cleft for Me."

The melody washed over Cathleen as she knelt beside the dog, and she could feel the easing of her tight shoulder muscles. But when she held the bowl of broth and beef under his nose, North gave it only a tiny lick, still not raising his head from the floor.

"Come on, boy." Her voice cracked on a sob, but she forced the emotion back down inside. What else could she try? One of her herbal teas from the kit Bryan left? While her mind played through the possibilities, she stroked the sweet dog's head over and over. He started panting again, although it was more of a gentle tongue lolling as his head still relaxed against the floor.

Had he gone into traumatic shock? If only she'd spent more time helping her brothers in the clinic these past months. She would know the signs better. She'd know what to do to help this poor animal who'd given of himself completely to protect Mrs. Scott.

A noise sounded on the porch, and Cathleen's shoulders tensed. For the quickest of seconds, the image of that wild animal flashed through her mind, skulking back for revenge.

But no. It had to be Reuben. The waning daylight through the small window meant it was time for his return. And maybe...just maybe he'd know what to do to help this hurting dog. A glance at the animal's cloudy gaze revealed the depth of his pain, and it brought a fresh burning to her eyes. She was supposed to be the nurse here, but she had no idea what else would make him feel better.

The cabin door opened, and she glanced up to catch Reuben's expression. How could she tell him she'd allowed his ailing mother to wander through the snowy woods, be attacked by a savage animal, and now his courageous dog may not live because of it? All because of her.

His gaze swept the room as he pulled off his hood and gloves. His focus stalled when he saw her crouched over the furry mass of North's body. The concern that settled over his face—nay, the fear—broke through the defense she'd built against her tears.

"I'm sorry, Reuben." Her words were barely audible even to her own ears, and she turned back to the dog as the depth of her anguish spilled down her face.

He was by her side in a second. "What happened?" He stroked the dog's head, pushing back the thick white fur to examine each wound.

"It was a wild dog, or wolf, or some kind of creature. I'd just gone to the barn to check the mare while your mum was asleep." Sobs interrupted as the story poured out of her. "I wasn't out long, I promise. But she was gone and I looked everywhere. Then I heard this awful commotion."

Emotion wrenched from her as she told about the creature attacking North and how long it had fought until finally skulking away through the woods.

Then the extent of North's injuries. She sniffed hard to control some of her tears and steady her voice. "I washed and treated his hip with cayenne powder, but he seems to be in so much pain. I just..." Another sob broke through, and she closed her eyes against the flow.

Her tears might seem irrational to him, maybe childish and unnecessary. But the weight of all the uncertainty she'd fought since coming to this homestead pressed down on her. She'd worked so hard, yet still there was so much she didn't know. So many things she still got wrong. She should have never left Mrs. Scott alone. That one choice could have cost the sweet woman her life.

And now that the torrent had started, she was powerless to stop it.

"Hey."

Strong fingers touched her chin, and her eyes flew open. Intense blue met her gaze, earnestness smoldering there.

"It's not your fault, Cathleen. You've done everything he needs." A softening found his eyes. "I'm not even sure I would have thought of using the pepper."

She inhaled a sob, wiping underneath one eye with a sleeve. The heat from his hand warmed her face. "It's a remedy I used a lot in Boston."

A single raised brow. "You have a lot of wolf attacks in Boston, do you?"

Something about his tenderness washed through her like a warm, soothing tea. The perfect blend to ease her frayed nerves.

With a final stroke of his thumb on her chin, he removed his hand and turned to the dog. "How ya feelin', boy?"

North raised his head a few inches, and his tail thumped twice.

"You're enjoyin' the attention, eh?"

Reuben's hands probed over the dog, hovering at his neck before moving on to the remainder of him. "His pulse seems strong and steady. No broken bones that I can tell." His hand stroked the animal's head again, pressing the hair back to reveal the dedication shining in North's eyes.

"He's going to be all right." Reuben's gaze found hers once more. "Everything's going to be all right."

Cathleen eased out a long breath. If only she could be as certain. *Lord, please let him live.*

CHAPTER 9

*R*euben stole a glance at the woman beside him. Seeing her so devastated about the dog had cut deeper than he ever would have expected. And she talked like she thought she was responsible. This woman did so much to keep the place going, then used her last spare moment to check on Tashunka for him, and now she thought Mum's wandering was her own fault?

The image she'd painted of beating off the wolf had formed a vivid picture in his mind. Snarling teeth. The animal must have been half-starved to attack the way he did. Wolves were usually skittish around people, only attacking weak or feeble animals. And usually they traveled in packs. A burn squeezed his chest. If the animal was rabid though, that would explain the fierce attack.

He turned to the woman. "Did it bite you? The wolf?" His eyes roamed her figure, searching for blood or torn fabric.

"No. I'm fine. Only North." She leaned close to stroke the dog's head and murmured soft words in his ear. If fear wasn't surging through his veins, he might have been jealous.

"Did it foam at the mouth? Or maybe have blood in its spit?"

She looked up at him, confusion clouding her eyes. "I don't…" And then understanding slipped over her, and she sat up straight. "You think it was rabid?"

The fear that touched her face didn't settle well in his gut. "I don't know. Probably not, but we need to make sure." He softened his voice as much as he could. "Tell me what it looked like."

Her forehead scrunched as she rocked back on her heels. "He was sort of a mottled gray. Not as big as North. He probably came up to here on me." She touched a spot not far below her hip, and his mouth went dry as his gaze followed her motion. If he let his mind go there, he'd be in real trouble.

He swallowed and forced his eyes back up to her face. There was a bit more pink on her cheeks than a moment ago, and she didn't meet his gaze.

He cleared his throat. "Tell me what the animal did."

That furrowed brow again. "He and North were both growling and all tangled up in a snarl. When I got close, his jaw was locked on North's rump. I took the stick from your mum and started beating his head. I made contact a few times, and he finally broke loose."

"Did he turn on you?"

"No. He acted stunned at first, then growled. I kept swinging the stick at him and screaming, and he finally turned and ran away."

He did his best to hold back a grin at the picture that formed in his mind. For a city girl, this woman had spunk. For that matter, she had spunk for a mountain girl.

"What do you think?"

He met her gaze, which was solemnly fixed on his face. "If he didn't go after you, and you didn't see any of the rabies signs, he was probably just a hungry wolf separated from the pack. This winter's been hard with all the extra snow and cold. Not as much game to feed on. He probably sensed Mum was an easy target, then once he got started with the attack, couldn't bring himself to give in till he knew he was beat." By a sassy slip of a city girl, at that.

Her shoulders relaxed a bit. "You really think so?"

"I do." At least he hoped it. They'd need to keep a close eye on North these next few days to be sure.

Something like a smile touched her eyes, playing with one corner of her mouth. He wasn't one to use big words, but *intriguing* was the only thing that properly described her look.

"What?"

"I think that's the most I've heard you speak yet."

The heat that flushed through him lit his face like fire. He turned away and slipped off his coat, both to chase off the warmth and to conceal his color from her sparkling eyes. This woman knew how to unravel him like no one else.

She rose to her feet, leaving the space beside him empty. And cold, without the warmth of her nearness.

"I need to get started on dinner." She spoke loudly, most likely to include Mum in the conversation. "Mrs. Scott, would you like to come into the kitchen? I could use your help to make sure I get everything right."

Mum patted her hand, then allowed Cathleen to help her up. "Oh, you do fine, dearie. But I'll be glad to come if you need me."

The pair shuffled along toward the kitchen area, Cathleen moving with the patience of Job.

Then her step faltered, and she spun to face him. "Your horse. I forgot. She's losing all her milk. Is there something we can do to stop it?"

His chest surged. Tash was getting close to her time, probably tonight. But the worried look on this woman's face did something even more unusual in his chest. "That's good she's leaking. Means she's almost ready."

Those lines appeared on her forehead again. "But don't we need to stop it? Or catch the milk and save it for the baby? What if she runs out?"

Her sweet innocence. He had the sudden urge to close the distance between them and fold her into his arms. Definitely not what he should be feeling toward his mother's nurse.

"Reuben?"

He pulled himself back from his thoughts and turned away so he didn't have to look into those expressive eyes. "Tashunka usually leaks the day before she foals. I'll go check on her."

"Tashunka? That's her name? What does it mean?"

He met her gaze then, studying her expression while he spoke the next words. "It's Sioux. Means horse."

Her eyes widened a bit, and she tilted her head. "Sioux Indian? Do you know the language?"

"My Crow friends have taught me some."

He had to give her credit for controlling her reactions. It wasn't fear that registered on her face, not even shock. Maybe curiosity. Maybe there was a tinge of fear, but nothing like most people who came here from the East. One more point for courage on her long list of abilities.

Rising to his feet, Reuben grabbed his coat. "I'll go check on Tash." A bit of cold air might be what he needed to clear his head.

The mare nickered when he approached her stall, and she *was* dripping milk like Cathleen had said. Her muscles seemed relaxed, though, so she hadn't started the foaling process quite yet. It looked like he'd be sleeping in the barn tonight, despite what their stubborn nurse might demand.

After tossing the mare a bit of extra hay, he headed out to the edge of the clearing. It wasn't hard to find their tracks from earlier that day. Both the long running strides of the woman as she ran toward the attack, then the deeper, unsteady prints where she carried North back to the house, tracking beside Mum's lightweight tread. It was a miracle Cathleen could even lift the dog. North was about the size of a small bear. And just as fiercely protective as a mother bear with her cubs.

What would have happened during the episode if North hadn't been there? Mum would have been killed by the wolf, most likely.

That thought sluiced pure fear through him.

At last he came on the scene, and the gore of it churned his gut. Blood had been tromped into the snow in a wide circle. The snow was so thoroughly churned in the area, it took a moment for him to find the tracks of the attacking animal.

There, heading away from the house, he found the prints it left as it retreated. The paw seemed a little smaller than a full-sized wolf. Maybe the animal wasn't quite full-grown, or maybe it was a wolf-dog mix. But it had to have wolf blood running through it, because it tracked in a straight trotting line, both as it had seemed to follow Mum and North's trail, and again as it had fled the scene. The steadiness of the tracks tended to confirm the animal wasn't rabid. Right?

He could only hope.

~

Cathleen sank into the strains of *Silent Night*, harmonizing her soprano over Mrs. Scott's steady alto melody. She'd only sung this tune at Christmastime before coming to the mountain, but it was one of Mrs. Scott's favorites, and it seemed to soothe North now as Cathleen sat beside him.

With the potatoes simmering into soup on the stove, supper would be ready whenever Reuben came in. She'd finally gotten the dog to drink a bit of willow bark tea. He seemed much more relaxed now, and the music worked its magic to calm all three of them. She'd noticed that about Mrs. Scott lately. Any time the woman's nerves were especially on edge, singing one of the old hymns helped soothe and refocus her.

The cabin door opened, and Cathleen spun to face the intruder, stopping her song in the middle of the word "heavenly." She'd not heard a tread on the porch. Could it be an animal had pushed the door open?

But it was Reuben who stepped inside, and her sense of relief at the sight of his hooded fur coat was perhaps a little stronger than the situation warranted. Her nerves must be worse off than she'd thought.

She kept her hand moving in steady strokes over North's head and back as she watched Reuben shed his gloves and coat. She was getting used to his towering presence now for the most part, but from this angle, he may as well have been a giant. But a gentle one, quiet and contemplative. And every so often, she glimpsed a depth of feeling in his penetrating blue eyes that intrigued her more than a little. What would it be like to really know this man? To hear his thoughts and understand his deepest emotions?

"How's he feeling?"

Reuben's words pulled her from her daydreams. Good thing, too, because she'd been staring. "He drank some willow tea, so he seems to be resting better now. How's the mare? Tashunka?" The word felt strange on her tongue. Hopefully she'd pronounced it correctly. With the high-low sounds Reuben had used.

He stepped closer and crouched beside her, his presence extracting all the air from the room. At least from her lungs. "I imagine she'll foal tonight. I'll go check her again in a bit."

She swallowed to force moisture into her mouth. "You were gone a long time. I was about to come check on you both." A silly thing to say. As if she could do anything to help this man, with all his skills and innate understanding of animals.

He slanted a look at her, those blue eyes twinkling and his mouth tipping in a smile. That look was worth embarrassing herself any day.

"I went out to check the area where the wolf attacked."

The smile left her spirit as quickly as his words sank in. She searched his gaze. "You're sure it was a wolf then?"

"I think so. A small wolf or wolf-dog. I'm pretty sure it wasn't rabid. Just hungry and not willing to give up a meal without a fight." He tapped her chin with the lightest of touches. "You were more than he bargained for, though."

Whether it was the warmth of his touch, his words, or just the power of his nearness, she almost melted right there on the floor. Sheer will power alone kept her upright, but it couldn't stop her from soaking into his gaze.

A gurgling sound from the stove finally broke through her awareness, jerking her from the pleasant warmth of the moment.

"The soup." She scrambled up and scurried to the pot, which was, indeed, bubbling over. The stove's surface seared the thick liquid, sending a scorched aroma through the room. After yanking the lid from the pot and stirring vigorously, the liquid eased and settled into a rolling boil.

She turned back to face Reuben and his mother, both watching her with varying degrees of humor and curiosity. Even the dog had raised his head to watch her flurry of activity. She forced the brightest smile she could muster. "Supper's ready."

Reuben helped his mum to the table, and Cathleen couldn't resist watching the pair as he settled her in her chair and tucked the serviette in her lap. He was remarkably gentle with his mum, the depth of his love reflected in each action. Such a kind man. Who would have thought?

CHAPTER 10

*W*hen they were all seated, Cathleen glanced at Reuben to find his head already bowed. Thus far, she'd prayed to bless the food at each meal, but maybe it was presumptuous of her to do the honors every time. "Reuben, you're welcome to say grace if you'd like."

He raised his head just enough to peer at her from under his lashes. "No. Thanks. You do fine."

Hmm… She'd have to examine that response later. For now, she closed her eyes and breathed in the peace that always soaked through her when she spoke with the Father. Along with a blessing over the food—such as it was—she sent up a heartfelt plea for North's recovery, as well as the mare preparing to give birth in the barn. The deep tenor of Reuben's "Amen" joined her own, along with the quiver of Mrs. Scott's sweet voice.

When she opened her eyes, she sent a glance toward Reuben and caught his gaze on her. She often found him watching her over their meals, and it would be easier to distract herself if he didn't sit directly across from her. But this look seemed different. Curious. Like he wanted to ask something, but didn't know how.

She met the look with a smile. "Everything all right?" She half expected him to drop his focus to his food and shrug off the question.

But he didn't. If anything, his gaze intensified. "I've never heard anyone pray like you."

For once, she had no idea how to respond. But she could feel the heat creeping up her neck, and she glanced down at the bowl in front of her. "I just talk to God. It's nothing special."

He was quiet, and when she finally chanced another look at him, he was still watching her. His eyes had a bit of a squint to them, like he was calculating something. For the thousandth time since meeting this man, she wished she could see into his mind. Have some inkling of what he was thinking.

But that wasn't to be, apparently. She took a spoonful of soup, and he did the same.

He downed his first bowlful in seconds, then reached to fill it again from the pot in the center of the table. "I'll check Pa's rifle tonight and make sure it's clean and loaded. Then I want you to carry it when you leave the cabin. Every time. Even if you're just going to the privy."

Cathleen forced her bite of soup down so she didn't choke on it. "A rifle?" She studied him, but nothing about his features looked like he'd jested. In fact, he was still spooning soup down his throat like she might jerk the bowl away before he finished.

He must believe she actually knew how to shoot the gun. Would he think less of her when he learned the truth? Maybe she should keep her mouth shut and try to learn on her own. Mrs. Scott might be able to teach her the basics. The woman seemed able to recall most of the tasks that were deeply ingrained in her memory. Although she was a bit shaky with them, and sometimes left out steps.

It might not be a good idea to take chances with an instrument that could so easily end a life. Her life. Or Mrs. Scott's.

She summoned courage and tried her best to keep her voice level. Casual. "I've actually never shot a rifle before."

That stilled him. He slowly raised his head, those dark brows lowering so they almost covered the blue of his eyes. "You haven't?" His voice dripped with sheer disbelief. Maybe even a hint of irritation.

And that last bit did more to raise her hackles than if he'd laughed out loud at her.

She squared her shoulders. "No. I haven't. You may remember, I lived in Boston until last fall. We didn't have much cause to hunt our own game or fight off rabid wolves."

The expression in his eyes disappeared, covered by that mask he wore so well, and he dropped his focus back to spoon a potato from his bowl.

His silence alone was enough to chastise her, and it stretched for long minutes. She knew better than to spout off when someone was trying to help her. And with this man especially…who'd just started opening up to her.

She took in a steadying breath. "Reuben, I'm sorry—"

"Don't worry about it." His voice didn't sound angry, but the clipped words spoke a clear end to the subject. Should she try again to soften the tension that now hovered between them? Or maybe he didn't feel it. Who knew with this man?

And did it really matter if she knew how to shoot a gun since she'd be going home soon? Even though the thought made the food roil in her stomach. She'd have to face the inevitable soon. But not yet. Mrs. Scott and her son weren't ready yet.

As soon as she finished her soup, Cathleen rose from the table and filled a plate of broth for North. He licked most of it before dropping his head back to the floor. She stroked him, staring into those mournful black eyes. They didn't reflect as much pain as they had earlier—probably the willow bark helping—but the sight of such a magnificent animal reduced like this, closed off the breathing in her throat.

"Guess I'll get started on these dishes. Quinn, you do make more mess than one o' those hogs." Mrs. Scott's grumbled words pulled Cathleen's attention from the dog. The woman was already rising, stacking plates and shuffling around the table.

Cathleen needed to help, especially before Mrs. Scott tried to heat water on the stove. She couldn't afford another burn. After a final stroke over North's head, Cathleen positioned her hands to push herself up.

North raised his head too, then scrambled in an effort to stand.

"No, boy." She lowered herself back to the floor and reached to help the dog lay down again. He'd not quite gotten his haunches underneath him, and seemed relieved to sink back in the softness of her coat that still padded his bed. "You have to stay here."

Once he was settled, she tried again to ease herself away, but the dog started to rise again. "No, North." Frustration and worry were starting to mingle in her chest. She had to go help Mrs. Scott before the woman burned herself, but she couldn't chance North rising and injuring himself further.

She darted a look at Reuben, still sitting at the table. As usual, he was watching her. What was the man waiting for? He could have stepped in to help any time. Dare she ask him to?

She forced a smile. "Would you mind sitting with North while I help your mum?"

He raised a brow, one corner of his mouth twitching. "I think he's playing on your sympathies." But he rose and came over.

While he knelt beside the dog to distract it, Cathleen was able to scoot away. "I'll get some water heated for those dishes." She stepped beside Mrs. Scott and helped ease the plates from her hands into the dry sink.

The two of them settled into their normal after-dinner routine, with Cathleen gently guiding the older woman in small tasks where she wouldn't injure herself.

"Is this your coat?"

Reuben's quiet comment caught her up short. She'd almost forgotten he was still in the room. She turned to study him as he held up what looked to be a sleeve from under North. "Yes. I need to get him some better bedding, but that's what I carried him back in."

It was dim in the corner of the room where Reuben sat, so she couldn't see the nuances in his expression, but those looked like scowl lines across his forehead. Without another word, he rose to his full, massive height and headed into his mother's bed chamber. Peculiar.

A rustling noise drifted from that room, but she did her best to ignore it as she scrubbed the soup pot. This was his mother's home—or his really, since he was the man of the family now. If he wanted to dig around back there, it wasn't any of her business.

But she'd never been good at containing her curiosity.

He finally returned a few minutes later, and she tried not to be obvious as she craned her neck to see what he would do next. Something large and fluffy draped across his arms, as he came to stand by the table. "Here's something that might help."

She dried her hands on a cloth, then turned to study the object. "What it is?" Some kind of fur. A blanket, perhaps?

He held it up, and the mass began to take shape. And what a shape. Tan buckskin formed a coat. Darker fur lined the inside and peeked out at each opening. Some kind of beading formed designs on both side panels, and she stepped closer to get a better look.

The beadwork took the shape of animals. A bear, standing tall on its hind feet in front of a cave. A mountain lion prowling on a leafless limb. The amount of detail in the art was remarkable.

Reaching out to touch the handwork, her skin brushed across the leather. So soft, she had to catch her breath. "Reuben." Her gaze wandered up to his and found those blue eyes watching her—their intensity stronger than usual. "This is… I've never seen anything like it. Whose…?" She wasn't making sense of her words.

He cleared his throat. "I made it last winter for Mum. I don't think she's used it, though. Said she wanted to wait till her old coat wore out. You need something heavier than what you've been wearing." He glanced over his shoulder at the dog. "I'm not sure it'll come clean anyway."

Cathleen swallowed down the lump forming in her throat. "I can't wear this, Reuben. It's exquisite." He must have spent weeks on the detailed work.

"That's why I remembered it. Reminds me of you."

The way those blue eyes drilled into her… If she'd had trouble breathing before, it was nothing compared to the pressure on her chest now. She might have a better chance if she could only look away from their intensity.

"Please. I want you to wear it."

She fingered the thick fur lining. Even softer than the buckskin on the outside. "But it's your mum's."

"She would want you to wear it too."

Again, she had to swallow. He sounded certain. "All right."

He held it toward her, shifting his hands so they gripped each shoulder of the coat.

As she slipped her left hand into its sleeve, then her right, it seemed almost like she'd fallen into a dream world. The sheer luxury of the fur inside muddled her senses.

"The lining is red fox."

She turned back to face him, extending her arms as she assessed the look and feel of the coat. It reached partway down her thigh, and fit perfectly through her shoulders. Not too restricting, despite its thickness.

"Perfect."

She didn't try to hold back her smile as she looked up at him. "It is, isn't it?"

But something in his eyes didn't seem like he was talking about the coat. Surely, he didn't mean her. But she'd not seen this look of male appreciation in his gaze before. And it sent a heat surging through her that certainly wasn't helped by the coat.

Slipping out of it, she carefully smoothed the sleeves. "It's lovely, Reuben. I'll take special care of it. Thank you." She couldn't quite meet his gaze this time.

Which meant she didn't have a chance to read his expression as he turned and walked out of the cabin.

CHAPTER 11

*I*t must have been an hour later when Cathleen heard Reuben's tread on the porch. Darkness had fallen outside the little window, and with the kitchen set to rights, she and Mrs. Scott had taken up their usual places by the fire.

Mrs. Scott's fingers worked at a blanket she was crocheting. Cathleen tried to keep her focus in the passage she'd been reading from First Corinthians, but her wayward attention drifted to the doorway as soon as Reuben's footstep sounded on the porch.

He entered and shucked his winter things. He didn't glance her way. "Animals are bedded down for the night."

She licked her lips to bring moisture to them. "How's…Tashunka?" Hopefully, she remembered the name correctly.

"Looks the same. I'll get my things and sleep out there tonight."

She opened her mouth to protest, then closed it again. Maybe that was necessary for the horse. She'd never been privy to the foaling process. But she couldn't help asking, "How's your cough?"

"Fine." The glare he sent was likely meant to put her in her place, but it only riled her nurturing instincts.

Laying her Bible on the side table, she pushed to her feet. "I'll get some extra quilts."

"I'm fine."

The bark in his words stopped her forward motion, and she eyed him.

"I'll be fine." A much softer tone this time, almost apologetic. "I'll sleep in my coat, and I have a good bearskin to cover me. You don't need to worry."

Her lower lip found its way between her teeth. Did he think her overbearing? "All right."

He moved to the corner where his gear formed an organized stack and started rifling through it. She had to give the man credit for neatness. Every morning when she came in from the outhouse, his bedding was folded and tucked in that corner. Certainly not something her brothers would have done. Dad either, despite the way he kept his shop organized.

She slid a glance toward Mrs. Scott. The woman was busy with her needlework, humming a tune Cathleen hadn't heard before. She didn't look like she'd be starting her usual evening doze any time soon. That meant if Cathleen was going to get a walk in, this would be her only chance. And after all the events of the day, she desperately needed time alone with God to sort through her thoughts.

"Reuben, would you mind staying with your mum while I step outside for a minute?"

"Go ahead."

Slipping into her new coat, she pulled it close around her neck to luxuriate in the silky softness. "Thanks again for letting me use this."

His gaze jerked to her, then lowered again to the pack in his hands. "You're welcome." The tone of his words was hard to decipher. Not angry or short-tempered, but brusque. Like he was trying to cover emotion?

She slipped outside on that thought, grabbing the extra lantern to take with her. She'd had an inkling all along there was a man with feelings under that stoic façade. Maybe it was high time to uncover him. But how to do that?

Inhaling a deep breath, she pulled the sides of her coat together and fastened the hooks as she stepped from the porch. Even the buttons were carved into intricate animal shapes. They looked like some kind of polished horn or bone. And the loops were woven from tiny leather strips. The amount of craftsmanship in this garment was fascinating, even more so as she thought about the man who'd put such detail into it. Where had he learned such skills?

A nicker from the barn grabbed her attention. She should check on Tashunka before heading to her normal prayer spot at the corner of the corral fence.

As she stepped through the barn door, the aroma of animals, musty hay, and mud seeped into her nostrils. The smell had such an earthy, intoxicating tone to it. Relaxing, yet invigorating at the same time.

Another nicker and shuffling sounded from the Tashunka's stall. Cathleen glanced into the milk cow's pen as she passed, but the animal snoozed in a back corner. When she raised the lantern to peer through the wooden slats of the expectant mare's enclosure, Tashunka seemed to be stomping something into the dirt floor, walking in a tiny circle. With a groan, the mare eased down to lay on her side, stretching all the way out so her head pressed into the ground and her legs went straight.

The poor horse looked miserable. Cathleen slipped into the stall and eased closer to crouch beside Tash's head. "Hey, girl. You all right?"

When she stroked a hand down the mare's glistening neck, dampness soaked her skin. This horse was sweating profusely. Did that mean it was her time?

The mare lurched up, pulling her feet underneath her so her position was more like sitting. A groan emanated as she arched her neck. Then a whoosh sounded, like water pouring from a bucket.

That was a sound Cathleen had heard before. This mare's time had definitely come.

Easing away from the horse, she slipped out of the stall. Reuben needed to know. Needed to be here to help. She'd assisted the midwife with a few human births, but that hadn't come close to preparing her to aid a horse in her time of need.

As soon as the barn door closed behind her, Cathleen clutched her skirts in one hand and the lantern in the other, then sprinted through the snow toward the cabin. By the time she pushed open the door, her breath was coming in jagged spurts.

Reuben stood by the hearth, one hand on the mantle as he gazed into the fire. He jerked around at her dramatic entrance, and his hand flew to the knife in the sheath at his waist. "What's wrong?" His voice was low—likely so he didn't disturb his mother's snores in the chair beside him—but the note of panic was clear.

"Tashunka." Cathleen gulped in enough air to speak. "It's time."

In long strides he joined her at the door, reaching for his coat from the hook and his gloves from the shelf by the door. "Let's go."

Cathleen touched his arm, eyeing Mrs. Scott. "But your mum." She should keep her mouth shut and go inside to sit with the woman, just like any good nurse. But she craved seeing the birth of this new life. Of all times to be a martyr, this was not one she could willingly submit to.

Reuben followed her gaze to his mum, and his voice dropped. "She's sleeping soundly."

"But...she was sleeping earlier too. Before the accident." Enough. No matter how much she wanted to see the foal born, she wouldn't risk Mrs. Scott's life in such a foolish way like she'd done earlier.

Cathleen slipped around Reuben to enter the cabin. She hung the lantern on the hook, then shucked her gloves and laid them on the shelf. "I'll stay here."

"No."

His strong hand on her arm brought her up short, and she turned to study him. Those blue eyes were dark in the night shadows, but the firm profile of his chin bespoke determination. "Mum'll be fine. I'll move something in front of the door so she can't leave the cabin. You should see Tash's foal. In fact, I might need your help."

Might need your help. If only this strong, self-sufficient man ever really needed her help. But he was asking for it now, and she'd be bound and gagged before she'd let him down.

With a final glance at Mrs. Scott lounging in her upholstered chair with snores pouring from her open mouth, Cathleen let out a breath. "Let's go." She picked up the lantern again and stepped out the door.

Reuben reached for a trunk along the wall, lifted it, and followed her outside. After she'd closed the door tight and pulled the latch string into place, he positioned the trunk. "That should work for now. Tomorrow I'll fix a bar here so we can secure it from the outside."

Secure it from the outside? It seemed unkind to lock the woman in the cabin, but as a safety measure, maybe it was necessary for rare occasions. And if it allowed her a trip to the privy while Mrs. Scott slept, well… A sliver of weight rolled off Cathleen's shoulders. A few stolen moments of freedom would be nice. When she could be sure Mrs. Scott would be safe.

Reuben shortened his long strides to match hers as they crossed the snowy terrain to the barn. She could tell he itched to move faster, so she did her best to hurry.

He held the barn door open as she slipped in first and crept toward Tashunka's stall. She gripped one of the rails and peered through.

The mare was lying on the ground still, but facing a different direction than when Cathleen left her. This view gave them a somewhat awkward view of her abdomen, with all four feet facing toward them as the mare lay flat and grunted. She seemed to be pushing, and a glimmer of white appeared by her tail.

"There it is."

She almost jumped at Reuben's deep voice, so close beside her. He stood with one hand on the stall door, peering through an opening as she did. Less than a foot of space separated them, and a smile touched his mouth as he met her gaze. Then he turned back to watch the mare.

She should do the same, no matter how hard it was to focus with Reuben beside her. So close. His height loomed at the edge of her vision, sending a comforting warmth through her. Something about him made her feel safe. Protected. When he was near, all would be well.

A grunt from the stall finally pulled her attention toward its interior. The mare was obviously straining, the rippling muscles easily seen where sweat plastered her thick coat.

Cathleen kept her focus on that white bubble at the horse's tail, larger now than before. As she watched, the white glimmer expanded, inch by painful inch. One end darkened, and a tiny black hoof broke through the slippery bubble. She sucked in a breath. So little.

She waited for the hoof to move. But nothing happened. At least a minute must have passed since her first view of the foot, but no more activity. Her eye tracked back to the mare, up to her shoulder. Tashunka bobbed her head against the stall floor, then raised it, tucking it tight to her chest. Veins rose across her shoulders and abdomen. Everything in the horse fought to expel this new life.

Cathleen grabbed Reuben's arm as her gaze trailed back to the still immobile baby hoof at the mare's tail. "Something's wrong." The panic she heard in her voice was only slightly less than what pulsed through her veins. "We have to do something."

"She's all right." The deep voice beside her rumbled calm into her ear, but the feeling warred against the fear in her chest.

She cut a glance at him. "The baby's not moving. She can't get it out. What if it's twisted inside?" One human birth she'd attended had been that way. Aunt Arlene had served as midwife and fought for what felt like an hour to get the baby unwrapped from the birth cord. It was only by the grace of God that both mother and child survived the ordeal.

Warmth closed over her hand where she'd squeezed Reuben's arm. A welcome warmth, since she'd forgotten her gloves. But where were his? He met her gaze for a fraction of a second, before focusing again on the mare. "She's just trying to push its shoulders through. That's the hardest part. Once that's done, the little one'll start moving."

Cathleen followed his gaze and cringed as the mare gave an awful groan and pressed flat against the ground. With a whoosh, the foal spewed out, the white bubble pulling away to reveal a tiny chocolate head. The muzzle was long and more delicate than she'd thought possible, only as thick around as her own forearm. A splash of white lay between the pink skin around each eye—eyes that still hadn't opened.

She gripped Reuben tighter. "Is he breathing?" She couldn't tell.

Maybe the nostrils flared the slightest bit, but that could be her imagination.

He squeezed her hand, and only then did she realize she clutched his. Not his arm, but his hand. She didn't dare look at him but couldn't bring herself to release it. His large grip enveloped hers. Protecting. Calming.

With her gaze glued to the tiny foal on the floor, she almost missed the mare's movement until Tashunka planted her front hooves and struggled to her feet.

Cathleen gasped. The foal was still half inside its mother. She was going to snap its back letting it hang upside down from her.

She reached for the door to intervene. Reuben may not realize there was a problem, but he'd brought her here to help. She had to protect that new life, if she could only get there in time.

CHAPTER 12

*A*s Cathleen tried to surge forward, the grip tightening around her hand held her back.

"He's fine." Reuben's voice held enough strength to still her.

And sure enough, the mare's rising had pulled the foal from her completely. It lay perfectly still on the stall floor. Tashunka circled and nuzzled the little head, then ran her tongue over its muzzle in short strokes.

The foal came alive. Sitting up, it shook its head, and those pink eyelids opened to reveal dark eyes. Both ears flopped as it rocked with the pressure of its mother's persistent licking.

The scene was magical, now that the foal looked healthy and Tashunka nurtured the new life she'd brought into the world. Yet Cathleen's heart hadn't quite slowed its racing.

A gentle stroking against the back of her hand worked its way into her awareness. She still gripped Reuben's hand. Or rather, her hand still nestled in his stronger one. And the touch of his thumb as it slid across her skin sent a shiver up her arm.

She swallowed. The urge to say something forced her to clear the muddle from her throat. "You were right. He's beautiful."

A soft chuckle drifted from beside her. "Tash is a good girl. Knows what she's doing. Any time I try to help her, I usually end up making things worse."

She couldn't help a glance at his face. "I can't believe that's true."

He gave a half shrug, almost self-deprecating. "We have a sort of mutual respect, I guess. She knows I'm here if she needs me, but I give her the respect of dignity if she doesn't."

As those words soaked in, clarity washed through her mind. That was the way he interacted with his mother, too. All those times she'd wondered why he stayed distant. Why he didn't step in and help his Mum but left the older woman to do it herself. He was allowing Mrs. Scott the dignity to try things on her own while he stayed close enough to help if needed.

Except Cathleen probably ruined that for him most times. She'd developed a habit of hovering over Mrs. Scott any time the woman wasn't ensconced in a chair doing something safe—sleeping or crocheting or just buttering bread at the table. Was she hindering the older woman from living fully in her remaining days? Not giving her the respect she deserved? Not allowing her dignity during every moment possible?

They'd shared some rather *uncomfortable* situations due to the incontinence challenges of Mrs. Scott's condition. Dignity was hardly a word she often associated with the woman.

But now the unfairness in that approach glared at her. The cruelness even. Moisture burned her throat as it traveled up to sting her eyes. "I'm sorry I've not had faith."

The pressure tightened on her hand. "Everything worked out just fine." And when Reuben said it like that, it made her believe things always would.

With a final squeeze, he released her hand and bent low to gather a quilt from the ground. She'd not even noticed it there.

"I need to help dry this fellow off before he catches cold." Reuben slipped into the stall, leaving a void greater than even his large frame.

"I should go inside and help your mum to bed."

He glanced up from where he crouched by the foal. Disappointment touched his eyes. "If you come back out later, you can see him stand. Maybe pet him a while."

Did he want her to stay? Oh, she'd love to stand here all night and watch him interact with the horses. His touch was magic. As if he spoke their language. Even now, Tashunka nuzzled his shoulder, affection clear in the easy way she allowed him to stroke her foal.

But Mrs. Scott needed her. The woman depended on her, and that wasn't something she could set aside. But she could help Reuben's mum age with dignity.

~

*I*t felt so strange to carry Pa's tools without the man walking alongside him.

Reuben glanced toward the edge of the woods where the cross rose above the unblemished snow. What did his father think about things now as he peered down from heaven? Mum's condition surely saddened him. Had he seen it coming before his death? He had to have. He and Mum were like two sides of the same coin. Always looking out for each other, filling in the gaps where needed, even when the need wasn't spoken. True helpmates.

As he mounted the porch steps, he eased the tools and wooden pieces onto the floor. They made a sizable *thunk* when they landed.

He straightened and tugged at his collar. The chinook wind that blew in earlier had driven away the cold faster than he'd seen in years. If this warm temperature kept up, the snow would be gone in a day.

Only in Montana could the weather change from snow to balmy in a quarter hour.

But he'd been through too many mountain winters to trust how long this warm spell would last. A day. Ten days. They'd best enjoy it while they could.

Noises drifted from inside the cabin. Cathleen was likely deep in some project by now, with all the chores finished from breakfast. She was a whirlwind, that one. Got more done in a day than he'd ever have suspected from a city girl. Kind of like Mum during her younger days. And it was a wonder what she accomplished while still caring for Mum. Maybe she'd like a break?

Pushing the cabin door open, he stepped inside and allowed his eyes a moment to adjust to the shadows.

Cathleen sat at the table, bundles of dried, leafy plants spread out around her. She looked at him with one of those smiles that sent a warmth through him. The woman was pretty at any time, but those smiles lit her whole face and made it hard to keep from stepping closer. Close enough to touch. Maybe even taste.

He looked away quickly before that line of thought could take hold. "Is, uh, Mum around? Thought she might like to sit in the sun while I work on the porch."

Cathleen stood and started toward the back room. "Isn't this weather terrific? I never imagined February could be so warm in these mountains. Your mum's in her room, but I'll see if she wants to join you."

While voices murmured from that chamber, Reuben grabbed one of the kitchen chairs and carried it to the porch. Only a minute passed before Cathleen's voice drifted louder toward him.

"Wait till you feel this weather outside. It's almost like summer."

"Really?" Mum's voice seemed strong this morning. "Must be a chinook blowin' in. Too bad Quinn's out in the fields. He always likes to sit on the porch with me an' whittle when the weather turns nice."

Reuben met them at the door and took Mum's hand from Cathleen. "I've got a nice spot ready out here, Mum."

Cathleen gave him that smile again, then turned back toward the house. "Would it be all right if I leave the door open? The cabin could use a good airing."

"Of course." Not that he'd deny her anything, but with him working in the doorway itself, this might give him occasional glances of her.

Mum mostly hummed while he fitted boards together to form brackets and a brace to hold the door shut. She seemed to do a lot of humming these days. He could remember times from his upbringing when she would sing while she worked, but not nearly as often as these last few weeks. Maybe she'd always done it and he hadn't noticed.

At last, he stepped back and studied his work. Fairly simple really. A wooden brace and pockets for it to rest in, one on the door and two on the frame. Pa would have built something more elaborate. More precise, too, with the wood lining up exactly. Perfectly level.

Reuben had spent his first eighteen years trying to follow in Pa's shoes. He'd not been successful then, and he wasn't likely to accomplish that miracle now. He eyed his handiwork again. This would get the job done.

A glance inside showed Cathleen standing at the work counter, her back to him as she stirred something in a bowl. What was she working on now? Would she think him nosy if he asked?

"How were the animals today, dear?"

Mum's voice turned him away from his thoughts, pulling him back to the sunshine and the glitter of melting snow dripping from the trees around the yard. He eased down on the porch step near her chair.

"The animals all seem fine, Mum. We had a foal born last night. A sorrel colt. I'll take you out to see him, if you want."

She gave him one of those rare smiles, shining with pride. "You always were good with the horses, son. Just like your pa."

He had to swallow down the lump in his throat formed by those words. "It's Tash's baby. She gives us the good ones." He turned back toward the scene in front of them. The opening in the trees on the left still afforded a view of the distant mountains, rising in splendor. His winter camp lay out there somewhere. Cold and vacant unless some other trapper had taken up residence for the rest of the season.

And that was likely the way it would stay if he took on his father's responsibilities here. As he should. The conversation with O'Hennessey yesterday filtered through his mind again. The man had given him a nice option out, but should he take it? Could Mum be happy anywhere other than this place where she'd made a home for over three decades now? Could he really ask her to leave it all and go with him on his trapping routes? Later, he could decide. There was time.

He glanced at her again. She'd stopped humming, but pleasure lined her face as the sun's rays splashed across it. Maybe now would be a good time to test the waters. "Mum, I went to check on our cattle yesterday. Mr. O'Hennessey's been feeding them for us with his own stock."

Her eyes turned a bit glazy as she looked at him. "Oh?"

He kept on but watched her for signs of understanding. "The animals look good for such a cold winter. He's offered to keep them on till spring." For payment of a decent chunk of the herd, but he didn't need to go into that now.

Besides, it felt like he was needed most here, not out feeding livestock half the day. Even though he wasn't as useful as he'd like to be, there was still plenty to be done to restock the place.

Not to mention their safety. After the wolf attack yesterday, he hated to leave the women alone for even an hour. And he'd been dead serious about teaching Cathleen to shoot a rifle. That was one critical skill she was sorely lacking. And one of the only areas he could actually help.

Another glance at Mum showed her eyes drifting shut. He'd not finished what he needed to say, though.

He cleared his throat. "Mum, I was telling you about Mr. O'Hennessey's offer to keep up with the cattle through spring."

She blinked and stared at him.

He trudged on. "He also offered to buy us out if we're open to it."

The lines across her forehead deepened. "Buy us out? What d'ya mean?"

"Just the cattle. I'm not saying we have to sell. I'm just saying that might be an option to make things easier around here."

If it were possible, those frown lines deepened, spreading around her eyes and mouth. "Quinn, are you sick? I know that fever was hard on you, but if you're feelin' poorly you should say so."

An arrow to his chest. Reuben swallowed. How did he break the news gently, so she didn't fall apart like she'd done last time? "Mum, it's me, Reuben. Pa's not here."

Her eyes fogged over. "Not…here? Where is he?"

Dare he say it? Was it better for her to live in a lie? He softened his tone as much as he could. "Mum, Pa didn't make it through the fever. He's in heaven now."

Her chin quivered, and she drew in air with a raspy breath. "What?" The childlike fear in her voice reached into his chest and squeezed it like a vise.

Water formed in her eyes, then rolled out in huge tears. "What do you mean?"

What did he do now? He should have kept his mouth shut, but now he had do something to fix this.

But before he could move, Cathleen was there. Kneeling beside Mum, stroking her hand and wrapping an arm around those frail shoulders. Mum leaned her head on Cathleen's shoulder and sobbed, while this angel of mercy murmured sweet sympathies in her ear. It was the balm he needed, too.

No matter how inadequate he felt, at least Cathleen was there, tending to Mum. Being the daughter she needed. The thought didn't stab like it had the first few times he'd felt it. Not as much anyway.

After a minute, Cathleen started to hum a song. One he'd heard them singing last night when he came in from the animals. That seemed to pull Mum from her sorrow more than anything, and she leaned back in her chair and hummed along. Cathleen's voice rang like an angel's compared to Mum's shaky vibrato, but the joined harmony seemed right.

They'd only gone through a verse or two when Cathleen straightened and patted his mother's hand. "Do you know what?"

Confusion washed Mum's eyes as they roamed Cathleen's face. "What is it, dear?"

"There was a baby foal born last night." She cut a glance at him, a pert smile on her lips. "I was hoping Reuben would take us to see him. Shall we ask him now?"

That he could do. Rising to his feet, he stepped closer and extended a hand to each of them. "Let's go."

Cathleen slipped fingers into his, her gaze finding his, then sliding down a notch. Surely that wasn't embarrassment pinking her smooth cheeks. From what? The warmth of her touch flowed up his arm, and he didn't let go right away, even after she'd stood and turned to help Mum from her chair.

At last, she gave a little tug to pull from his grip. He stroked his thumb across the back of her hand before releasing it. Something about this woman brought to life places inside him he'd not known existed. Like the desire to touch her so often. Last night as they watched Tash foal. And now.

He had to squelch that urge. She came from a different world, and would be going back to that place. He'd better keep his hands—and emotions—in check.

CHAPTER 13

*R*euben fumbled with his clumsy hands around Mum's frail arms as he and Cathleen got her up and positioned between them. Down the steps they hobbled as a threesome, then they continued a painfully slow walk toward the barn.

Cathleen kept up a steady conversation with his mother as they walked, but it wasn't incessant babble, just light banter. And Mum responded with rapt attention, answering and commenting in the slow cadence she'd developed since he'd left in the fall.

As they entered the barn, Cathleen's voice dropped to a loud whisper. "Wait till you see this young man, Mrs. Scott. He's all legs."

The colt was napping when they drew near his stall. Tash stood over him and had probably been enjoying her own rest but perked her ears at their approach.

Reuben stepped into the pen to pet the mare while Cathleen stood with Mum at the fence.

"He is good-lookin', son. Let me come see that boy." Mum pushed through the stall door before Cathleen could stop her, like a woman ten years younger.

Cathleen shot him a wide-eyed, worried look, but he could only grin. This was the Mum he was used to seeing. Full of zest and ready to charge through wherever she aimed to go.

The colt scrambled to his feet, and Mum slowed her approach. "Hey, boy. You are a tall fellow."

He sniffed one of her extended hands and let her come close enough to stroke his neck. "You're a fine lad, aren't you, son." Mum kept up a steady monologue to the horse as she scratched the itchy spot at the base of his neck, then the top of his back. "You jest need some lovin' is all." That hint of Irish brogue had drifted back into her voice, just like he remembered from his youngest childhood days. It was good to hear. Good to see her come back to life as the woman he'd always known.

His gaze wandered up to Cathleen. She'd stepped into the stall and hovered beside Mum. Probably to jerk her away should the horses put her in danger. Ever the stanch defender, the loyal caretaker. *Thank you, God, that she's here.*

She met his gaze, a half smile lighting her eyes even in the dimness of the barn. A streak of dark brown lined her left cheekbone, marring her usual flawless face. Cinnamon, maybe? She smelled faintly of the rich aroma.

Tashunka was the only barrier between them, and with the mare's head lowered, he could just reach across to brush the mark from Cathleen's cheek. Her eyes widened as his hand approached, but she didn't back away.

The touch of her skin was every bit as luxurious as he'd imagined. His hand cupped her cheek while his thumb stroked it clean. Her eyes held the faintest look of confusion, and he tried his best not to let the bliss of the touch show too strongly on his face. "You had a streak of something. There." He stroked the spot again, and if he wasn't mistaken, a little tremor unsteadied her. Did she feel the tension between them? Could she possibly care anything at all for him?

It wasn't possible, was it? He dropped his hand but couldn't do the same for his gaze. This woman deserved far better—was worth far more—than a back country trapper like him. He was fooling himself to let these thoughts meander through his brain.

He turned away, and Cathleen didn't speak. Soon enough, she gathered Mum and coaxed her toward the house. "I'm making a vinegar pie for tonight and was hoping you could help me with the crust. I never can get the thickness right like you do."

He stood at the stall door and watched the two of them, arm in arm, as they walked away. If he didn't do a better job of guarding his heart, he was going to be in a mess when she walked away for good.

~

*R*euben sat on a crate in the barn, cleaning his Sharps rifle while his mind filtered through his upcoming task. As much as he had to keep his distance from Cathleen—Miss Donaghue. It would be easier if he thought of her that way. She had to learn how to shoot a rifle. Without that skill, she'd be easy prey in these mountains. He'd lost himself in his work on the furs for a couple hours that morning, but he couldn't put this off much longer.

He'd just have to get it over with and try to keep the damage to his heart contained. She'd need to learn how to load and fire Pa's old Springfield breech-loader eventually, but this first time should be with his Sharps. The queen of rifles with its dead-on accuracy, even at long distances. Not to mention how quick and simple it was to load. She'd be spoiled for sure, but she deserved it. This first time anyway.

Once he had the rifle fitted back together, he grabbed the pouch holding his cartridges and propped the gun over his shoulder. As he passed Tashunka's stall, the colt inside startled at his appearance, jumping the way foals always did until they figured out this new world.

"It's all right, fella. You're in good hands." He had the sudden urge to whistle as he stepped from the barn into warm sunlight. He shouldn't be looking forward to this at all, much less so much that the beat in his chest quickened like it was. The prospect of spending time with his Sharps and a pretty gal, who wouldn't be excited? Maybe for just this next hour, he could forget about the future and enjoy the moment.

On the cabin porch, he propped his rifle against the wall and tapped on the door before pushing it open. He never knew what Cathleen and his mum would be up to, and sometimes it felt like intruding on their privacy to barge in.

Cathleen looked up at him from a chair by the table, the usual smile on her face. Maybe a little more subdued. Maybe. He wasn't so good at reading those things. She held a needle in one hand and a wad of frilly fabric in her other.

He cleared his throat as his gaze swept the room. Mum wasn't around. "I... If you're not busy, I thought this afternoon might be good to teach you to shoot."

The heat crawling up his neck certainly wasn't helping his rush of nerves. And why in the starry sky was he getting nervous? It wasn't like he was asking to court her or anything. Just teach her a skill she'd need to keep from getting killed around here.

She set down her needlework and leaned back in her chair. "All right. Now's probably the best time. Your mum's napping in her room."

He nodded, then stepped backward toward the porch. At least he could breathe out here. He sat on the steps with the rifle and pulled a cartridge from his pouch as Cathleen settled beside him. These steps were wide enough he didn't have to worry about his leg brushing her skirts. Especially since the dress she wore didn't seem as frilly and wide today. More sensible. But not as much like Cathleen, and he almost missed the old look. Although the lack of ruffles did nothing to lessen her beauty. A quick glance at her face confirmed that and picked up the speed of his pulse.

He focused on the rifle in his hands. "This is my gun. It's a Sharps, easier to shoot than the one hanging on the wall in there. You'll need to learn both if you stay here much longer."

As he explained how to load the gun, then how to aim for the most accurate shot with the variations he'd made to the sights, the tension in his muscles started to ease. Talking about guns was something he could do.

She watched with a wide, steady gaze, taking in each word and every move he made.

He held out the gun. "You want to load it?"

Twin lines formed between her brows as she took the rifle and cartridge, then started to follow his directions. "It's heavy."

Her fingers were clumsy, but she loaded the cartridge pretty much the way he'd shown. It seemed she'd absorbed most of his lesson with her intense scrutiny.

When the gun was loaded, she looked up at him with eager eyes. "What next?"

He looked to the woods at the side of the cabin. "I guess let's go shoot it. Just a couple times, though. I don't want to worry Tash and the foal." Tashunka was more than used to him hunting from her back, but a newborn at her side would make her jumpy. Not to mention his own mother, who might not appreciate gunshots so near the cabin.

Cathleen carried the rifle as they walked around to the spot where he'd target practiced in his younger days. The trees rose up on a hill, so the ground would cushion any stray bullets.

"All right. First, you'll line up your target in the sights. That biggest pine in the middle is a good mark. Then squeeze this rear set trigger, pull back on this to cock the lock." He pointed to the hammer, careful not to touch her with his oversize finger. Still, he was close enough to smell the cinnamon drifting from her. And it was more than a little distracting.

"So this first"—she fixed the set trigger—"then this?" She cocked the hammer, accomplishing what he'd directed. But she held the gun all wrong, barely balancing it with her hands close together and the butt resting too high on her shoulder. It'd take her teeth out if she squeezed the trigger holding the rifle like that, maybe even break bones in her chin.

"Here. You need to tuck it in tighter to your arm."

She adjusted it, but now the gun was too close to her shoulder, close enough to dislocate the bone on her first shot. "Like this?"

"Not quite." He had no choice but to reach in and help. He gripped the barrel and tried to do it without touching her, but to get the gun seated right, he had to press a hand to her back. Her muscle flinched under his touch, but no more so than his own. She was just the right amount of softness and strength, and for a second he let himself enjoy the feel.

"So...am I ready to pull the trigger?"

Cathleen's unsteady words pulled him back to the present, and he took in her stance. "You'll want to put your left hand out here to support the barrel." He pointed to the spot, and she did as he asked, but again, her effort was all wrong.

He supported the barrel himself, then slid his hand over hers and showed her how to position it correctly. He didn't breathe a whit through it all. No wonder his mouth went dry. Would he be able to speak, if it became necessary? He seriously doubted it.

Was she having the same trouble? From the way her shoulders rose and fell as he stepped away...maybe.

He forced his muddled brain back to what he was supposed to be doing. "All right. Now, match up the target between the sights, then squeeze the front trigger."

She followed each direction precisely and stared down the sights for several long seconds.

He should probably warn her about the rifle's kick before it caught her off guard. The moment he opened his mouth to do that, the blast of the gun filled the clearing, sending up a small puff of black powder.

Cathleen jerked backward, almost as if the bullet had struck her shoulder. She stumbled to catch her footing, but her skirts tripped her up.

He reached for her, missing her shoulder but just barely grabbing her arm with his fingertips. She was already falling, though.

He stumbled, trying to gain his own footing so he could keep her upright. His left boot caught on her skirt, his right tangling in her ankle.

And almost like he was watching from a dream, he tumbled forward, too.

At the last minute, he grabbed his bearings enough to twist sideways so he didn't land on her. Instead, his elbow hit the ground first, his side slamming close behind it.

A glance at Cathleen showed that she'd landed on her elbows, too, the gun resting across her chest. Those pretty brown eyes were wide enough to read a book through. Then they narrowed a bit, laugh lines forming at the edges. A giggle broke through, and her eyes met his with a sparkle.

Peas and carrots, but she was pretty.

Her smile was contagious. He tried to hold his back at first, but finally let out the grin that begged for release.

"I guess I should have expected so much gunpowder to be hard to hold." She released that clear laugh again.

A bit of black powder smudged the bridge of her nose, and he reached over to wipe it off.

She looked at him with both brows raised. "A mess, am I?"

Oh, she was too cute for words. "Not at all."

She reached over and touched his cheek, running a finger down his jaw. "You're not quite spotless yourself."

Her skin was soft as rabbit fur, her touch warm. And he couldn't stop the skitter that ran through him at the contact.

The smile that had lit her face faded into a very different look. Longing, if his eyes could be believed.

Then she blinked, pulled her hand back, and sat up straight. She stared toward the tree line. "Do you think I hit the target?"

Letting out a long breath, Reuben straightened, too, and pushed up to his feet. He extended a hand to help her up, but she placed the rifle in it, then scrambled up on her own.

Probably best.

CHAPTER 14

*C*athleen pressed a hand to her skirt as she rounded the corner of the cabin from the outhouse. Mrs. Scott had been knitting, with North lounging at her feet, when Cathleen took the opportunity for a quick outing. She probably should have put the bar across the door, but with the weather still so nice after three days, they'd been keeping the door open to let in the fresh air.

A movement at the edge of the woods caught her attention.

A rider? She stopped and shaded her eyes. Reuben was in the barn, working on the hides he'd brought, so it couldn't be him.

But that profile was familiar. Unmistakable.

Grabbing her skirts, she sprinted forward. "Alex!"

He nudged his horse into a jog and closed the distance between them, then reined in and swung down. She landed in his arms, relishing the warmth as they wrapped around her.

"You really are alive." His voice had a hint of a chuckle, but the way he held her overlong brought a rush of moisture to her eyes. She hadn't realized how much she'd missed this brother of hers.

Finally, he pulled back, gripping her shoulders like he was holding up a puppy for examination. "Two arms. Still standing and walking."

He grabbed her hands and raised them up. "All fingers are still there." The twinkle sprang into his eye in full force. "I guess you've done all right."

She jerked her hand away, then gave him a backwards shove. "Scamp."

He raised both hands in an *I didn't do it* gesture. "That's your name, not mine."

"Who's there?" A shaky voice from the porch pulled Cathleen back to her surroundings.

She slipped her hand through Alex's arm and pulled him toward the cabin. "It's me, Mrs. Scott. We have a visitor."

At the porch, Cathleen motioned to the rail. "Just tie your horse for a minute and come inside." She ascended the stairs first and took Mrs. Scott's hand in hers. "My brother's come to pay us a visit. Isn't that wonderful?"

"Oh. Yes, dear. I'm sure that's nice." The older woman used her confused voice, the one that meant she had no idea what Cathleen had just said, but she was trying to play along.

"Why don't we go in and cut some of the sourdough bread we made this morning? He's been riding a long time to get here, so I'll bet he's hungry." She turned the woman, and they headed into the house with Alex close on their heels.

She needed to find Reuben too. He'd want to know they had a visitor, and how wonderful it would be to introduce him to her brother.

As soon as she had Alex settled at the table with somewhat-fresh coffee and buttered bread, she stepped back and untied her apron. "I'm going to the barn to get Reuben. He'll be glad to meet you."

Alex's head tilted, and something about the way he held his jaw seemed to send the happy moment fleeing from the room. "Reuben?" His voice had gone dry.

She hung her apron on the peg. Alex might get his hackles up about her not coming straight back to town as soon as Mrs. Scott's son arrived, but he'd have to get over that. There was no way she could leave her patient just yet. "Yes, Reuben Scott."

"How long has he been back?" There was more of a steel under-tone in the words than she would have liked.

She turned to face him with a sigh. "I don't know. A few weeks, I guess. It's been a lot for him to adjust to, both about his pa and his mum's condition." She dropped her tone with that last sentence so Mrs. Scott didn't pick up on her words. "I've been needed here."

A muscle flexed in Alex's jaw. "Where is this Reuben?"

She couldn't quite hold in her exasperated breath as she turned and started for the door. "Drink your coffee, Alex. I'll get him."

After stomping down the stairs, she untied Alex's horse and led the tired creature toward the barn. From the flecks of white foam lining its neck and saddle blanket, and from its drooping head, she decided her brother must have ridden hard to get here. Of course, the horse could just be exhausted from the climb up into these mountains. She knew from experience it was a challenge.

The barn door was open, and Reuben looked up from his furs when she came in. He'd been rather distant since the incident when he'd taught her to shoot. A fact she wished she knew how to change. Had he been offended that she'd stroked his cheek? It wasn't much more than he'd done for her. Of course, he hadn't had black powder for her to wipe off, but he didn't know that, did he?

It had been such a delicious feeling to touch him. The first real contact since she'd cut his hair. And as she'd gotten to know him over these weeks, seen him day in and day out, watched his kindness and wisdom—not to mention his strong, handsome features—she couldn't have stopped her hand from touching his cheek if she'd wanted to.

But the way he'd frozen in place...he'd looked so shocked. Did he feel nothing at all for her? There were times, she thought maybe he did. But not when he looked at her with the wary expression he now aimed her direction.

He lowered the hide he'd been working with and draped it over his work table, then stood. "Whose horse is that?"

She put on her brightest smile. "My brother's come for a visit. Alex, the younger one. Do you mind if I put his horse in this first stall?"

The wary look disappeared from his face. In fact, his expression went void of any emotion. That stoic mask took over, the one that had gradually disappeared these last weeks.

He strode toward her and took the horse's reins. Almost jerked them from her, really. What had him on edge? Alex's visit? No matter how she examined the idea, that didn't make sense.

Maybe he wasn't comfortable around new people. Well, that she could help him with. "You'll come inside for coffee then? I made a dried apple pie for supper, but I think we'll eat it early." She kept her voice pleasant, but with an undertone of finality.

He mumbled something as he led the horse into the stall.

She'd take that as a yes for now, but if he wasn't in the house in a quarter hour, she'd be back for a stronger conversation.

$\sim$

*R*euben forced himself to climb the porch stairs, one at a time. Cathleen was leaving. Her brother had come to fetch her, and she would be leaving them.

Leaving *him*.

He'd known this day would come. Had done his best to put distance between them since that ill-fated shooting lesson. But facing the stark reality of it now....

Could he take care of Mum by himself? He'd have to. If Cathleen had been able, surely he could, too. There might be some awkward moments, but together he and Mum could work through them.

But would he be able to face the cabin without Cathleen's smiling face? He wasn't so sure.

He pushed open the door, and that bright smile he'd just been picturing turned its full force on him from her seat at the table. That look had so much more power in reality than it had in his mind. Power to make his stomach flip at the first sight of it.

He clenched his jaw and turned his gaze on the man rising to his feet from Pa's old chair.

"Alex, this is Mr. Reuben Scott. Reuben, my big brother, Alex Donaghue." Cathleen's voice had an awful lot of perkiness in it. She must be thrilled to finally escape this primitive mountain and get back to town.

Reuben shook Alex's hand with a nod and took a quick measure before meeting his gaze. The man was a decent height, maybe six feet. Hair a little browner than Cathleen's auburn. His eyes were dark and expressive like Cathleen's. And at the moment their expression held an extra heaping of distrust.

Well, the man didn't have anything to fear from him, if that's what he was worried about. He'd protect Cathleen to his dying breath— even if it meant protecting her from himself. But it didn't mean he had to look forward to her walking away.

"Scott." Cathleen's brother eased his glare as he pulled his hand back. "Didn't expect to see you here. Glad to, though."

Reuben nodded. He couldn't exactly say the same, and the best remedy to lying was usually to keep his mouth shut.

Cathleen rose from her chair and scurried toward the stove. "I was just telling Alex about the wolf the other day. I asked him to look at North to see if there's something else we should do for him."

Reuben glanced at the dog, curled by his food dish in the corner. He'd been up and moving around these last couple days, although he still stayed mostly in the cabin. Reuben had a strong suspicion that had more to do with the coddling he was getting here than anything. If they were still at the winter camp, North would have been jogging the trotline of his own accord two days ago.

Cathleen turned to face him with a smile and a steaming mug in her hand. "Here's some coffee. Have a seat, and I'll cut you a slice of pie."

As usual, that smile started a flip in his belly. Letting her leave was going to be so much harder than he'd ever planned.

He took the cup from her and tried to offer some semblance of a smile. The least he could do was let her know how much he appreciated the little extra things she did. How much he appreciated her.

She held his gaze a second longer, then turned to her brother. "Are you ready to check him?"

Reuben sipped coffee while the two of them knelt over North, Cathleen stroking the dog's head while her brother poked and prodded. The animal, of course, stared at Cathleen with devoted eyes. It was going to be a hard awakening for the dog when she left, too.

Finally, the doctor sat back on his heels. "It doesn't seem like any of his organs are damaged, especially if you say he's eating and drinking fine. There is some damage to the deep tissue on his haunches, but the area already shows signs of healing." He glanced back at Reuben. "I'll leave a tincture that should speed his recovery."

"Thanks." Reuben forced out the word.

Cathleen gave the dog a final pat, then rose to her feet. "Come sit again, Alex, and tell me how the babies are. I bet they've forgotten who their Aunt Cathy is."

The two jabbered back and forth across the table, Cathleen's face glowing as he filled her in on each family member. Her brother's responses sounded like she was quite a favorite among the group. And no wonder.

At last, Donaghue leaned back in his chair and eyed his sister. "Shall we wait till the morning or try to head back tonight? We'd have to ride a couple hours in the dark, but Miriam would thank you for getting me home sooner."

Reuben couldn't quite force breath through his lungs. And he couldn't bring himself to look at Cathleen either. So, he stared down into the collection of grounds at the bottom of his mug, swirling them in the last sip of coffee.

"Alex, I..." Cathleen paused, and it took every bit of control in him not to look up at her. "We haven't discussed when I'll be leaving, but I don't think it should be today or tomorrow."

The control fled from him. He scanned her face, taking in the hint of apprehension as she glanced at Mum. Her look changed when she turned it on her brother, though. That perfect little chin came up, and her brows rose, eyes sparking.

For half a second, he was thankful that look wasn't pointed at him.

And then she did dart a glance his way. Not long enough for him to read it, but a glimmer of hope lit in his chest. Maybe, just maybe, he wouldn't have to say goodbye quite yet.

"We'll talk about it in a bit." Alex's voice had definitely lost its light-heartedness. He shot a penetrating look toward Reuben, then he turned his attention on Mum and leaned forward on his elbows. "And how are you feeling these days, Mrs. Scott?"

"Oh, just fine. Just fine. Enjoying this nice weather." Mum fiddled with her sleeve as she gave a bit of a toothy smile. "How about you?" Mum likely had no idea who the man was, but at least she sounded somewhat competent.

As Alex kept her in light conversation, that penetrating look replayed itself in Reuben's mind. Was the man worried about his sister's reputation, up here on the mountain with only him and his confused mother? He hadn't given much thought to that, as far removed from town gossips as they'd always been.

But Pa and Mum had tried their best to instill a good sense of morals in him, and spending excessive time alone with a lady was definitely on the *Not Proper* list. The thought hadn't occurred to him at first because Cathleen was here as Mum's nurse, but the more time he spent around her, the harder it was to keep his distance. Maybe he *should* encourage her to leave with her brother.

The thought churned bile in his stomach, but he'd do what was best for her.

Cathleen rose and started stacking their used pie plates. He needed to speak with her now, before she picked a fight with her brother on the topic.

He pushed his chair back and stood. "Cathleen, I need to show you something in the barn if you have a minute."

She paused mid-stride on her way to the dry sink. "Certainly." She glanced at the stack in her hand. "I can finish these in a bit, I guess."

Good. He nodded and waited by the door for her to precede him. He didn't have to glance at Donaghue to feel the man's stare pierce his back. If only he knew they were on the same side, no matter how begrudgingly.

Cathleen walked beside him in silence to the barn. They could have had the conversation standing on the porch, but it would have been too easy to be overheard. Or even watched through the cabin window.

And he desperately needed privacy for this baring of his soul.

CHAPTER 15

$\mathcal{I}$nside the barn, Reuben slowed as he and Cathleen approached Tash's stall. He propped a hand on the top rail and peered in. The colt slept with his dam standing over him, head drooped as she rested, too. So peaceful.

Quite opposite to the battle raging in his chest. But he had to say this before he lost his courage. "Cathleen, I think you should go back with your brother."

She'd been standing quietly beside him, but she stiffened at his words, and the air around them seemed to disappear with the intake of her breath. She didn't speak right away. The burn of her scrutiny seared him, but he kept his focus forward.

"You want me to leave?"

There was the faintest amount of hurt in her tone. Or was that his imagination? He tightened his jaw. No, he didn't want her to leave, but he didn't want to keep her here if it would tarnish her reputation. Didn't want her to regret coming to help them. Regret him.

He had to be honest. At least, as much as he could.

Turning to face her, he did his best to meet her gaze, but couldn't quite muster it. His eyes landed on her perfect little nose, and he locked them there. "You've been a lifesaver around here. Helped Mum and me both, and we'll always be thankful. But if your brother thinks you should go, that's probably best."

He kept his gaze trained on her nose, and it didn't move for a long moment. Then the nostrils flared, and he forced his focus up to see the rest of her reaction in those big brown eyes.

Their intensity drove deeper inside him than any person had probed in years. Through his thoughts, his motivations, maybe even as deep as his yearnings. The power of it started beads of sweat rolling down his back, and he looked away. Had she seen how he felt about her? Not that he really knew himself, but that look could have split bone from marrow and stitched it all back together again.

He propped both arms on the wooden rail and cleared his throat. Was she going to say something? For once, the silence was making his skin itch.

"I think I'll stay."

Those soft words brought his head up, and he whirled to face her. "You will?"

Her eyes had softened, even crinkled at the edges in the hint of a smile. "Yes. If you don't mind. I'd like to help your mum."

The relief that washed through him would have dropped him to his knees if he hadn't been gripping the rail so tight. He inhaled a long, steadying breath.

"All right."

～

*R*euben straightened saddle on Alex's gelding before reaching under its belly for the cinch. The man would come to the barn shortly to begin his ride back to Butte, but hopefully he'd appreciate these few private moments with his sister.

The evening before had been tense, especially before Cathleen invited her brother out for a walk under the stars. Whatever she'd said, the man had been a little more genial after that, although chores kept Reuben away in the barn most of the evening after they returned.

It was plain Cathleen loved her brother, although she certainly wasn't afraid to speak her mind when she disagreed with him. That was a side Reuben had only seen a few times—like when she insisted he sleep in the cabin instead of the barn. Those pert brows arched, and her eyes sparked. She was even more distracting in these moments than when she flashed that smile that heated his insides.

But as relieved as he was that she'd chosen to stay, was he making the wrong decision in letting her? Mum would certainly be better off with her here. He would do his best by Mum if Cathleen left, but she had a special way that his mother adored. Like the daughter she always wanted. The daughter she would have had, if only his twin sister had lived. He'd worked his hardest to fill the void Nora's death had caused, but they'd all felt it. Even now it lodged a longing in his chest.

A shadow shifted in the barn doorway as Reuben pulled the cinch strap tight. He patted the gelding and turned to face the doctor. "He's all ready."

As Alex moved closer, the sun shifted from his back, so his features were more distinguishable. The softness in his profile when he'd spoken with Cathleen at breakfast was gone, replaced by stiff shoulders and a firm jaw.

Did the man hold something against him? Or just the situation in general? Was there anything he could say to help Donaghue feel better about leaving his sister here? It was worth a try.

He stepped back as Alex tossed his saddle bags over the rear of the saddle. After licking his parched lips, he started in. "I appreciate all your family's done for my parents. I know it's not been easy, but Mum would be much worse off without Cathleen's help."

If it were possible, Alex's shoulders stiffened even more, but his back was to Reuben as he tied the leather straps to secure the bag. It was a long moment before the man responded, but he finally let out a long breath and turned to look Reuben in the eye.

"I can't say I like it, Cathleen staying up here. We didn't think she should come in the first place, but your mother was in a bad way. So, we let her help. But now that you're here, well..."

The man's brows rose in that same pert way Cathleen's did when she expected to be obeyed. Yet coming from this man, it definitely felt more like a challenge.

What could he say to ease Donaghue's concerns? Forthright had always been his approach with the Crow. Maybe it would suit him here, too.

He met Alex's gaze. "I understand your worries. Your sister's been a godsend for my mother. I don't know what we would have done without her. And if she stays here, you have my word I'll protect her with my life. But if you think she should go home with you, we won't hold her back."

Alex stared at him for a long scrutinizing moment. Gone was the challenge in his gaze, replaced only with searching. At last, he let out a breath and scrubbed a hand through his hair. "I don't know, Scott. I don't like her being up here, but Cathy tends to think more with her heart than her head. And she's a bit stubborn besides. Once she sets her mind to help someone, it'd take a man stronger than me to change it. I'm not sure I could get her to leave unless I tied her on a horse and led her down the mountain."

Put that way, it made him and Mum sound like a charity case. But he forced down his wayward pride. "I'll make sure she's safe. And if I can talk her into going home, I'll bring her there myself."

Another sigh leaked from Alex, and he moved around to the other side of the horse to fasten the pack there. "I suppose that's the best I can hope for."

Reuben stepped closer to the gelding, stroking its forehead. Just one question remained, but he wasn't sure he wanted to know the answer. But if he was any man at all, he had to ask it. "So, doctor. What about my mum's condition?"

Donaghue didn't answer right away but finished fastening his pack. Then he turned to Reuben with clear deliberation, propping an arm on the saddle to face him across the horse. "She has senile dementia. More severe than a lot of cases I see. I'm a bit surprised it's come on so quickly."

Reuben swallowed. "You think it's because of Pa's death? She's trying to forget?"

The doctor shook his head. "This form of the disease isn't thought to be something triggered by intentional memory blockage. The general consensus is that the arteries leading to the brain harden, so the brain doesn't receive the blood flow it needs. Over time, portions of the brain stop working from lack of nutrients."

His own head pounded, but he forced the doctor's words to make sense in his mind. So this truly was a medical condition. Not that he'd questioned that for a while now. But it sounded so...irreversible. "Is there anything we can do to make her mind start working again?"

A glimmer shone in the doctor's eyes. Not pity, thank the Lord, but sadness. "I wish there were. A lot of great minds have worked to find a cure for dementia, but no proven treatment has been discovered yet."

He swallowed to force moisture into his dry mouth. Just one more question had to be asked. "How much longer? Is this something that'll kill her?"

The doctor's gaze didn't waver. "We all die eventually. She could have a few months. Maybe even several years. But God calls us all home in His time."

There was truth in the man's statement. Everyone did die eventually. But bringing God into the mix? Reuben had long ago resigned from believing God cared about what really happened in his life. If others wanted to believe a Supreme Being helped them each step of the way, that was fine. But throughout his life he'd not seen one whit of difference in the outcome of things whether he'd involved the Almighty or not. And it was easier to make his way on his own.

"I've left Cathy some herbs that may help open the arteries and lessen the progression of damage. Beyond that, enjoy the time with your mother. Try not to argue with her when she gets confused. Help her remember pleasant memories from the past. Do things with her she enjoys. That will help stimulate her brain function as much as anything."

Reuben nodded. At least it was something. Something he was capable of, certainly.

The two of them walked from the barn together, Donaghue

leading his horse. When they reached the open yard, Reuben glanced toward the house. "Shall I go tell Cathleen you're headed out?"

Alex followed his gaze. "I guess so." The words escaped on a sigh.

Reuben started that direction, but Cathleen must have been watching for them. The door opened, and she stepped outside, leading Mum by the hand. She raised her other hand to shade her eyes as Alex stopped in front of the porch.

"You sure you don't want to go with me?" His voice held just a hint of hope.

She gave him a sweet smile. "I'm sure. Give my love to everyone. And snuggle the babies for me."

He raised a brow. "There's not much snuggling with William these days."

A soft chuckle flowed from her. "I guess there isn't. Well, remind him Aunt Cathy loves him."

Alex mounted and gave her a final look. "Last chance."

Something that sounded like a grunt issued from Cathleen. "Are you hedging for more food, Alex? I already packed a half dozen cinnamon rolls for you."

Now it was her brother's turn to chuckle. "No. The pack feels like I'm taking out as much food as I brought in." His gaze swept the three of them. "So long, then. Don't be strangers."

Reuben raised a hand in farewell as the three of them watched the man ride off. He could feel the angst as clearly as he could see it in the set of Alex's shoulders. Probably the same as Reuben would feel if he were in that saddle and his baby sister stood on the porch waving goodbye. Maybe even the same empty place Reuben had carried all these years for his lost twin.

Except Alex had the hope that he'd see his sister again. Soon.

And until his dying breath, Reuben would make sure she stayed safe and happy for that meeting.

CHAPTER 16

*R*euben slipped through the cabin door the next morning after barn chores, determination flooding every pore inside him. He'd spent the night wrestling with how to help both Mum and Cathleen. The doctor said spend time with Mum. And getting her away might free Cathleen up some, but she still worked so hard around the place, he wanted to help them both. His hides were all to the final softening phase, and half of them were done with that already, so he could afford to leave them alone for a day or two.

Now was his chance.

Cathleen looked up from the sink, and her smile took a second longer to form than usual. "I didn't expect you back so soon. Want another mug of coffee? Alex brought me a fresh supply of cinnamon sticks, so I can brew a special blend if you like."

A grin tugged at his mouth. He'd never smell cinnamon again that he didn't think of this woman. Just the thought of the stuff made him want to step close and nuzzle her neck, take another whiff from the aroma that always seemed to cloak her.

But...that wouldn't do just now.

"No coffee. I came back in to help."

Her brows rose, and she turned toward him more fully, raising an arm to wipe her forehead with the back of her wrist. She held a scrubbing pad, and the edges of the big cast iron pot peeked out of the sink. "Help? I think we're all right for now. Thanks for checking, though."

He glanced toward Mum, who sat at the table with her hands covered in floury white dough. She smiled her wrinkled, toothy grin at him. "You always were a good lad."

A frown tightened his brow. He'd come in here to help, not be shooed off like a boy not capable of anything. This felt too much like all those times growing up when he'd tried to assist his parents and failed miserably. But his mother wasn't the same woman she'd been then, and he was going to get it right this time if he had to die trying.

He stepped farther into the kitchen and peered over Cathleen's shoulder. "I can scrub that pot."

She glanced up at him from the corner of her gaze, and he suddenly realized how close he'd approached. A mere foot separated them.

She dropped her focus back to the pot and swished a handful of water around its base. "It's all right, Reuben, really. I'm done here. Once I get the floor swept, we were going to make soap. I know you have a lot of work to do on your furs. You don't have to worry about us."

Something about the way she wouldn't look at him sent a ribbon of frustration through his chest. He was asking to help, why wouldn't she let him? In two strides, he grabbed the broom from the corner and started whisking the dust and food scraps out from the corners and under the table. North jumped up from his bed when Reuben's broom neared, and the dog padded to the far side of the great room. His efforts might have been a little overzealous, but at least he was getting the job done. Helping.

"Reuben...?" Cathleen started her question, but didn't finish.

"What?" His voice rang with a little more impatience than he should have let show, but if she thought she was going to send him to the barn when there was work to be done here, she'd best adjust her views on the matter. And she could raise her brows and stomp her feet all she wanted. Wouldn't change a thing.

But she didn't.

While he swept out the kitchen and sitting area, she clanged dishes around for a while, then pulled packages down from the shelves. When he came back in from sweeping the scraps off the side of the porch, he saw she'd sat at the table with Mum.

"So I melt the lard first, then combine the lye and water?"

"Yes, dearie. That way they can both cool at the same time. Don't worry, I'll show you." Mum patted Cathleen's hand as affection spilled from her tone.

Cathleen always took such pains to make his mother feel needed. That was probably one of the reasons Mum adored her so.

Cathleen shot a glance at him as he replaced the broom in the corner, but then she turned back to Mum in a lower tone. "So I heat the lye and water mixture on the stove, too? When do I know it's ready?" Twin lines formed on Cathleen's forehead. She was certainly pressing deep with her questions. Maybe she was trying to coax Mum's memory back to life like Alex had said.

Mum shook her head. "No, you don't heat the lye. It gets hot on its own when you add it to the water. An' ya gotta make sure you add the lye to the water, not the water to the lye. Else ye'll blow up the kitchen."

The memory work seemed to be effective. Mum was speaking more clearly than he'd heard her in weeks.

Cathleen pushed back from the table and turned to scan her ingredients.

He eased forward a step. "Just tell me what to do." He kept his prodding gentle, but he wanted to make sure she knew he was here to work.

She tossed a distracted glance his way, then peered over a pot on the work counter. "Could you get some fresh water from the stream? Make it as clean as you can."

Good. That was work he could handle without feeling awkward.

When he returned with a full pail, Cathleen was bent over the work counter, peering at the old scales Mum used for soap-making.

The mess of dough still sat on the table, but his mother was nowhere in sight.

"Here you go. Where's Mum?" He set the bucket down by the stove.

"She needed to rest." Cathleen didn't take her focus from the scales she studied.

"What are you weighing?"

"Lard. She said five pounds, but this scale only goes up to two pounds. Which means I have to transfer the stuff again until I get everything measured out."

He studied the dial on the scale as she spooned more of the thick, gelatinous stuff into the bowl on the scale. She slowed her scooping as the dial neared its two pound limit.

As he did the calculations in his head, he was missing one important number. "How much does that basin weigh?"

She darted a wide-eyed glance up at him. "Um. I don't know."

The look on her face, like a frightened deer, bubbled up a chuckle in his chest. With all her other talents, arithmetic must not be as high on the list. "All right, then. Let's get this to the two pound mark, then we'll weigh the bowl by itself."

As they finished weighing the lard and got it transferred into the smaller black pot, an easy split of roles developed. He handled the measurements, and she handled the thick, messy ingredient.

At last, he stepped back. "All right. Five pounds of lard. What's next?"

Cathleen shifted the pot to the stove. "Now a little less than two pounds of water."

He frowned. "How much less?"

She shrugged. "A little less is what she said."

"How do *you* normally do it?"

Her mouth pinched. "I don't."

"You don't use water?" Why weren't they making soap from her recipe, the one she was familiar with?

She turned in a flounce of skirts and faced him dead on. "I don't make soap. I've never made soap. I have no idea what I'm doing here, other than praying your Mum's memory is strong enough to give me all the details. And it doesn't help that part of the instructions included something about not blowing up the kitchen." With that last sentence, she threw her hands into the air, making a bit of an explosion herself.

He stood mutely as her words sank in. Then he couldn't help but cock his head as he studied her. "You've never made soap?"

Now she glared at him. "No, Reuben. We bought our soap ready-made. I've never needed to cook the stuff from scratch."

He should hold his tongue, but the questions kept prodding him. "But you're an apothecary's daughter. Didn't you make soaps to sell in the shop?"

Another withering glare. "I could mix any salve we carried, and perfectly recreate Lydia Pinkham's Herb Medicine, but Dad always purchased the soaps we stocked."

As her spurt of anger subsided, a vulnerability he'd not seen before glimmered in her eyes. Her lack of ability—or at least knowledge—really bothered her. Was that because she was so competent in most other areas of keeping house and nursing? Or maybe she wasn't as experienced as she let on. How many other times had she fumbled her way through a task since she'd come to the homestead? If that were the case, she was sure accomplished at hiding it. And that was a challenge he could relate to.

He offered Cathleen a grin. "Well, I guess that makes this the first time for both of us. Do you think Mum's memory was good enough to get this done?"

She nibbled one corner of her lip. "I think so. I hope so."

An idea came to him. "Maybe I should head down the mountain and buy it. I'm sure we could use some supplies anyway. With all the snow melted, this might be our only chance."

Her brows lowered and her teeth worked harder on her lip. "I... really need soap today."

"Today?" What was the rush?

She nodded. "We've been low for a while, and your mum's had several accidents lately. When Alex brought the supplies I thought we'd be fine, but it turned out there was no soap in the lot. I should have made it yesterday, but…I guess I just couldn't work up the nerve to try."

The way she prattled on, he almost had to laugh. "So there's no soap left at all?"

She shook her head, dejection drooping her shoulders. "Not for a few days now. And your mum's out of clean clothes."

He reached for his left shirt sleeve and started to roll it. "Let's make soap then."

~

"*Y*ou want to pour the lye or stir?" Cathleen held the wooden spoon toward Reuben.

"I'll stir." His hand brushed hers as he took the spoon, and a tingle shot up the nerves in her arm. Being near this man did funny things to her, no doubt about it.

"All right." She examined the pot of water and the bowl of lye crystals on the work counter. "I guess we just mix. She said we had to let it cool, but I'm still not clear on how it gets hot to begin with. She did say to make sure we pour the lye into the water. That was where the part about not blowing up the kitchen came in."

He stepped up behind her, and his warm hand touched her back, pressing a little to ease her forward. "Let's do it then."

His hand stayed at the small of her back a while longer. The warmth and protected feeling that settled over her made her want to sink against him. But all too soon, his hand fell away, and she was left with a bowl of lye in her hands, longing for that warmth again.

While she poured the lye crystals into the water, he stirred the cloudy mixture. With every rotation of the spoon, his upper arm brushed against hers. Did he feel each touch as strongly as she did? She should add more distance between them, but truth be told, she didn't want him to stop.

"How do we know when it's cool?" His voice came out a little husky, so close to her ear.

She forced her mind away from Reuben and back to Mrs. Scott's instructions. "She said stir until it gets clear. Maybe by then it will have cooled?" She hazarded a touch to the outside of the pan. Heat definitely warmed the surface, and a noxious odor permeated the air around them. It tickled her throat, and she turned away to cough out the fumes.

"Strong stuff, huh?" Reuben coughed too, then snatched up the handle on the pot. "I think I see why Mum always made this outside."

With long strides, he carried the pot toward the door and out onto the porch, holding it as far away from himself as his long arms would allow.

The smell followed him out, and Cathleen coughed again to rid her lungs of the wretched stuff. Something bubbled on the stove, and she stepped closer to peer into the pot of lard. It was a clear amber liquid, and while she watched, another bubble rose to the surface and popped. Definitely time to let it cool.

After she'd moved the pot to a leather pad on the work counter, she headed toward the porch to check on Reuben.

He sat on the top step, still stirring the lye mixture. She settled beside him. "How's it coming?"

He raised a brow at her, not stopping the motion of the spoon. "I never realized how much went into making soap." A twinkle slipped into his eye. "It's kind of fun."

And she felt the same way, although she had a strong inkling it wouldn't be half as pleasant without him there.

The rest of the process was fairly uneventful. After they poured the lye mixture into the lard, Reuben stirred for what seemed like half an hour.

Cathleen kept her post seated beside him, absorbing his nearness. "So are you finished with the hides you've been working on?"

"Almost. Just a half dozen or so to finish softening."

"What will you do with them then?"

He shrugged. "I usually take them down to the mercantile or the dry goods in Butte. Sometimes trade them to a freighter when the wagons start coming through in the spring. The hides are usually enough to restock supplies around here for most of the year."

Such an interesting job. Some men were doctors or dentists, others worked in the mines, but this man helped provide for his family by trapping.

Reuben cleared his throat. "So you have a niece and nephew in Butte?"

She glanced up at his face, but he stared casually into the mixture he stirred. He was making small talk?

"Yes. Amanda's just three months old, but William's a year now. That's actually why I came west. Both my brothers' wives were expecting, and Mum was in a fit about someone being there to help. Dad wouldn't leave the shop, and she didn't want to leave him, so...I was the likely choice."

She shot him a smile, and he glanced up at her but didn't return the expression. "You miss Boston?"

Did that thought bother him? Because his face certainly looked troubled. She chose her words carefully. "I miss my parents. The city's nice, but...not anything as special as these mountains."

Those blue eyes pierced her, probing past her words. "You like the mountains?"

She met his gaze squarely. "Very much. I don't think I've ever seen anything as beautiful as the view from this front porch when the trees and the far mountain range are covered with snow."

"One day I'll take you to a spot that's even prettier." The tenor of his voice dropped, turning husky again. "You can see mountains for miles and miles. It's like you're standing at the top of the world."

Something fluttered in her chest. "I'd like that."

He reached to brush a finger along her temple, tucking a strand of hair behind her ear. His touch left a tingle everywhere it landed. She couldn't help but lean into the sensation, and his palm slid around to cup her cheek.

"Cathy." The hint of a smile played at his mouth as his gaze searched her face. "That's what your brother called you. Do you like it?"

She liked it too much, when it came from his lips. Like warm cinnamon tea flowing through her. "Only my family calls me that. Makes me feel loved." Her words came out like a breathy whisper, though she couldn't seem to summon enough air with him so close. Touching her.

"Cathy." His gaze flickered down to her mouth, which had gone as dry as cotton. "I like it."

Her eyes sank closed as he drew closer. The touch of his breath gave warning just before his lips brushed hers. The gentlest of kisses. But...oh...so perfect.

She slid a hand up to his neck, and he came back for another, deeper this time, yet still so tender. She rested her other hand on his shoulder.

Oh, mercy. Who would have thought a kiss from this mountain man would be so exquisitely gentle?

~

She even tasted of cinnamon. Reuben pulled her closer, every bit of her filling his senses until he couldn't breathe, couldn't think, could only crave. His hand slid from her cheek, into her hair. So soft. So perfect, every part of her.

He had to stop this madness. Even as his mind gave the command, his body said no. But he didn't want to scare her. Except, considering the way she kissed him back, fear seemed to be the last thing on her mind. But still...

Gradually, he eased the intensity of his kiss, moving into quick light kisses on her bottom lip, the corners of her mouth, then touching his mouth to hers for one final memory.

He finally pulled back a few inches and let his eyes take in her beauty. Those full lips now bloomed rosy red, the same flush filling her cheeks. And her lashes... As they fluttered open, he saw how truly long they were. Elegant, just like every part of her. Those brown eyes were cloudy as they lifted to his, and the look almost made him come back for another taste.

Instead, he pulled her to his chest. He had to get a handle on his breathing. And his racing heart.

She molded to him, wrapping her arms around his waist and planting a feeling in his chest that almost burned from its intensity. "Cathy." He murmured the word as he pressed a kiss into her hair.

Her response was a contented sigh, and she pressed even closer. That definitely wasn't helping slow his galloping pulse. He'd better get her down the mountain soon, before he did something they'd both regret.

CHAPTER 17

*L*ater that afternoon, Reuben stopped scraping the hide to listen. Was that a scream he'd heard?

No sounds drifted from the yard now. All the animals were out enjoying the last of the temperate weather, since it looked like the chinook had blown through. Snow would come again soon.

Dropping the pelt to the work table, he touched his hip to make sure his knife was in its holster, then grabbed his Sharps and sprinted toward the open barn door.

The cry could have been the squeal of a horse, but it sounded like it had come from the direction of the house. He couldn't take chances.

When he reached the yard, two figures on horseback drew him up short. He'd recognize the horses and the beadwork on their blankets anywhere, but seeing his good friends here—in the yard of his parents' homestead—gave him pause.

Gathering himself, he strode toward the men. They saw him right away and turned their animals to close the distance. Akecheta sat proud and tall on his horse, the warrior worthy of his name. But Mato...something was definitely wrong there. His frame had always been slighter than Akecheta's and most of the other braves, but the way he slumped over his horse... Was the man injured? Sick?

Dread snaked through Reuben as the horses stopped in front of him. He raised a hand to greet the men and spoke in their native language. "Welcome, friends. It's a good surprise to see you here. All is well?"

Akecheta gave the sign of greeting, then nodded toward Mato. "We came to your mountain for hunting, but this one is sick. He needs a resting place."

Reuben studied Mato closer. Yes, the man had lost most of the color on his usually tanned face. Could be due to blood loss from an injury, but Akecheta had used the Crow word for illness. What did the man suffer from? One of the diseases spread from the white people? He'd seen yellow fever rip through an Indian band and kill more than half of them. If that was what Mato suffered from, his friend was in a bad way.

He stepped around the sick man's horse and raised a hand to touch his forehead. No fever that he could feel. Looking over to meet Akecheta's gaze, he asked, "What is he sick with?"

Akecheta spoke a word Reuben hadn't heard before, and mimicked vomiting something from his belly.

No fever, but there was vomiting. That would explain some of the man's pallor. "Can he drink water?"

"A little."

Well, that was a good sign. He needed to get the man bedded down and try to feed him broth or something. Maybe Cathleen would know what else to do. But he couldn't let the illness get close to her or Mum. Not until he was certain what the man suffered from.

He pointed toward the barn. "Make a bed for him in the hay. I'll get food and drink for you both. Feed your horses in the stalls."

As his foot touched the first step of the porch, Cathleen jerked the front door open. "Who are they, Reuben. What's wrong?"

His chest did a little flip at the sight of her, his body remembering their kiss from that morning. He'd secluded himself in the barn purposely to let those feelings settle, but just the sight of her stirred everything anew.

But the angst on her face helped to sidetrack him a little, and he stepped closer. "Everything's all right." He couldn't stop himself from brushing a wayward strand of hair from her cheek, but he did refrain from swooping down for another kiss.

"Do you know them?"

He had to blink to pull himself back to the cause of her worry. "Yes. It's Akecheta and Mato, friends from the Crow band that winters near my cabin. They said they came this way for hunting, but Mato's pretty sick."

She started to push past him as she craned her neck to search the yard. "What's wrong with him? Are you bringing him inside?"

He grabbed Cathleen's arm before she ran out to meet them, then guided her through the cabin door. "They're settling in the barn. I don't want them near you two until we figure out if it's catching."

She gripped his wrist with her free hand, slowing their forward progress just inside the doorway. "What is it, Reuben?" She searched his eyes, lines creasing her forehead.

"Some kind of stomach illness. He's vomiting, but I don't think he's feverish."

She paused for a moment, her gaze drifting as her thoughts took over. "I'll make some ginger root tea. Can he eat? Is he drinking? Do you think it's typhoid?" She whirled and headed for the kitchen shelves.

Reuben followed in her wake. "I don't think so. A little. And I have no idea."

She fluttered about like a whirlwind, pulling herbs from a box, clanging pots on the stove, stoking the fire.

"What can I do?" Anything to keep from standing there like a bump on a log.

"We need to get him in the house where I can tend him. Get some extra blankets from the trunk in my room."

"I'll get the blankets, but he's not coming in. Not until I know it's safe."

She shot him a glare, but it turned into a thoughtful look as she stirred the pot on the stove. "Your mum could be susceptible, I suppose. Get the blankets, and we'll go see him in the barn."

He had to lock his jaw in place to keep from telling her—once again—that she wouldn't see the man either until they were sure it was safe. But he'd wait to argue the point when he was ready to take the supplies to the barn.

When he stepped into her chamber—his old room—a wave of nostalgia swept over him. Every aspect still looked the same. Same rough cut wooden boards on the walls. Same pegs mounted in the corner near the washstand. Even the same bedposts where he'd carved his name that time he'd been sent to bed without supper for sneaking off to fish when he was supposed to be checking the cattle.

Yet the whole place was so very different, with one of Cathleen's frilly dresses laid over the bed, and several fancy combs and bottles on the dresser. At least no white underthings peeked out at him from anywhere.

He stopped at the old trunk by the foot of the bed, the one where Mum always kept the spare blankets and bits of cloth. Inside, familiar quilts lay like old friends. Some he could even remember helping Mum stitch.

Pressing those memories aside, he gathered the three from the top, then lowered the lid and left the room exactly as he found it. Yet the sight of very womanly things—Cathleen's things—in the midst of his familiar domain left an impression burned in his mind.

When he returned to the main room, Cathleen was piling cloth bundles into a basket. "I have a stew simmering for supper, but it's not ready yet. I suppose I can come back for it."

She looked up at him, her brow knit. "I put your Mum down for a nap when I first saw the Indians. Do you think she'll be all right for a while if we bar the door?"

Now was the time to put his foot down. "She'll be fine, because you'll be here with her. I don't want you exposed to whatever Mato has."

Her chin jutted forward the slightest bit. "He needs someone to care for him, Reuben."

He kept his voice steady, but laced a bit of steel through it. "That's what I plan to do. And Akecheta can help. Won't be the first time I've nursed an Indian through a white man's disease."

That determined look in her eye didn't fade. "So you think you're less likely to get sick? Why? Because you're the strong man and I'm just a weak female?"

Ouch. That wasn't what he'd been thinking at all. He cared too much about her to let something happen to her. Something he could prevent. He'd rather die a thousand deaths than watch her suffer the way the Crow had suffered those years ago.

He took a step forward, relaxing his posture the way he would with a frightened horse. "Cathy. That's not..." How could he tell his reason for protecting her without revealing everything inside him?

She inhaled a long breath, loud enough he could hear it even with several feet between them. Her eyes softened the tiniest bit, and glimmered with sincerity. "Helping people is what I do, Reuben. Please don't try to stop me."

"Cathleen. I...I just don't want to see you hurt. I don't... I couldn't..." He scrubbed a hand through his hair. Why couldn't he find the right words?

She stepped forward, closing the gap between them. Her hand touched his arm, the gentlest of touches, yet the pressure drove deep. "You don't have to keep me safe, you know."

"I do." His hand dropped from his hair, and he straightened. How could he explain this fierce craving in his chest? "I want to."

Her thumb stroked his arm, the pressure warm, even through the wool of his shirt. "I'll be careful. I promise."

He didn't like it, not one bit. But with those luminous brown eyes pleading that way, he was powerless to say no. "Please. Be careful."

That smile bloomed on her face, making him feel that—just maybe —giving in had been worth it. But it couldn't quite squelch the churning in his gut.

~

*C*athleen peered into the dim light of the barn as she followed Reuben inside. She'd watched the Indians speaking to him in the yard, but that had been at a distance through the tiny window. And it was before she'd known for certain they were friendly.

The idea that Reuben not only interacted with the Indians, but counted some of them as close friends, was still a marvel to her. He paused by the threshold, struck a match, and lit one of the barn lanterns, then they proceeded toward the back corner where he'd slept those first few nights.

A rustling sounded in the hay as one of the dark figures rose to his feet.

"Cathleen, this is Akecheta and Mato." Reuben motioned first to the man standing, then the smaller Indian curled in the hay. The poor brave on the ground let out a moan and coiled into a tighter ball.

Her gaze roamed his body for symptoms, but she couldn't see much of him, covered in his blanket. She glanced up at the tall Indian and nodded. "How do you do?"

The man grunted a word. Not English that she could tell.

Reuben spoke a string of Indian words, and the other man nodded, answering with a few words in the same language. The cadence was rhythmic, with alternating high and low sounds. So foreign to her ears.

When it sounded like the men were done speaking, she looked to Reuben for interpretation.

He touched her arm and spoke in a low tone. "I told him you were a healer, here helping Mum. He said you could check Mato."

She nodded and eased the basket down beside the man. She should kneel and check his symptoms, but a sudden shyness held her back. Not only was this a strange man she'd never met before, but an Indian, no less. *Lord, give me strength.*

He moaned again, and the sound loosened the concern holding her back.

Dropping to her knees by the man's head, she stroked his black hair away from his brow. The braid that must have been intended to restrain the locks was losing the battle. His forehead didn't feel warm, at least not very.

She peered up at the Indian looming behind his friend. "What are his symptoms?"

He answered in the sing-song Indian language, and Reuben spoke after his friend finished.

"He's casting up his accounts."

She glanced up at Reuben. "Runny stools, too? How long has he had the symptoms?"

It might have been her imagination, but in the glow of the lantern he still held, it looked like his ears turned red. He looked to Akecheta, who spoke words in rapid succession.

"He, uh, said the symptoms have been there since yesterday morning."

She turned back to the patient and pressed two fingers to the pulse in his neck. "And the other?"

"He cannot dishonor his friend by speaking of such things."

She sent Reuben a sharp look.

He held up his hands, palm out. "I know. I'm just the messenger."

She sent that same glare to the Indian standing over her but didn't give voice to her frustration. If she had any chance of helping his friend, she needed to know what they were dealing with here.

Mato's pulse was steady, if a little light. When she shone the lantern into his eyes, the pupils shrank evenly as they should. He opened his mouth when Reuben translated her request, but no bright red bumps marred his tongue or gums. Good.

"I'm going to move this blanket so I can see your arms now." She spoke to the man on the ground, but loud enough for the guard above her to hear.

As she eased the cloth back, her gaze took in every bare patch of skin she could find. His neck, left arm from the elbow down, the skin of his right hand. Everything looked to be a normal light-brown color. Not yellowed. No rashes that she could see, although she needed to verify that.

"Mato, have you developed any red bumps or a rash?" Maybe she

137

would have better luck asking the patient directly than going through his bodyguard.

Reuben squatted beside her, his hand resting lightly on her shoulder. In a low tone, he repeated the words in the Indian's language.

The protective warmth of Reuben's touch stole her attention so it was hard to focus on Mato's faint answer. As she tried to comprehend the response, she finally realized it was spoken in Indian. Of course. She needed to forget about the strong presence beside her and focus on caring for her patient.

"He doesn't think so."

Well that was a good start. She'd need to have the men check him over in a little while, when she went to get the broth. They had to rule out typhoid, which would surely show itself in a rash at this point. For now, though, the poor man needed to drink something before his muscles seized up.

She poured a mug of ginger tea and slipped her hand behind his head to prop it a little. "This is going to taste bitter."

Reuben translated beside her, and the man took two sips, then grunted and sank back against the blanket. It was interesting that Reuben interpreted her words for Mato, but not when she spoke to Akecheta, yet both men responded in their native language. Either Akecheta could understand English better than he could speak it, or he chose not to give voice to the words.

She ran a cold cloth over Mato's head, even though he wasn't feverish. After a bit more encouragement, he finally downed the remainder of the tea in the small mug. If this was a typical stomach ailment, the ginger would help a great deal.

Easing back onto her heels, she settled the blanket under Mato's arms. "I'm going to get food for you both." She turned to Reuben. "I need to know for sure it's not typhoid. Can you check under his clothing to make sure he doesn't have a rash?"

Reuben only raised a brow. She ignored it and pushed to her feet. He gripped her elbow and helped her rise.

She hurried with her basket to the house, and within a quarter hour, had the foodstuffs loaded in a crate and was headed back to the barn. The wind whipped at her hair, pulling it from its pins. The temperature had dropped substantially, and the clouds loomed low and gray. That Chinook wind that had brought such wonderful balmy days must be gone. Did that mean more snow was coming soon?

CHAPTER 18

The protection of the barn was a welcome relief, and Cathleen blew at a tendril of hair that plastered itself in her mouth. What a sight she must be. Maybe she could cover her dishevelment with a bright smile.

Reuben appeared from the shadows, striding toward her. His tall form and broad shoulders set off butterflies in her stomach as it usually did these days. Especially after that kiss. She could still feel the memory of it when she closed her eyes. It was hard to believe a man like Reuben, so vibrant and larger than life, could have any feelings for someone like her. Just a simple apothecary's daughter from Boston.

He met her halfway across the barn and took the crate from her grip. His eyes searched hers, apprehension in their blue shadows. Was he worried about his friend? Or that the sickness would spread to his mother?

She forced a soft smile. "It's getting really cold out there. Windy, too."

He nodded, and turned toward the back corner where their visitors were settled. She tried to straighten her hair as they walked, but so many wisps had pulled loose, there was no hope.

He still didn't speak, so she switched to a different topic. "Did you check Mato for a rash? I meant to tell you to look at his hands and feet especially."

"We looked but didn't find anything."

Relief eased through her as she let out a breath. "That's good. Really good." No apparent signs of either typhoid or yellow fever. And with his temperature not elevated, could the man's problem be that he'd gotten hold of bad food? *Lord, please let that be the case. Give me wisdom.*

Akecheta sat by his friend and quickly downed the stew and sourdough bread she'd brought. Mato wasn't nearly as eager, but he did keep his eyes open now and had uncurled a little from the ball he'd been in before.

"Are you feeling better?" She poured another half mug of tea for the man.

He spoke a single word, and Reuben offered the meaning. "A little."

"I'm glad." She kept her attention focused on her patient. "See if you can eat this bread with more tea."

It took several gentle urgings, but the man finished the drink and ate half a slice of bread. They were making progress.

She finally straightened and glanced around the barn. Even though the structure kept out most of the wind, she could hear it howling outside, and the temperature had dropped, so she couldn't stop shivering. These men couldn't sleep out here. They'd freeze to death with no fire.

Cutting a glance at Reuben, she rose to her feet. "Would you help me carry this box back to the house?"

If she could assure him Mato didn't have a contagious disease, maybe he'd let the men sleep in the cabin. But they couldn't discuss it in front of their guests.

As she turned to leave, Akecheta grunted a word at her. She paused and looked at the man, then at Reuben.

"He says thank you." Reuben's low tone was accompanied by the hint of a smile playing at the corners of his mouth.

She looked back at the Indian, sitting tall beside his friend. "You're welcome. I'm glad you both came to us."

He nodded, then looked away. Effectively dismissing her.

But it didn't stop the elation in her chest as she and Reuben left the barn.

The moment they stepped outside, the wind attacked with ferocity, and she pulled her thin shawl tighter around her shoulders. She should have worn her coat, but how could she have known the weather would change so quickly?

"Reuben, those men can't sleep in the barn tonight. It's getting too cold."

He shot her a glance as he huddled against a gust. "I'm not bringing them inside to infect the place."

"But I'm fairly certain he doesn't have typhoid or yellow fever." She rested a hand on his arm. "Reuben, I think it may have been something he ate. It will pass soon, maybe even by morning. We can't let them freeze to death out there."

He slid a look at her but didn't answer.

She knew better than to push him, so she left it alone until they reached the cabin.

Mrs. Scott was just shuffling from her room when they stepped inside, her white-gray hair mussed but her eyes bright. "There you are, dear. I was just gonna get supper started."

Cathleen followed her toward the kitchen and bent down at the cook stove to add another piece of wood. "I made some Irish stew for us. Would you like to butter the bread?"

～

*R*euben wiped his mouth on a serviette, then pushed back from the table. "Food was good."

He needed to get out to the barn and settle the animals for the night. And maybe he could make it outside before Cathleen started pressing to bring his friends into the house again. Akecheta would be fine in the elements. The brave knew how to survive in the coldest temperatures. Especially with a few extra furs he could take them.

Normally, he wouldn't worry about Mato either. But would the man's weakened condition affect his ability to withstand the cold? What exactly was wrong with him? Cathleen seemed to think it was nothing more than bad meat. Would that lay the man so low? Reuben had suffered that malady himself once or twice at his winter cabin, when the hunting had been poor and he'd been forced to eat something he normally wouldn't touch. And he did remember being sick enough to wish for death. Could their fiery nurse be right? Maybe.

"Reuben?"

He made it to the door before her word caught up to him. "Yep." He didn't turn, just slipped his coat on and fastened the hooks. But it didn't stop his full awareness as she stepped close behind him.

"I'll have your mum in bed in about an hour. Will you please bring your friends into the house then? I can scrub things well tomorrow, so she won't risk getting sick. Please?"

He clamped his jaw against the pleading in her voice. Why did she care so much about those men anyway? She only met them a few hours ago. And they were Indians, for mercy's sake. Eastern city girls were supposed to be shaking to their toes at the mere thought of Indians. She cared far too much for people.

His traitorous body turned for a glimpse of her, and it had the exact effect he'd known it would. He melted. This caring spirit was exactly what he loved about her, exactly what drew him to her in the first place. That and her magnificent smile.

He breathed out a sigh. "All right."

She rewarded him with one of those smiles, then grabbed his arm and pulled him down to plant a kiss on his cheek.

The warmth of it sluiced through him. She started to back away, but that absolutely wouldn't do. He grabbed her hand and pulled her back as he lowered his lips to hers. He kept it short and light. Just a memory of that kiss from earlier.

Still, when he backed away, all the blood seemed to have emptied from his head, leaving him blinking to regain control. He turned toward the door so she couldn't see her effect on him, as he grabbed his gloves and struggled them on. "I'll bring them inside in an hour."

"Thank you, Reuben."

If he didn't know better, he'd have said there was a touch of laughter in her tone. Most likely because she'd seen through what he'd been trying to hide. Knew exactly what his reaction meant. This woman could read him far too well.

As much as that should scare him—and it did—a small piece of him felt the relief of knowing someone cared enough to try to understand him. That *Cathleen* cared that much.

~

The next morning in the cold wind, Reuben stood at the base of the porch stairs, stroking the muzzle of Mato's horse. He looked over at Akecheta, who sat tall on his own mount. "You are welcome to stay longer, my friends."

The brave shook his head. "Our people wait for us. Your kindness will be long remembered."

Cathleen stepped from the cabin then, saving him from having to mentally translate an answer into Crow. She took the stairs gracefully and moved up beside Akecheta's horse. That hint of nerves he'd detected when she first met the Indians in the barn yesterday was long gone now.

She lifted a hand to shield her eyes from the sun as she raised a cloth bundle toward him. "This will give you something to eat on the trail. I put some ginger root in there, too. If either of you feels sick, steep it in water and drink."

She glanced over at Mato, and Reuben followed her gaze. The smaller man still looked weak, but most of the color was back in his face, and he sat straighter on his horse than when he'd arrived. He'd not vomited since the effort to move him to the house last night, and he'd eaten both bread and potatoes this morning. Not to mention all the tea and water Cathleen had plied him with.

It'd been good to see his friends, to hear news about the rest of the band as he and Akecheta had talked last night. He was sorry to see them go, although he did feel some relief that they were taking away the risk for contamination to Mum and Cathleen.

Akecheta raised a hand in farewell, then spoke in his native language. "Take care, Napayshni."

Reuben bit back a grin at his old Crow name. Akecheta had dubbed him Courageous One when Reuben saved him from a brawl with a mountain lion the first time they'd met. He opened his mouth to reply, but Akecheta spoke first.

"The next time we meet, you will have made this woman your squaw. My people will like her. They will show kindness as she has done."

It took everything in Reuben not to choke on the breath he'd just inhaled, but he struggled to school his features. It was a good thing Cathleen couldn't understand a word the man said.

He did his best to stay solemn as he answered the man. "She is not my squaw. She comes from a far land and must go back there. She does not fit with the life of a trapper."

Akecheta raised his brows the slightest bit, but it was more than enough to show how little he believed Reuben's words. "She looks to me like she fits well."

The man turned to Cathleen and said in clear English. "Thank you, Kitsakike." Then he reined his horse around, and Mato followed suit.

Cathleen stepped back beside him as they watched the pair ride from the yard. After a long moment, she spoke. "What did he say?"

Akecheta's words about Cathleen being his squaw rang in Reuben's ears, but he kept his tone casual. "He called you One Who Heals."

She cut her eyes to him. "What did he say before that?"

A smile tugged at Reuben's mouth, but he held it back. This woman was far too insightful. But if she thought he'd divulge Akecheta's comments, she was sadly mistaken.

"Reuben?" Her voice had an insistent tone, but it only prodded the smile he was trying to hold in.

"He said Thank You." And with that, he turned and headed toward the barn.

As her frustrated grunt followed him, he could picture the image she made. Hands on her hips, that pert mouth pinched. Adorable.

~

*R*euben worked with his furs the rest of the morning, scraping every spot until the leather was as soft and pliable as a newborn babe. As soft as the flawless skin on Cathleen's face. But that line of thinking would only get him into trouble.

Unfortunately, the hours working by himself gave his mind too much time to think. He'd spent the first part of the morning playing back Akecheta's words and wondering if he had half a chance of really winning Cathleen's heart. She seemed open enough to him, but would she really be satisfied with life as a trapper's wife? Even if he gave up his winter camp and took over this homestead for the rest of his life, could she be happy here, so far from any form of civilization? It was different from everything she knew. She may think she liked it now, but she would grow tired of it soon. The endless work to accomplish the simplest of tasks—like cooking a meal, or making lye soap. It was hard. Even though he'd never experienced life in a big city like Boston, things had to be easier there.

He couldn't ask her to leave all that. It simply wasn't fair to her. And if he forced her to choose, her answer would surely be the life she'd been raised to love.

So that left him with two options. He could leave these mountains that were so much a part of him and move to the city with her...or he could let her go. And that decision was what he'd been sorting through as he worked the last three skins.

Staying tied to the homestead would be bad enough, but leaving the mountains? Other than a few trips to the eastern edge of the Montana Territory, he'd never been out of sight of these peaks. Did they even have mountains in Boston? Probably not. Cathleen had said something about a beach, which must mean it was beside the ocean. Mum had told stories of seeing the Atlantic when she was a girl, and the thought of that much water all rolling and pitching made his skin shiver.

Could he do it for Cathleen? Leave these mountains and live where he had to look at that much water every day? Yes, if that's what she wanted, he would do it. But how could he support them? Certainly not by hunting and trapping, or even farming the way Pa'd tried to teach him. With all those people packed together, there wouldn't be room to run enough cattle to earn a living. So what then? He was decent at fishing, but he had a feeling a trotline wasn't going to work in the great Atlantic Ocean.

He allowed a long sigh to leak from him as he rubbed harder at a thick spot on the Marten pelt in his hand.

None of this really mattered if Cathleen didn't want him. And why would she? A homespun mountain man. Uncultured and uncivilized. He'd probably embarrass her the first time they stepped off the train.

No. Their worlds were too far apart. It wouldn't ever work. Even if she thought she had feelings for him now, they would die away soon enough when she saw how he didn't fit in her sphere.

So that left him with only one remaining option. He had to let her go.

Even though the thought of her leaving pressed his heart rate faster, it was the only choice left. The right choice, if he set his own desires aside and focused on what was best for Cathleen. He swallowed hard. That's what he had to do.

As frustration mounted in his chest, he pushed up from the work table and grabbed his rifle. He'd had too much time alone with this thoughts. Maybe some fresh air would clear his head.

And if he brought home a couple grouse for supper, Cathleen might appreciate the variety.

CHAPTER 19

Cathleen pushed the door closed on the chicken shed and set the bar, then grabbed her empty slop bucket and hurried back toward the house. The temperature was dropping quickly again. She'd been wrong about snow the other day, but Reuben had commented on the possibility of a winter storm this evening. She pulled her coat tighter around her neck.

He was still in the barn, where'd he'd spent most of the time since his Crow friends left the morning before. Except for that unexpected hunting trip he'd made yesterday. The fresh meat had been nice, but with the huge stock pile of meat he'd brought when he first arrived, they hardly needed it.

It had probably been good for him to get out by himself though. He'd been extra quiet since Akecheta and Mato left, and she couldn't find a clue why. In time, though. He'd share in time.

As she pushed open the cabin door, warmth from the cook stove blasted her face. Had she put too much wood in the firebox? Hopefully her cornbread wasn't burning.

She slipped her coat off and turned to hang it on a peg, but movement from the stove caught her attention.

"No!" She lunged forward to stop Mrs. Scott from reaching her bare hand into the oven.

But she was too late.

"Ahh." The woman pulled back from the opening, dropping a cast iron skillet full of cornbread onto the oven door with a clatter. "Oh."

Cathleen reached the woman and grasped her shoulders, pulling her back from the intense heat pouring from the opening.

"My hand." Mrs. Scott's voice held a hint of disbelief as she raised the palm that had gripped the skillet's handle. Bright red marred the skin, and there was a faint smell of burning flesh.

A sob climbed into Cathleen's own throat, but she swallowed it down. Water. She had to stop the pain that was surely starting to radiate through the dear woman's hand.

A bucket of fresh creek water sat near the counter, where she'd been planning to boil beans for supper. She sloshed some into a bowl and whirled back to the table.

"Sit here, Mum. Put your hand in this water to stop the burning."

Mrs. Scott's shuffle to the chair was painfully slow, and the groan as her hand sank into the clear liquid tightened the knot in Cathleen's chest. How had she let this happen? Mrs. Scott was her responsibility, and she couldn't seem to keep the woman from injury.

What else could she do for the burn? Maybe her brother had packed a burn salve in the medicine box. *Lord, show me what to do.* If she didn't have salve, what should she put on it? Lard? She'd heard a midwife mention that one time, but she'd never tried it as a remedy for burns.

"Sit here and keep your hand in the water, all right?" Cathleen pressed a palm to Mrs. Scott's shoulder until the woman looked up at her.

"I'll be fine, dear." But her eyes were glassy, and her chin quivered with the words. She was most definitely not fine.

Near the bottom of the wooden box, she found a small tin of salve, and the sight tightened her already-tense emotions. *Thank you, Lord.* She grabbed the medicine and a rolled bandage, then turned back to face Mrs. Scott.

~

*R*euben pulled off his leather work gloves as he stepped onto the porch. When he'd seen Cathleen hurry from the chicken shed a few minutes ago, it had been the final straw of guilt to force him out of the barn. As much as he needed to keep his distance from the bewitching woman, he still couldn't shirk his duty to help around the place.

She'd had almost sole care of his mother for two days straight now, and she deserved more of a break than a quick trip to see the chickens.

When he opened the door, heat hit his face. The two women sat at the kitchen table, and the stove door hung open. No wonder it was so hot in there. He left the cabin door ajar and shrugged out of his coat, then turned to hang it on the wall peg.

"Reuben, I..."

Something about the catch in Cathleen's voice spun him around to face them. She was crying. Her hands held a white strip of cloth she'd been wrapping around Mum's hand. As he peered closer, large tears rolled down his mother's cheeks, too.

"What happened?" He reached the table in two strides, then touched Mum's bony shoulder. "What's wrong?"

Cathleen inhaled a shaky breath. "She burned herself...pulling cornbread from the oven."

He turned to glance at the stove door. A cast iron skillet lay cock-eyed, half on the rack and half on the door. The pan still held a dark brown chunk that must have been cornbread. It was a wonder the stuff hadn't caught fire yet, so near the flames. He grabbed a leather pad and scooped up the pan, then set it safely on the work counter. Once he'd shut the oven door, he turned back to the women.

Cathleen's teary gaze met his. "I was coming in from feeding scraps to the chickens. She'd been knitting. I didn't think she'd try..." Her words trailed off as another big drop ran down her cheek.

A small voice in his mind warned against it, but he couldn't stop his body from skirting the table and kneeling beside her. When he wrapped an arm around her shoulders, she leaned into him, more tears slipping down her cheeks and splashing onto his shirt.

She sniffed hard, then straightened in her chair. "I'm sorry. Your mum's the one who's hurt. I just can't believe I let this happen. I gave her something for the pain, and now we're doctoring it to keep out infection."

He turned to focus on his mother. "How you doin', Mum?"

"All right, honey. I'm all right." Her voice quivered more than usual, but that was surely to be expected.

He looked back to Cathleen, stroking a finger across her shoulder, where his hand still rested. "What can I do?"

She sniffed again, then focused on wrapping Mum's hand. "I'm almost done here. I'll make her some willow bark tea so she can sleep. That will probably help more than anything."

Tea. He could at least get the water started for that. He pushed to his feet and got to work.

∼

*R*euben sat by himself at the supper table that night, eating beans and piping hot cornbread—a fresh batch Cathleen whipped together. The murmur of voices sounded from Mum's room as Cathleen helped her eat supper from bed. It was Mum's right hand that had been burned and was now bandaged tight, which meant she'd have even more trouble doing simple tasks, like feeding herself.

So he sat alone. Being alone shouldn't bother him. Not the man who spent his life on his own.

But the two women who meant the most to him in the world sat on the other side of that door, and he was excluded. Make that the one woman who meant the most to him, and another he was trying to force his stubborn heart to ignore.

The door squeaked on its hinges, and Cathleen stepped through, carrying a tray.

"How's she feeling?" The question gave him an excuse to turn and watch her as she moved to the work counter.

"Holding her own. I can tell the hand pains her, but she's keeping a cheerful spirit." A sigh leaked out of her. "I just hate she's suffering from it."

"Cathy, this was *not* your fault." He'd not meant to use the nickname, but it slipped out.

She didn't turn to look at him, but her shoulders stiffened as she paused from unloading the tray. "I shouldn't have left the cabin."

He scrubbed a hand through his hair. Obstinate woman. "You're not here to be a prisoner. I put the lock on the door so you could step outside when you need to. Mum may not be of sound mind anymore, but she's still her own person. You can't keep her wrapped in a safe cocoon all the time. It's just not possible." His voice rose more than he'd intended, and he clamped his mouth shut. Maybe something he'd said would sink in.

She didn't answer. Didn't turn to face him, just went back to putting used dishes in the wash bucket.

He pushed up from the table. He wasn't getting anywhere here, so he might as well move on to evening chores.

$\sim$

Cathleen stared out the cabin's little window as the white glimmer of snow flurries fell in the darkness. Reuben had been silent when he came in from feeding the animals. Now he was in his Mum's room, and the rich tenor of his voice drifted occasionally through the open door. She could only hear its rumble though, couldn't distinguish what he said.

His words had been painful earlier, even though he'd probably meant them to help her feel better. Was she trying to bundle Mrs. Scott in a safe little cocoon where the world couldn't affect her? Whether she was trying or not, she obviously wasn't succeeding.

What happened to her lofty goals of letting the woman age with dignity and grace? There'd been nothing graceful about the incident earlier. How did she find the balance between allowing Mrs. Scott independence and being there when the woman needed her?

"I think Her Highness is asleep."

Cathleen whirled at the masculine voice as Reuben closed the chamber door behind him. His hair had an untamed look to it tonight, and a shadow of two or three days' stubble covered his jaw. It all made him look so attractive, her insides tightened. She forced the thoughts aside to focus on his words. "Her Highness?"

His mouth tipped a little at one corner. "I called her that sometimes when I was young. Not when she was around, of course. Pa would wrap an arm around her and call her his queen. So it became a little joke between me and Pa. Anytime she wasn't nearby, that's what I called her."

She couldn't help a little smile at the image of a half-size Reuben with his Pa. "You're lucky, you know. Having so much alone time with your parents. With four kids in the house, the only moments I ever had dad to myself was in the apothecary shop. And there he was always distracted with customers."

His gaze narrowed as it met hers, something undefinable in the dark blue shadows cast by the lamplight.

Thinking over what she'd said, she realized she probably sounded ungrateful. "My folks were good parents, mind you. I didn't mean it to sound like they weren't. There just wasn't a lot of quiet time. Especially with two brothers." She scrunched her nose to lighten the mood, but Reuben's expression didn't change. "You're lucky, is all. That's what I was trying to say."

"Yeah, lucky."

She almost missed the mumbled words as he turned away from her.

~

The next day, Cathleen watched the shirtwaist swirl amidst the soapy bubbles in the water bucket at the sink. Peaceful quiet had fallen over the place this afternoon, except for North's gentle pant as he lay at her feet. The cabin was likely too warm for him with his thick winter coat, but he'd become such a dear friend. If he didn't complain about staying in the warmth, she certainly wasn't going to force him outside.

Did Reuben miss the dog as a constant companion? It didn't seem to bother him that she and North had bonded. Of course, Reuben had kept himself secluded in the barn for days now. How would she know if he was upset or not, when he stayed so distant?

He probably did have a lot of work to do out there. And the two snowfalls they'd had in the last few days surely added more chores with the animals. But it was more than that. She could feel his distance when he came in for meals. The way he stayed outside until the last possible moment, then wouldn't meet her gaze at the table. He'd come in several times to sit with his mum, always making sure Cathleen spent the moments outside for a breath of fresh air.

So what had changed, that he didn't want to be near her anymore? After that first kiss, she knew he felt at least *something* for her. Had she offended him? Maybe it was the way she'd argued against his wishes about not bringing his friends into the cabin that night. But he must know that if someone needed her help, she had to give it.

His concern for her and his mother had been real, which was just like Reuben. He cared deeply for those close to him. So different from what she'd expected of the bear-man who'd first walked into the cabin almost two months ago.

So different from any man she'd ever known. His strength, his gentleness, the thoughtful way he examined a question from all angles. Even his artistic side, with the beadwork and the furs.

She'd never met a man she could respect so completely.

It was obvious when he'd first arrived that he struggled with his mother's condition. But with the shock of finding his father deceased and his mother almost a different person—his struggles proved he was human. Over these last few weeks, he'd made efforts to help far beyond what she'd expected. He was truly a good man.

A man she could love. And maybe she already did.

So why was he distancing himself from her? Did he really feel nothing? Or maybe he couldn't reconcile himself to a woman not from these mountains. He'd been raised here. Was used to living off the land, in harmony with nature, the way God intended. And she was sadly lacking in those abilities. No wonder he thought she wasn't suitable.

Beside her, North's ears perked, and he rose to his haunches with a guttural growl.

"What is it, boy?" She strained to hear outside as she transferred the shirtwaist to the bucket of clean rinse water, then dried her hands on her apron. She could hear nothing through the cabin walls, but North growled again and padded to the door.

Something was definitely not right.

Her gaze found the rifle mounted beside the door. Would she have to use it? Reuben had said this one was harder to shoot than the gun he'd taught her with. Would this rifle load and fire the same or was it completely different? Could she even remember the steps he'd showed her?

Striding past the gun, she peered through the cabin's small window. The leafless branches at the edge of the clearing swayed, and a rider emerged through them. Her shoulders eased.

Bryan. What was he doing here? Alex had just left a couple weeks ago. Surely her oldest brother hadn't come to try to talk her into leaving too.

A smile found her mouth as she sprinted toward the door. Her brothers. Always over-protective.

North growled again as she pressed the latch and pulled it wide, the animal trying to nose out in front of her. "Stay, North." She spoke the command as sternly as she could, pointing a finger at his black nose.

He whined but dropped to his haunches in the opening.

"Good, boy." Reuben had done a remarkable job training this animal.

She left the door open so she could hear if Mrs. Scott awoke, then gathered her skirts and ran down the steps. Reuben had cleared the snow from the stairs, so they weren't slick, but when she reached the ground, the icy white thickness slowed her quickly. She had to lunge through it with each step. North let out an excited bark from the porch but stayed where she'd left him.

A dozen yards out, she slowed to a walk, shading a hand to watch her brother's approach. He didn't push his horse, just kept the animal in a slow, steady walk. It was Bryan, though. No doubt about the set of his shoulders and the hat she'd seen him wear a hundred times.

So why wasn't he eager to see her? Maybe his horse was too exhausted from the climb. She picked up her pace again.

"Bryan. What are you doing up here?"

He was within ten feet now and reined in his gelding, then slid to the ground. A slower movement than normal, maybe because his muscles ached from riding in the cold.

When he turned to her, he opened his arms, and she flew into them. No matter his reason for coming, it was so good to see her oldest brother. Moisture stung her eyes as she soaked in his solid strength. Bryan had always been the quiet, steady one in the family. The pillar that supported them all.

She clung to him now, and he returned the embrace. Maybe a little tighter than she would have expected. Was something wrong?

Leaning back, she peered into his face. Sorrow lined his eyes in creases. "What is it, Bryan? What's wrong?"

He only met her gaze for a moment, and red rimmed his brown eyes as he looked away. "It's Dad, Cathy. He's gone."

CHAPTER 20

athleen's eyes followed the Adam's apple at her brother's throat as it bobbed. Down, then up. What was Bryan saying? Their dad? Gone where?

"What?"

As the word left her tongue, Bryan turned those glassy eyes on her, and his full meaning came rushing in. Dad was dead? No... It wasn't possible.

Her vision blurred, and she vaguely felt Bryan's arms wrap around her. How could Dad be dead? He'd been in full health when she'd left Boston. Just months ago.

A quiver shook her shoulders, but she breathed out a long breath. Her vision gradually came back to her, and she pushed away from Bryan to look at him.

"What happened? How?" Her throat had grown impossibly tight, her eyes gritty.

The bump at Bryan's throat bobbed again. "Some form of dropsy, they think, probably in his heart."

His heart. An image formed in her mind, one she'd seen a couple times in the final days before she left Boston. Dad, perched on the stool at the apothecary shop counter, peering intently at his ledger.

His right hand rubbed his left shoulder. She'd thought it was just sore muscles from too much focused work. Had it been the first symptoms of a heart condition?

Her body went even more numb, and her upper lip tingled. Bryan pulled her back against his chest, and she didn't try to stop him. Probably couldn't have stood much longer under her own strength anyway.

Male voices sounded around her. Bryan's rumbled deep under her ear. Then Reuben's, the sound of it infusing a tiny bit of strength. She pushed away from her brother again, sniffing, even though tears had yet to come.

There was so much to ask. So much she needed to know. "Mum? How is she?"

He released a long sigh, slipping an arm around her shoulders, and moving them both forward toward the cabin. "I don't know. Her telegram seemed like she was holding her own. Said friends have been nearby to help her."

Probably Mrs. Branson. And the Stamey family. Dad and Mum had always been mainstays in their little community there on Chesapeake Street. And Mum was always taking care of other people. Of course the group would flock to help her during a need.

They reached the porch, and Bryan's arm loosened around her as they ascended the steps. Reuben walked on her other side, his strong presence telegraphing a bit of comfort. His worried gaze found hers, and she tried her best to pull together a reassuring smile. But what she managed probably wasn't close.

She sniffed again and swallowed to clear her clogged voice. "Reuben, have you met my oldest brother Bryan?"

Reuben offered a deferential nod. She couldn't see Bryan's face, but his grip at her shoulders tightened.

She pulled away, forcing some strength into her backbone. That initial shock had struck hard, but she had to pull herself together. "Come inside for coffee, Bryan. I'm sure you're hungry." Her voice didn't sound like her own, but at least it had come out clearly this time. She pushed through the open doorway, running a hand across North's head as she passed him.

She had to keep busy. For a few moments, at least. Until the burn in her chest subsided enough that she could speak without breaking down.

The coffee she'd made at lunch was still warm, but she moved the pot to the hottest part of the stove anyway. She stuffed a skillet of biscuits in the warming oven, then set out plates, butter, and blackberry jam. Then mugs for the coffee, serviettes, and forks.

She pulled out the biscuits, and her hand shook a bit as she set the pan on a leather pad on the table. She steeled her grip on the coffee pot while she filled the three mugs with the dark brew. Good thing she'd stuck in a cinnamon stick earlier to simmer with the grounds. When she turned back to set the pot on the stove, she almost lost her grip on the handle. It clanged onto the stovetop, the vibration echoing through the room.

"Cathy."

She didn't turn at Bryan's voice, only inhaled a long steadying breath as she faced the stove.

"Who's there?" Mrs. Scott's quivering voice drifted through her closed bed chamber door.

Cathleen whirled and headed for the larger of the two back rooms, dodging glances from the two men on her way. "I need to help Mrs. Scott up." At least this would give her something to do.

The older woman was sitting on the bed when Cathleen entered the dim room. Her hair was sleep-rumpled, but her dear face lit when she saw Cathleen.

Cathleen pressed a hand to the blanket to check for dampness, but for once it was dry. She sank onto the mattress next to the older woman and pulled her sweet wrinkled hand into her lap. "Did you get a good rest?"

Mrs. Scott covered Cathleen's hand with her free one and smiled softly. "You're a good girl. Always trying to help."

The words started a burn in the back of her throat, which crept up into her eyes. Moisture filled them, but she was able to hold back the flow. "Thank you." Her voice came out in a hoarse whisper.

Lord, I need Your strength. She inhaled a deep breath. While they sat in silence, a bit of calm seeped over her. As terrible as the news was, God had control of the situation. Dad was in a better place now.

She finally rose and refastened Mrs. Scott's hair, then straightened the bed covers. Finally, there was nothing left to do but go out and face the others. Yet, now she felt strangely...fortified.

Both men watched as she led Mrs. Scott from the chamber, but she ignored their scrutiny. After she had the woman settled in her chair at the table with a mug of coffee and a biscuit before her, Cathleen took her own seat.

She raised her gaze to her brother, making sure it was as solid as she could make it. "So...did Mum say what she plans to do next?"

His jaw tightened. "Alex is going back to Boston to sell the store, then bring her here to Butte."

She nodded. "Mum always has wanted to come here. She said she wants to know what was so wonderful about this place that it stole her children away."

Bryan's mouth pinched. "I came up to get you, so you can travel with Alex. I'm sure Mum will need you."

The words struck hard. In the back of her mind, she'd been wondering if she should leave this place and go to her mother. But hearing the thought spoken out loud...she wasn't ready for it.

She opened her mouth to answer. Then closed it. Of course she should agree. Mum might need her.

But Mrs. Scott needed her too. It was too much for one person to try to keep up with the homestead and the animals and still watch over Mrs. Scott the way her condition required. The burn she'd obtained the other day was the perfect example. As competent as Reuben was, it would require divine ability to be in two places at once in order to accomplish the task.

A glance at Bryan showed he waited for her response.

She opened her mouth again. "I...I need to think about it, Bryan."

His brows lowered, twin creases forming on his forehead. "What's there to think about? Mum needs you, Cathy."

Emotion welled in her chest, threatening to spill over from her eyes. She pushed against the table to stand and whirled to face the cook stove. "Please. Just give me a bit." She had to get control of herself. Needed to sort through her emotions.

She bent to stuff another log into the fire box, then poured clean water into the large pot. After a long moment, shuffling sounded from behind her.

"Guess I'll go put up my horse." Bryan's voice. He sounded begrudging, but at least he was giving her a few minutes alone. She almost wilted from relief.

"I'll help you get him settled." Reuben's tone was quiet, reserved. She hadn't meant he needed to leave, too. But maybe it would be best for her to clear her mind if they were both gone.

~

The tension in the air was thick as Reuben strode beside Cathleen's eldest brother, who led his gelding to the barn. Should he say something to break the silence? He could at least offer his condolences. "I'm sorry about your Pa."

No immediate answer, so he kept going. "I know it's not easy to lose your father. Especially so suddenly."

Bryan shot him a look. Not angry. But aware. "I guess you do. And you're right, it's hard."

The other man didn't speak again, but the tension between them had loosened a bit.

In the barn, Reuben reached for the reins. "I'll get him settled and fed. There's a new colt you might like to see in that stall that opens to the corral outside."

Bryan nodded, then handed over the reins without speaking. It was refreshing to find someone who didn't feel a need to cram words into silence when none were needed.

The gelding settled into the stall with a sigh and immediately started into the hay Reuben had piled in the corner after he'd last cleaned the pen. It was always handy to keep an empty stall cleaned and stocked.

After he'd stripped the saddle and bridle from the horse, he found Bryan standing at the pen where Tashunka and her colt stayed during the day. He leaned against the rail, staring inside as the colt nursed from his mother.

Reuben propped his own arms on the rail and settled in beside the man. It seemed like something specific was bothering Bryan. Maybe he'd open up with a bit of time.

It only took a couple minutes before Bryan's first words came. "I don't understand why my sister would even consider staying here instead of going to help our mother in her grief."

Nothing like getting to the point. Reuben took some time to think through his response. The problem was, he didn't have a good answer. Straightforward would have to do.

"I have yet to figure out what Cathleen's thinking. I do know she has a special way of caring for people. It's different from anything I've ever seen. Like an angel of mercy. I don't know what Mum would have done without her these last few months."

He could feel Bryan turn a solid gaze on him, and Reuben met it.

"But that's *your* mother. Why won't she do the same for her own? What's holding her here?"

And that was the question, wasn't it? One he'd contemplated—and forced himself to stop contemplating. He had no idea why Cathleen would want to stay here. Except that she must think him not competent to care for his mother alone. Was that the reason? The thought struck him like a blow. Did she think him incapable?

He raised his brows, still meeting Bryan's gaze. "That's a question only she can answer."

Bryan turned back to the horses and didn't speak again. But the man's words replayed in Reuben's mind. *That's your mother.*

He was right. And no matter how much Reuben wanted to keep her here, he had a duty to his mother, and Cathleen had the same to her own family. It was time he step in and relieve her of any misguided priorities.

CHAPTER 21

*R*euben took a bite of potato, then glanced at his mum, then Bryan. Both ate in silence, heads ducked over their food. Cathleen's empty chair sat like an omen, feeding the tension hovering over the room.

Occasional sounds of shuffling drifted from her bed chamber. What was she doing in there that she couldn't share the meal with them? Packing? She'd not said more than five words since he and Bryan came in from the barn. As soon as she had the food on the table and Mum settled in her chair, she'd motioned for them to go ahead, then disappeared into the back room.

He understood the need to be alone to sort through her thoughts and emotions, but this silence and withdrawal wasn't like Cathleen. It just didn't fit with her nature.

Her door opened, and she strode across the room toward the front door. "I'm going for a walk." Without glancing their way, she grabbed her coat from the peg and slipped out the door.

Enough. He couldn't sit there and leave her to grieve on her own. Besides, he needed to talk to her about leaving. Her family needed her, and he suspected she needed them just as much.

He scooted his chair back and rose. "I'm going to talk to her."

Bryan didn't object, not that Reuben waited around for his approval. He grabbed his fur and headed outside.

Cathleen had made it halfway across the yard, but her skirts in the snow slowed her down, and he caught up with her before she reached the barn. She didn't stop to greet him, but allowed him to fall into step beside her as she kept walking past the building and stopped at the corral fence on the far side.

He'd often wondered where she went on her evening walks, and the familiar way she settled into position against this post answered the question for him.

He propped an arm on the fence nearby but held his tongue. He could almost feel her mind churning beside him. She'd talk when she was ready. And if he knew Cathleen, it wouldn't be long.

At last, she spoke softly. "I think I should stay here, Reuben."

That was the very last thing he'd expected. Not *I can't believe my father's dead.* Or *I have to leave.* How could she even consider staying?

He had to understand what she was thinking. "Why?"

She turned to him then, those brown eyes glimmering in the moonlight. "I want to be with my mother, I do. But I don't have a peace about leaving. It feels like my place is here. If Alex brings Mum to Butte, I can visit her there. Maybe your mum would be willing to go to town with me for a week or so."

The knot in his gut wound tighter. Her place was with her own grieving mother. Not guilted into staying on this remote mountain with a confused old lady and her incompetent son. No matter how much he loved her.

He turned back to face the corral, because he wouldn't be able to speak the words if he looked at her. "Cathy, I think you should go. Your family needs you." He barely got them out without his voice cracking, and he had to clamp his jaw before he ended with *But I need you, too.*

He had to do what was best for her.

Cathleen didn't answer for a long moment. And when she did, it was only a slow sigh as she turned back toward the house. "I need to get inside and clean up."

He let her go without following, but he couldn't help watching as she picked her way through the snow.

Her chin dipped toward the ground, and her steps were slower than usual. But her shoulders didn't sag, and her back held its normal erect posture, as if she'd made up her mind.

A fist reached into his chest and clamped hard. She was leaving. He'd just told the woman he loved to walk away. And something in his gut said, once she left this mountain, she'd never be back.

~

Cathleen's tears soaked into the worn cotton of her pillow, plastering the fabric against her cheek. If only crying could release the ache in her chest. Images of Dad swam through her mind, assisting customers in his shop, peering over his spectacles as he sat at the counter with mortar and pestle. His proud smile and the way he'd slip his arm around her when they discussed herbs and remedies. He'd loved his work, but he'd loved his family, too.

It gave him such pride when both his sons became physicians, even though she'd seen the lines on his face deepen as he bid each of them farewell. She could only imagine the pain of a parent, sending their child away to pursue his dreams.

The way Reuben was sending her away.

Had it caused him any pain? She'd seen something in his eyes before he turned to hide them.

But despite whether he thought she should leave or not, the decision was her own. Should she abandon Mrs. Scott, knowing it was too much for one person to see both to her care and to the homestead? How badly did her own mother need her? Mum had always been strong, even after losing Britt so young. She surely mourned Dad, but Alex was the more sensitive of her two brothers and would do Mum a world of good.

So which was the right choice? Comfort her mother in her grief and assist with the move to Butte? Or stay here to attend a woman who—without Cathleen's care—might very well meet a tragic death?

She knew which decision her heart said was right. But her head couldn't come to terms with it.

But then, did her preference really matter? Reuben had sent her away.

~

*W*hen Cathleen woke the next morning, grit clogged her eyes, tightening the skin around them so much it was hard to force her lids open. But she had to. Bryan would want to leave this morning, and she had so much to do to prepare.

Her brother accepted her news with a nod, although it looked like his shoulders sagged a bit from relief.

"Just give me a few hours after breakfast, and I'll be ready." She spoke while she cracked eggs into a skillet for breakfast. So much to do.

Her mind scanned a mental list. They would need food to carry them for a few days, at least. She wouldn't have enough time for bread to rise, so maybe she could make pans of biscuits, and cornbread, too. It'd be nice if she could leave something sweet. Maybe a cake? That might take too long. Cinnamon crisps? Yes. And Mrs. Scott's soiled clothing needed to be laundered, so Reuben could start fresh. Maybe she'd have time to wash some of his clothing, too.

What else should she do for them? What else *could* she do? Once she rode her horse out of the clearing, she would have to turn them over to God. *Lord, give me strength.*

Even with all her hurrying, the sun was about an hour shy of high noon by the time she had the essentials on her list completed. Bryan had been pacing for a while, but he'd been nice enough not to push too hard. The two men had finally headed out to the barn to look at Reuben's crop of furs.

She stirred the pot of beans she'd put on to cook for their noon meal, then turned to face the empty room behind her. The sounds of shuffling drifted from Mrs. Scott's bed chamber. She should go say goodbye to the woman. But the burning sensation in her eyes that she'd been pushing back all day threatened again.

How could she make Mrs. Scott understand she'd be leaving? Did she even want her to realize it? The poor lady had lost so much over the past few months. Yet she'd kept such a sweet spirit. Would she believe Cathleen hadn't wanted to abandon her?

She inhaled a long breath. *Oh, God. Strength.*

Boot treads sounded on the porch, and she bolstered her defenses as she turned back to the table. Out of the corner of her eye, Bryan's form appeared first.

She grabbed the bundle with her personal effects and shoved it his direction. "I guess you can saddle the horses."

He took the pack, then stepped back out the door without a word.

When the cabin door closed and quiet settled over the place, a motion grabbed her attention. She looked up.

Reuben stood there, in front of the closed door, watching her. The expression on his face, those piercing blue eyes, brought back memories of the first few days after he'd returned. The way he always seemed to be watching, his face never giving away his thoughts.

She swallowed down the burn in her throat. So much she needed to tell him. And not just about the household. Yet sharing her thoughts and emotions would be pointless.

He'd asked her to leave. That meant he didn't love her, not the way she loved him. Because she did love him, she had no doubt of it now. But the feeling was apparently unrequited, and because of that, she *did* need to leave.

The only way she would get through these next few minutes would be to keep her mind focused on tasks.

She whirled toward the stove. "I have beans cooking for your lunch, ready in an hour or so. And cornbread under this cloth. There's fresh biscuits in this tin." She motioned toward the freshly restocked crockery. With each sentence her voice lost some of its quiver. "These are the herbs I give your mum each morning and night. I think they might actually be helping. Some days anyway. Just steep them together in a tea and add a stick of cinnamon. It cuts the taste, and she doesn't like the sweetness of honey."

A memory slipped in, of Mrs. Scott when she'd first served the tea mixture with honey. The woman had actually turned up her nose at the stuff and dumped it in the fire.

Cathleen's jaw started to tremble. *Keep your mind on the work.* She averted her face from Reuben as she stepped toward the corner shelves and pulled out the medicine box. "There's bandages here, and this is the salve I've been putting on her burn. You shouldn't need to wrap it anymore unless it looks infected, but put this on at least three times a day."

"Cathy."

She jumped at Reuben's voice so close. Only a couple feet away. Her shoulders tightened, and she almost hunched over the box.

Then warmth touched her shoulder, soft and strong, those hands she loved. The hand she'd held the night of Tashunka's foaling. With the memory, her defenses allowed a single tear to slip past her barriers. *God, if you don't want me to leave, please stop me now.*

Another hand touched her other shoulder, the thumbs of both easing into circular movements. Her traitorous muscles responded, relaxing into the rhythm as his thumbs worked magic against her knots.

"It's going to be all right." His words were almost a whisper, hoarse and throaty. And the way he said it, she could almost believe him.

But it was a lie. He and his mum may be fine, if God sent an angel to help them each step of the way. But she would never be the same after knowing this man. Even if, after the months and months it would take to travel to Boston, settle her parents' affairs, and make the return trip, she returned, would he and his mum still be here?

Not likely.

He didn't belong tied to a homestead like this. As hard as he'd tried to do it for his mother, he would be miserable. And she had no doubt he'd eventually find a way to make a life for himself and his mum where he could freely live out God's calling for him. Using the gifts the Lord had infused within him in great measure. God had so much planned for this man's life, if only he would stop running and fully accept the Almighty's gifts.

But those plans were not to include her, apparently.

"Hey, it's going to be all right." Reuben must have felt her shoulders stiffen, for this time he turned her to face him.

A second tear slid down her cheek, and a third. She couldn't look at him, couldn't let him see how much this was killing her. So she stepped forward into one last forbidden comfort.

Into his arms.

Her barriers broke loose the moment her face pressed against the beat of his heart. And her tears flowed. It didn't help that he wrapped his strong arms around her, stroking her back, pressing his cheek against her hair. Comfort swaddled her in his embrace. *Lord, I can't do this. Please.*

After long moments of releasing the pain, the tears finally began to subside. She sniffed them back, doing her best to rebuild her defenses. She didn't lift her face from his soggy shirt yet, couldn't quite face him. If she were lucky, he would think her collapse was only because of her father's death. And that surely was the root of her emotional upheaval. Yet with this second loss right on the heels of losing Dad... She bit her lip against a fresh wave of tears.

Bryan's voice called from outside the cabin. Her name, possibly.

As she breathed in one final breath, she soaked in the aroma of man that was so uniquely Reuben's. Then she pushed back from him.

Without meeting his gaze, she turned to the side, wiping her cheeks with the heels of her hands. "I need to say goodbye to your mum." His grip fell away as she stepped around him, and the depth of the chill that replaced his warmth almost brought on her tears again. Her teeth sank hard into her lower lip to ward off the emotions.

She tapped a soft knock on Mrs. Scott's door, then slipped inside. Snores from the mattress sounded before she saw the tiny mound of raised covers. The older woman didn't often put herself to bed, but she'd not had a nap that morning, so exhaustion must have taken over.

Cathleen crept around to the side of the bed where the quilt covered the lower half of the wrinkled face. Such a dear face, full of kindness and wisdom. She didn't deserve to grow old in this way, but the dementia hadn't stolen her sweet spirit.

Cathleen leaned forward and pressed a kiss to her temple. The older woman likely wouldn't remember anything she said if she woke her for goodbye. It was possible she may not remember Cathleen had been here at all.

With that awful thought, she stroked the soft gray hair from her brow, then whirled and escaped the room. Tears once again broke through her barricade and streamed down her face. She pressed through the front room, charging toward the door, forcing herself not to glance at Reuben where he still stood by the medicine box.

If she looked at him, even once, she was too likely to tell him the true state of her heart. And that would never do.

He'd told her to leave.

~

Reuben watched through the tiny cabin window as Cathleen and her brother rode away. He'd not gone out to see them off. There was too much chance he'd grip her horse's reins and beg her to stay. Tell her the truth.

But she deserved more than that. More than him. Her family needed her now, and as soon as she was back in the world she'd been raised for, she would see that was her place. She was born for greatness, and keeping her here would mean cheating her out of what she'd been created for. And he loved her too much to do that to her.

That was the only thing that kept him rooted to the floor as he watched her leave.

CHAPTER 22

The trip down the mountain went much faster than the ride up had seemed. With every steady plodding step, the horses carried them farther from Reuben. Farther from Mrs. Scott.

What were they doing at that moment? Had Mrs. Scott been worried to awaken and find her missing? The woman always went straight into the kitchen after her nap and started tinkering around the stove. Would Reuben be there to stop her? Would he help her find something safe to do with her busy hands? Now that his mum seemed to be feeling better after those initial weeks, she did best if Cathleen kept her active with small tasks.

Of course, the burn had been a setback. Would Reuben remember to apply the salve three times a day? Infection was still a risk. Maybe she should have wrapped it once more before she left. But if Reuben didn't change the bandage regularly, it could get soiled and cause the infection it was meant to prevent.

"Finally home."

Bryan's eager words brought her attention up to see the outskirts of Butte. It wasn't a very pretty town as a whole, although the church in front of them did paint a nice picture, with its whitewashed walls and the rose vines climbing the picket fence around the perimeter.

Bryan had aimed their horses to the left where his and Claire's house could just be seen in the distance. They had a nice view of the mountains from their western windows. She'd enjoyed more than one fiery sunset from the kitchen window as she cooked supper or washed nappies in the wet sink. But the view couldn't compare to that from the Scott's front porch, with layers of snow-capped mountains peeking through the break in the trees, stretching as far into the distance as the eye could see. Sheer majesty.

She swallowed the knot in her throat and nudged her mount to catch up with Bryan. He'd pushed his horse into a longer stride, no doubt eager to see his family after a night away.

Claire must have seen their approach from a window, for she stepped onto the porch, then rushed down the stairs to meet them in the yard. Bryan was off his horse and into her arms within seconds.

Cathleen took her own time dismounting, as much to look away from the reunion as to allow her stiff muscles time to unfold and support her weight on the snow-packed ground.

"Cathleen, I'm so glad you're home. Safe." Claire's arm slipped around Cathleen's shoulders, and she turned to embrace her brother's wife. Her friend.

The warmth of the hug brought moisture to threaten her eyes again, but little Amanda squirmed between them, and Cathleen pulled back to tickle the babe's neck. "And how's my favorite niece? Do you remember your Aunt Cathy?"

She took the child from Claire, slipping her thumb into the little chubby hand. It was remarkable how straight the baby held herself, gurgling about something as her big round eyes stared at Cathleen. Not an infant anymore. Soon she'd be walking. Cathleen rested her head on the little mop of hair, mostly to hide the glimmer of tears that surely shone in her eyes.

"Let's go in. You both must be starved." Claire slipped a hand around her shoulders and guided her forward.

While Claire scurried around the kitchen, Cathleen tried to focus on the child. But Alex and Miriam soon came in, and they all sat around the big table in the kitchen for supper. The meal felt so strange, so different from the quiet suppers with Reuben and Mrs. Scott. Like she was watching the gathering through a window—on the outside, staring in.

She didn't want to be here. It wasn't her place right now. She belonged on the mountain, caring for that sweet old woman. Wrapped tight in Reuben's arms.

The burning sensation flooded her eyes, this time more than she could hold back.

Slipping out of her chair, she mumbled an apology and fled the room. She grabbed her coat from the rack in the parlor and stepped out the door.

Outside, a gust of cold whipped into her. A welcome blast to clear her mind. She desperately needed some time with the Father to settle her roiling emotions. Before going up to the mountains, she used to walk down the street toward the church in the evenings. Yet now, the handful of wagons and people passing seemed to invade the peace she sought.

She skirted the house and headed toward the meadow behind it, toward the trees and hills that led up to the mountains. Almost as if they called her. It was where her heart longed to be.

Now that she gave them free access, the tears wouldn't come. Instead, her feet crunched through the snow, on a determined march she had neither the power nor the will to stop.

At the base of the hill, she pressed her hand against a tree. *Lord, what am I doing?* A large rock stood in the snow beside her, and she sank onto it, still gripping the tree as if she needed the support. And she did.

She inhaled several deep breaths, allowing the cleansing air to fill her pores. Then, she let her eyes sink closed. "God, I need Your direction now more than I ever have. Show me which way is right."

With her eyes pressed shut and the chilly air clearing her mind, she focused on listening to her Creator. He'd never failed her yet. Not in her earliest memories when Britt died, not when He'd led her to this place. He had a plan. She just needed to wait for it.

As she sat in silence, the refrain of a hymn crept into her spirit. "It is well with my soul." She hummed the tune, the words filling her mind, settling peace through her as she mentally moved through the second verse.

> *Though Satan should buffet, though trials should come,*
> *Let this blest assurance control,*
> *That Christ hath regarded my helpless estate,*
> *And hath shed His own blood for my soul.*

Tears pricked her eyes as realization of the truth washed through her. Whether she was in Boston with her mother, or on a remote mountain homestead, what mattered was the Father. The sacrifice He'd made for her, and her need to share His love with those around her. The freedom that only came from living with Him.

She pressed her lips together. "I'm sorry, Lord." Sorry for losing sight of Him in the midst of her troubles. Even in the midst of her love for Reuben. If God had been her focus, would she have ever left the mountain to begin with?

In that place of meditation, she lifted a prayer to the Father. *What would You have me do? I'm willing.* Her mind immediately stole up the mountains, images playing there that she'd tucked into her heart.

The wild beauty of the cliffs seen from the cabin porch.

Sitting with Mrs. Scott in the evenings, singing hymns while they both did needlework.

Reuben.

The warmth of his arms around her.

The utter peace of it all.

But didn't she owe it to her family to help in her father's death? Didn't her own mother need her? She pictured Mum, so strong in spirit as she raised four children. Even when they lost Britt, Mum had grieved, but she'd always had such inner strength. The same strength she'd passed on to her offspring.

The Lord's strength that now flowed through Cathleen's veins. It was a wonderful legacy from her mother. A legacy she wanted to share. With Reuben, if he'd let her come back.

For another long moment she sat there. *Am I hearing You right, Lord?* She pushed every thought out of her mind, focused on listening. No words impressed themselves on her, either audible or in her spirit. No bolt of lightning. Only relaxing peace.

Lord, if it's Your will, let my brothers agree to allow me to stay.

After a few more minutes of relishing the peace, she pushed up from the rock and headed back toward the house. It seemed colder now than it had on her way out, as if she were experiencing the world around her more deeply. Her mouth hummed the final verses of "It Is Well," and her heart sang along.

~

When she stepped back into the kitchen, her brothers still sat around the table while Miriam worked at the sink, her hands in soapy water. Little William perched on his papa's lap, chewing on a carved horse. No sign of Claire and the baby, so she must be putting the little one to bed.

All eyes turned to Cathleen at her entrance, but she ignored the expectant faces and took her seat.

Miriam stepped away from the sink. "I saved your plate, Cathy. Here you go."

Cathleen accepted the dish as Miriam pulled the cloth covering from it, but she had no intention of eating.

Alex cleared his throat and looked at Bryan as if he was about to pick back up on the conversation she'd interrupted. "So there's a chance we might have to wait in Fort Benton until the steam ships start running again."

Bryan squinted into the distance, the usual sign he was calculating something. "If there's one docked at the Fort, you might be able to get out of there at the end of March. Or early April, maybe. The only other way to get to the train in Dakota is overland, and you might as well wait for a boat than try to travel the mountains in the winter."

The more they talked, the worse the trip sounded. Wait in Fort Benton for weeks or months, just for a boat? It'd be winter time again

175

before they ever settled Dad's affairs and made it back here with Mum.

She leaned forward, resting her elbows on the table. Both brothers turned to look at her.

"Fellows, I think I've made a decision." Her mouth had gone dry, but she pressed on.

Bryan only raised a brow at her, but Alex leaned back in his chair and glared. "What?" The younger of her brothers certainly didn't mind showing his thoughts.

She'd gone too far to turn back now, though. "I don't think I should go with Alex. I've prayed about it, and feel like the right thing for me to do is stay here. To help Mrs. Scott. I'm sure Mum would appreciate me coming, but..." She glanced from one to the other, willing them to understand. "I just don't have a peace about it."

Silence stretched across the room. Even little William stopped his babbling and eyed her, still gumming the slobbery horse.

After a long moment, Bryan finally let out a long breath. "I guess I can't say I'm surprised. Had a feeling all along you would decide this."

She turned pleading eyes to her big brother. "It's not that I don't want to be with Mum. I do. It's just that I'm needed more up on that mountain with Mrs. Scott." She sank back in her chair. "I can't explain it. I just feel...that's where I should be right now."

She looked to Alex. "Mum will be so glad to have you there. And as soon as you get back here with her, I'll spend time with her here."

Alex's eyebrows drew low in a thick line. "Just how long do you plan to stay up there with that man and his mother?"

She shrugged, offering her brother a gentle smile. "Until God tells me I'm finished, I suppose."

Alex looked over at Bryan. "I don't know. What do you think?"

Bryan studied her with a piercing gaze, sharp and searching. She met it squarely.

Without looking away, he said, "I guess we can't argue with God's will."

The relief that washed through her was more of a heavenly peace than anything. She could feel it bloom over her face. "Thank you."

Alex let out a long-suffering sigh. "All right, but you better go up and check on her regularly while I'm gone."

Cathleen turned to her younger brother. "I want to send a letter for Mum. I'll have it for you before I leave in the morning."

His brows rose high. "You're going back up tomorrow? Not by yourself."

She nodded. "As soon as I can gather supplies. Mrs. Scott needs me. And I know the way. I'll just follow our tracks from today."

∼

*R*euben kept one ear tuned to the sounds within the cabin as he scraped a deer hide on the front porch. Mum's snores just barely drifted over the sounds of his work as she slept in her chair. Today had been their first full day alone together. Without Cathleen.

He'd had great intentions of keeping Mum nearby while he worked most of the day, but the temperature dropped so cold, and her needs had been so steady, he'd ended up stuck inside the cabin except for the few times he'd stepped out to care for the animals. Now that she slept, he finally had a chance to make progress on his work.

A nicker sounded in the distance, pulling his attention to the barn. It didn't sound like the noise had come from that direction. A second whinny sounded, this one definitely from his stock in the corral—one of the wagon horses most likely. North appeared in the cabin doorway, tail raised as he stared off into the distance. Then the first horse whinnied again. Definitely from the direction of the trail down the mountain.

North let out a bark and wagged his tail, then sprinted in the direction of the new horse. Had one of his stock escaped? Maybe their stallion? Or did they have a visitor? The whinny had sounded frantic, like the horse was running free. The sound of hoof beats in the snow soon became audible.

Reuben dropped his fur and jumped to his feet. After a peek inside at Mum's sleeping form, he pulled the cabin door closed and settled the bar across the outside.

Once down the porch steps, he sprinted toward the barn. If one of their horses had gotten loose, he'd need rope and dried corn to catch the animal. But the sight of a prancing horse at the edge of the clearing stopped him in his tracks.

It wasn't one of his stock, but the horse was painfully familiar. He'd seen it ride out of the clearing wearing that same saddle just yesterday morning.

Cathleen's mare.

Fear gripped his chest as he took in the torn leathers dangling from its bridle. He stepped toward the chestnut, extending a hand and crooning to the animal. "Hey, girl. Watcha doin' there?"

She froze as he approached, then lowered her head and blew hard at him. But he kept up the monologue and made sure the fear racing through his veins didn't unsteady his movements. She let him approach.

What had happened to Cathleen? Had she and her brother been in an accident on their way down the mountain yesterday? The horse didn't show signs of having worn the saddle and bridle all night. No snow or branches caught in the leather that would signal she'd fallen or lain in the snow.

But it was clear Cathleen needed help.

North ran beside him as he jogged the animal to the barn and quickly stripped the tack from her while she dove into the fresh hay in the extra stall. What was he going to do with Mum? Cathleen needed him urgently. Could even now be freezing to death in the snow, but he couldn't leave his mother locked in the cabin. It might take hours or even a day to find Cathleen if she'd veered off the trail.

He'd have to hitch the sleigh and take Mum with him. There was no other choice.

CHAPTER 23

It took a painfully long time to get the sleigh hitched and Mum loaded, along with a few supplies they might need. Blankets, ropes, some food and water. Of course, his guns and knife. His mind ran through the list as he climbed up beside Mum, wrapped in a buffalo skin, and snapped the reins hard to start the team. With North perched in the back with the supplies, they looked like a family out for a drive to town. Except for the fear that pulsed through him.

He pushed the draft horses as hard as he dared over the icy hills. The tracks left by Cathleen's horse that morning followed roughly the same prints from when she and Bryan had gone down the mountain the day before. For about the first hour, at least.

Then the recent tracks split off, climbing up a steeper section where large rocks poked through the snow. He slowed the team, peering ahead to gage whether he could actually fit the sleigh through the trees. The path didn't look like an established trail. Was the ground safe for the horses? Maybe if they took it slow and kept to the prints left by Cathleen's horse.

"Are you sure we're going the right way, Quinn? I thought we would have been there by now." Mum had been prattling on for a while now, nagging really. If only she would be lulled to sleep by the sleigh. But the icy bite of the cold was probably keeping her alert.

"Yes, Mum. We're going the right way." It didn't matter that he had no idea where they were headed.

Every moment counted, and Mum's nagging stretched his last nerve thin.

He wove the horses and sleigh through the trees, often having to depart from the tracks left by Cathleen's horse for short periods while he found a way to get the sled through. If only he knew how much farther ahead she was, he might be able to leave the sleigh and trudge forward on foot.

They were skirting the edge of a mountain now, on an easy incline, but near a steep drop-off on their left. How had Cathleen gotten this far off the road? And where was Bryan's horse? Had they lost the trail and slipped in the icy rocks? Maybe both people had gone over the cliff, along with Bryan's gelding, leaving only Cathleen's mare to signal help. The thought tightened the ball of dread in his gut.

Dear, God. No. The prayer rose from his chest before he realized it was there. He meant it, though. If it took God to find Cathleen and save her, he'd gladly involve the Almighty.

The slope they traveled was only about twenty feet wide now, with a sheer drop on the left and a steep, rocky incline on the right. He was able to pick a route for the sleigh through the trees, but would he be able to turn the rig around if they couldn't get through?

What in the world had possessed the Donaghues to take this route?

"Cathleen!" His voice echoed over the chasm to his left.

"Where is that girl anyway?" Mum chattered on as if this weren't a dire emergency. "I haven't seen her all day."

He ignored her, ears straining to hear over the creaking of the harness and the rustle of the sleigh runners in the snow.

"Cathleen!" he called again. Maybe she would be strong enough to answer. He could tie the horses and run ahead to find her.

But there was no response. Over and over he called. Not that it seemed to help. He ground his teeth against the slow plodding of the horses, but he had no choice but to continue their course.

After what felt like another hour, a faint noise answered his call.

He jerked the horses to a stop. "Cathleen!"

He froze, listening. Mum started to say something, but he pressed a hand to her arm and for once, she held her tongue.

There it was.

A soft noise. A whimper maybe. But its tone was high enough it could have come from a woman. Maybe that was wishful thinking, but his heart clamored in his throat.

He set the brake and leaped from the sleigh and barely had the forethought to turn back and look his mum in the eye. "Stay in the sleigh, Mum. All right?"

She gave a look that he hoped was acquiescence.

He eyed the dog in the back of the sleigh. "North, stay."

The animal stared back at him with steady, dark eyes. The dog would care for his mother.

Reuben tromped through the snow to tie the horses to a tree, then spun toward where he thought he'd heard the sound. The snow was virgin through here, with only the tracks from Cathleen's horse breaking the white icy covering.

"Cathleen!" He charged through the stuff, following the prints but straining for the sound of her voice.

Up ahead, he saw a spot where the tracks veered dangerously close to the edge of the cliff. It looked like the snow had been churned there, with several long sliding marks. *No.* His pulse thundered through his ears, louder than his boots in the snow. His breath came in short spurts as he ran.

He reached the spot and dropped to his knees to look over the edge. His left knee landed on something sharp—a rock—and his movement pushed snowy powder over the ledge to float through the empty air below.

As he peered down, his mind strained to make sense of what his eyes took in. The cliff was steep, a vertical rock wall for hundreds of feet down before it leveled into another snowy slope. In a couple of places, outcroppings of rock jutted from the cliff face, covered by snow and an occasional scrawny juniper peeking out from the white.

The knot that had been growing in Reuben's gut turned to a sick ball of dread. "Cathleen!" He screamed her name.

She had to be alive. Couldn't be buried in a mangled heap in the snow so far below.

Something moved on one of the outcroppings about thirty feet down. The spot was just a tiny ledge really, with a juniper somehow struggling for life on its surface.

The tree shifted, and a noise drifted up from it. A moan.

His chest surged. Could it possibly be?

"Cathleen, don't move." Even as hope sprang inside him, fear threatened to strangle it when he made out her form. She was curled in a ball, but as she unfurled herself, one arm and both feet dangled perilously over the edge of the small ledge.

"Don't move!" Any slight shift could make her slide off into a free fall. And who knew how strong the rock was that supported her tiny ledge? The whole outcropping could give way.

She shifted again, and his heart seized in this throat.

"Please, Cathleen! Don't move. You're about to slide off that ledge. Can you hear me?"

Long moments passed as his pulse thudded in his ears.

At last, a soft voice sounded. "Yes." The word was almost groggy. Maybe muffled from the snow, or she might be just coming back to consciousness. How badly was she injured?

"Where are you hurt? Can you tell me without moving?" He had to know so he could figure out the best way to get her up.

Another pause. Excruciating.

"My arm. I think that's all."

Probably her head too, from the way her words slurred. If her arm was broken, though, she might not be able to tie a rope around her waist. Not tightly enough anyway. And he couldn't risk trying to pull her up, only to have the rope come loose. For a torturous moment, images of the possible outcome filled his mind. Her wide eyes growing smaller as she fell to her death. Snowflakes piling on top of her, unaware of the treasure they hid at the bottom of the cliff.

Oh, God, no. The picture seared in his mind, and he pressed his eyes shut against it. *God, you have to keep her safe. Please. For Cathleen.*

He opened his eyes again, forcing his mind to focus. "Cathy. I'm going to the sleigh to get a rope. I'll be right back. *Stay there.* All right? Don't move even an inch."

"All right." These words were a little stronger, like she spoke them through gritted teeth. Her arm had to be broken.

He sprinted to the sleigh, the distance seeming a little shorter than the first time he traversed it.

"What's wrong, dear?" Mum's slow cadence buzzed in the back of Reuben's mind as he scrambled to gather all the rope he'd brought.

"Nothing, Mum. Just stay put."

With the cord slung over his shoulder, he raced back to the spot above where Cathleen perched on the cliff face. There was a good stout pine about ten feet from the edge, and his gloved hands fumbled to tie the rope around it in a strong knot. He finally jerked the buckskins off his hands, but his fingers still shook, taking precious extra seconds to secure the rope. He still had another section of cord, but he tossed it aside in case he needed it later.

Crawling back to the edge with the secured rope in his hands, he peered over. Cathleen was exactly where he'd last seen her, and the wash of relief that flowed through him almost leaked the strength from his muscles. *Thank you, God.*

"Cathleen. I'm going to lower this rope down to you. Do you think you can tie it around your waist?"

For a moment, there was silence from below. Then the slightest bit of movement, although she still lay curled in a ball.

And then her weak voice sounded. "I can try. I can't move my left arm, but maybe with the other."

Her left was broken then. It could be worse, but he couldn't count on her being able to tie a secure knot with only one hand. And if she moved around too much, she could slide right off the ledge.

He'd have to go down and get her. But how? He turned and scanned his supplies. Two ropes. A good stout tree. He had the horses to help, but no one else to guide them if he lowered himself down to help Cathleen.

Could Mum play a part? She might be able to lead a horse, but she was still so unsteady on her feet. Even if he could get her to follow his direction, if she fell in the thick snow, she could easily be trampled by one of those huge draft hooves. And that would put Cathleen at risk, too.

No, he had to make this work alone. Maybe if he secured a rope around himself and the other end around the tree, he could lower himself down and use the other cord to lever Cathleen up.

He peered down again at the cliff face that separated him from her. It was mostly vertical, but had a tiny bit of slope, and some crags that he could use to climb back up. This could work.

As long as the ledge that held her could support them both.

"Cathy, does that rock you're laying on feel like it's going to fall any minute? Can it hold us both?"

Another moment passed, and he saw her arm shift. "It feels sturdy. I think."

That would have to do. The sooner he got the rope tied around her the better. "Don't move. I'll be down in a minute."

When he had the ropes fastened the way he wanted them and his gloves back on, he sidled to the cliff, lay on his belly, and slid his legs over the edge. Even though heights had never bothered him, lowering himself into that great abyss took every bit of his willpower.

With his elbows still pressed into the hard ground above, and with his lower body dangling, his left foot found its first purchase in a crack on the rock face. Then his right located a groove a little lower. He kept steady tension on the rope that secured him to the tree, but with one hand holding that rope, it made it hard to grip the hand holds he found in the cliff. Still, he progressed one painful step at a time.

About halfway down, he glanced below to check on Cathleen. She still lay huddled where he'd last seen her, yet her head was turned so she could watch him. She was close enough now that he could see her mouth move. Praying? Hopefully she was praying enough for them both.

He had maybe fifteen more feet until he reached her perch. He could do this.

His gaze scanned the little ledge. It was wider than it had looked from above, with a small place for him to stand near where it joined the cliff face. His gaze drifted to the side of it—to the empty chasm of space that dropped for hundreds of feet. The white far below swam in his focus. If anything went wrong, neither of them would survive that drop. His arms trembled, and he squeezed his eyes shut against the dizziness.

But it was too late. His left hand slipped, losing its firm grip on the rock. His fingers clutched at the cliff, but they couldn't find enough purchase to hold the weight of his body as it swung out. His right hand lost its hold, too. He clung tight to the rope, gripping with both hands as his body swung like a pendulum, dangling by only the strength of the cord.

CHAPTER 24

*R*euben's mind barely registered the cry from below him as every muscle in his body strained to hold tight to the rope. He had to get down to that ledge. Solid ground.

Sliding his hands carefully down the cord, he lowered himself, one handhold after another. Slowly at first, but then faster as his arms began to quiver.

At last, something touched his ankle—Cathleen's hand—and it guided his foot to an empty spot on the ledge. As his feet touched the solid foundation, he didn't loosen his grip on the rope with both hands. Truth be told, he wasn't sure he could pry his fingers from it. But weakness threatened his shoulders, and he sank back against the cliff wall behind him.

"Reuben." Cathleen shifted in front of him, and he looked down to assess their situation.

"Don't move." He had to get that rope tied around her, but his racing heart felt like it might beat out of his chest.

The rock beneath him felt sturdy enough, although the snow and ice made it slippery. It wasn't perfectly flat, but sloped down on either side. So easy to slide off. They'd have to be careful.

He eased down to a crouch, keeping one hand tight around his securing line. At this point, he should retie it around himself so it wouldn't let him drop any lower if he fell off the ledge. The gloves made it hard, so he jerked them off again. When he finally had his line tied so he could feel a little tension when he crouched, that small bit of security slowed the frantic pace of his chest by a fraction.

His gaze roamed Cathleen. She had been lying on her left side, but she'd shifted mostly onto her back to watch him. That left arm lay still in the snow. His focus wandered up to her face.

And that was nearly his undoing.

The strength and bravery that always shone there was almost overpowered by the glaze of pain. And fear too.

"How long have you been out here?" He brushed a hand across her forehead to feel for fever. He'd not even thought about hypothermia, but if she'd spent the night on this ledge, a broken arm might be the least of their worries.

"A few hours." Her voice still wasn't as strong as he'd like, but her words brought welcome relief.

He'd find out how she got here later. He needed to know about Bryan, too. But if the man had already met his fate down below, it would be better to question Cathleen once he had her on solid ground.

"I'm going to tie this rope around your waist, then pull you back up. Do you think you can handle that?"

Her chin tightened, and determination replaced a bit of the fear in her eyes. "Yes."

Her voice was stronger with that word. Good.

A bark sounded from overhead, and Reuben glanced up. He'd told North to stay in the sleigh, but it sure sounded like the dog was right above them.

The bark sounded again. Twice. That animal never disobeyed, but maybe with all the excitement, he'd not been able to stay put.

Then a voice echoed from above that sent cold dread through his tense muscles. Mum.

"Quinn? Are you here?" Her quivering voice drifted from directly overhead. Not from the sleigh where he'd left her.

Cathleen gasped, drawing his gaze down to her. Her brown eyes rounded. "Is she next to the cliff?"

"It sounds like it. But I left her in the sleigh with North. I told her not to get out." He could hear the panic in his own voice as his mind played through possible scenarios. Maybe if they were quiet, Mum wouldn't come near the edge.

"Quinn?" A brush of snow floated into the air above them.

His chest clutched. "Mum! Get back from the edge of the cliff."

"Quinn? Where are you?"

Dear, Lord. She was going to fall over the ledge. In one single, horrible moment, he might lose the last bit of family left to him in this world. *God, stop her. Help, please.*

"Mrs. Scott, can you hear me?" Cathleen's voice held a strength it hadn't had moments before. "Can you sit down and pet North for me? I think he's upset. Sit down in the snow and we'll sing *Silent Night* to him. All right?"

Silence for a long moment. Reuben strained to hear, but his heart galloped in his ears, blocking out any sounds.

At last, Mum spoke again. "Sit down?"

"Yes, ma'am. Sit down in the snow, and let's sing a song for the dog."

A shuffling sounded overhead. "All right. What do you want to sing, dear?"

Had she actually done it? While Cathleen started in on a shaky rendition of *Silent Night*, Reuben set to work.

Still lying on her back, Cathleen's eyes tracked his progress as he carefully tied the rope around her waist. The thick fur of her coat would help cushion the burn of the cord, but he had to make sure it was tight enough.

She never slowed the song, and Mum's shaky vibrato joined from above. He started to help Cathleen sit up, but the pained expression on her face stalled him. Why hadn't he thought to bring something to wrap her arm? He couldn't very well let it dangle while he raised her up the cliff side.

He slipped out of his coat, then peeled off his blue wool shirt.

Good thing he'd worn this instead of his buckskin tunic today. This would be more pliable to tie around her. He pulled his coat back on, then folded the shirt into a sling.

She was just starting into the second verse of the song when he slipped a hand under her back and eased her into a sitting position. Even though he held her injured arm close to her body, her voice broke on the word *shepherd* as her face twisted in pain at the movement.

"I'm sorry, love." His chest ached at her agony, but he had to keep moving. Had to get them back onto safe ground.

Her mouth twisted in a pinched smile, but her song never halted. This woman possessed a depth of strength he could only dream of.

From his position on her right side, he had to reach across to secure her left arm to her upper body. She leaned into him, and he gladly took her weight. He needed to check the break to see if it was a simple injury or if the bone protruded from her skin, but that would require removing her coat and cutting through the sleeve. With the slippery ice on the ledge, there was too much danger in staying here that long.

Finally, he had her arm secured. He checked the rope around her midsection again. It was tight, but with only one hand to hold onto the rope, it might put too much pressure on her thin little waist. He fastened another loop under her legs, almost like a swing.

Then he hunched low to look her in the eyes. "I'm going to hoist you up now. Just hold tight to this rope and let me do the work, all right?"

She gripped his arm, and her voice cracked again on the word *Savior*. For the first time, fear was the primary emotion in her eyes.

And it sliced through him.

But this was the only way he could see to get her to safety. He swallowed to force the lump from his throat. "Trust me, Cathleen. I'll do everything in my power to protect you."

He swallowed again. He was a mere man. Not capable of controlling this situation in the way he wanted. It was going to take a stronger Power than him to keep her safe.

He met her gaze, pouring everything from his heart into that look. "God will take care of you, Cathleen. It's up to Him." *Lord, please. Don't prove me wrong.*

Something calmed in her gaze then. And as she started into the third verse of *Silent Night*, she nodded, then released his arm and clutched tight to the rope with her good hand.

He found his gloves and slipped them back on. His mind sent a steady stream of prayers heavenward as he pulled on the free end of the rope that was attached to Cathleen and levered around the tree above. As his muscles strained, she lifted up off the ledge.

Her back stayed ramrod straight, and she clutched the rope tight to her chest as she dangled over the rock. But she didn't squirm, didn't cry out. Even kept up the song, although her voice faltered into a weak tone.

Foot by precious foot, he pulled her up.

Finally, finally… She reached the cliff edge high above him.

As her head disappeared over the corner, then her middle, and finally her feet, all strength seemed to slide out of him. Cathleen was safe. His body sagged in relief. If he hadn't had a rope tied to his own waist, he may very well have gone off the side of his perch.

The singing stopped overhead, and he heard a few murmured words. Then Cathleen's head peeked over the ledge. "Do you want me to pull you up?"

He almost laughed, but he didn't quite have the strength for it. That waif of a woman with a broken arm thought she could pull him thirty feet up the side of a cliff? He waved her back. "No. Just take Mum away from the edge. I'll be up shortly."

Her worried expression before she disappeared from view was enough to renew his strength. He needed to end this whole ordeal and get her arm splinted. The pain had to be excruciating with the stress she'd been under. And he still hadn't checked to see if she'd injured anything else in the fall, especially since it seemed like she'd been unconscious when he found her.

After gathering every bit of his remaining strength, he started the climb up. For the first third of the way, he was able to walk his feet up the side of the cliff. Then he lost his foothold, and ended up pulling himself up hand over hand on the rope.

Every muscle in his body strained. His focus narrowed to one grip after the next.

At last, a hand grabbed his upper arm. His fingers found the edge of the cliff. Then he reached over it, and gripped the rope where it strained in the snow. Digging in one elbow, he levered himself up. Then the other elbow.

His strength was almost completely spent now, but with his body dangling from the waist down, he gave one final heave and hauled himself up over the edge.

He barely had the sense to roll away from the edge. If it hadn't been for the hand that pulled him, he might not have. At last, he lay in the snow on his back, eyes closed as his breaths came in deep gasps. The blood coursed through his veins, and his body was drenched in sweat. There was no strength left in him.

But they were safe.

A soft hand brushed the hair from his forehead, and he cracked an eyelid to see the angel hovering over him. Her luminous brown eyes found his, then came closer as she planted a soft kiss on his brow.

If he'd had enough breath in his chest, he would have pulled her down for a real kiss, but instead he cradled her hand in his, gloves and all. His thumb stroked the inside of her palm.

No words passed between them as her glimmering eyes locked with his. There was nothing that could possibly be said. It all passed in that gaze. The depth of his love for her. The full extent of his relief that she was alive. They were both alive. Thanks to a Divine hand.

Finally, she eased back, and his exhausted eyelids sank closed. It was high time he acknowledge the One Who'd truly saved them.

"Thank you, Lord."

CHAPTER 25

athleen watched Reuben's exhausted face as his body recovered from the torture he'd just put it through. Love welled stronger in her chest the more she looked at him, overcoming even the pounding in her skull and the pain piercing her shoulder.

A shuffling sounded behind her, and she turned to see Mrs. Scott trying to rise to her feet.

"Gettin' all wet sittin' in this here snow," the woman mumbled as she tried to push herself to her knees.

Cathleen eased back from Reuben's grasp, but his hand closed around her palm.

"Wait."

She turned back as his eyes opened. "I need to help your mum."

"Mum, can you sit down for a minute?" His voice rasped across the little space, and his mother stopped her scramblings and looked at him.

"All right." She sank back to her haunches.

Reuben pushed himself up to a sitting position so he faced Cathleen, then turned those piercing blue eyes on her. Something about the grave lines on his face tightened her stomach. "Where's Bryan? Is there anything we can do for him?"

She had to blink to absorb the words, and it took a moment longer for their true meaning to register. "Bryan? No, he's at home. We made it fine yesterday, but I was coming back up the mountain on my own today. Somehow, I got off the trail. Then my mare spooked at a deer, and everything happened so fast. I woke up on that ledge."

As the words poured out of her, his eyes narrowed. "You came up here by yourself?"

She almost giggled at the steely tone in his voice. Maybe she was overwrought from pain and exhaustion. "You're missing the point. Bryan's fine."

After a long moment, the tension in his face and shoulders eased, and he scrubbed a hand through his hair. "Thank the Lord."

Then he straightened again. "Let's look at that arm. Do you think anything else is hurt?"

"Nothing else." Her head pounded almost more than her arm, but that was just from the fall. He didn't need anything else to worry about.

She allowed Reuben to unstrap the sling he'd made, but when he eased the arm out of her coat sleeve, it was all she could do not to cry out. He surely heard the intake of her breath, though.

When he got to the sleeve of her brown shirtwaist, he reached for the knife at his waist. "I'm going to have to cut this."

He seemed to be waiting for her to object, but she wasn't about to stop him if it would help. And they did need to know if the break was compound.

With the fabric slit open, a rush of frigid air raised goose skin on her arm, made even colder by the sweat that dampened her body.

"Where does it hurt?" His deep voice was the most soothing thing she'd heard all day.

She tapped the spot on her upper arm, a couple inches below her shoulder. The slightest touch seemed to sear through her, but she didn't feel bone protruding through the skin. Hopefully the break wasn't compound. She cradled her forearm and focused on deep, steady breaths as his fingers brushed the spot she'd pointed out.

"Doesn't look compound. Let's get you bandaged and back down the mountain." He reached for the shirt he'd wrapped her arm in before.

"Just get me to the cabin, so I can take something for the pain. I can splint it myself." She'd helped with the splinting of more than one arm through the years. Surely she could do this.

He didn't slow his movements. "I'm taking you to the doctor."

She was far too exhausted to fight another battle, but she had to ask. "What about your animals?"

"We'll stop at O'Hennessey's and ask him to look in on them."

And with that, she forced the worry out of her mind and sank into his care as he wrapped her arm and settled the coat around her shoulders.

"Do you think you can walk to the sleigh, or shall I carry you?" His voice rumbled close to her ear, and she wanted so badly for him to sweep her into his arms. But he was exhausted too. He'd already born her weight up the side of the cliff.

"I can walk."

But she was ever so thankful that he helped her to her feet, then wrapped a strong arm around her waist. With his other, he helped his mother stand, and the three of them limped along the path of foot-prints in the snow. North padded along in front, leading the way. A weary group, more than thankful to be alive.

Reuben settled her and his mum in the sleigh, then untied the horses. It took some doing, but he finally had the rig turned around, and he climbed up in the seat between them.

As they started on their way, Cathleen sank into his side, and he slipped an arm around her waist. It was a welcome relief to rest her aching head on his shoulder, but the pain radiating through her arm made it impossible to relax. A mug of willow bark tea would help a lot. If only...

$\sim$

*R*euben had forced aside the thoughts whirling in his mind while he'd had to focus on guiding the horses around the trees dotting their path in the forest. But now that they were back on the established trail and he didn't have to focus as much, his questions refused to be contained.

Cathleen lay against his shoulder on one side, and Mum did the same on his left. Mum's soft snores made it easy to tell she slept, but he couldn't be sure about Cathleen. He couldn't quite see her eyes from this angle.

At last she shifted, and he took the opportunity to speak. "Are you awake?"

"Yes." Her voice sounded a little strained. Most likely her arm paining her. He hoped that's all it was, anyway.

He forged on ahead. "Did you plan to tell me why you were coming back up the mountain? Alone?" He tried not to let any anger sound in that last word, but that was a tall order. What had her brothers been thinking to let her make that journey on her own? Of course, it was possible Cathleen had left without their agreement. She was just stubborn enough to try something like that if she felt she had a good reason. But still…

She slowly straightened beside him, leaving his shoulder cold with the loss of her nearness. And when he glanced down to see her face, the solemn expression, tightened a cord in his chest.

"I was coming back to care for your mum. I decided not to go to Boston with Alex."

He couldn't stop the explosion in his pulse. He'd been afraid to even consider that she was coming back to them for good. But now to hear her say it…

He turned to face her and nearly knocked Mum off his other shoulder in the process. "You were?"

She met his gaze solidly. "I prayed hard about it, and feel like this is where God wants me right now."

She could surely hear his heart rate triple in speed. Had God actually answered his prayer? The prayer he'd been afraid to pray?

So what did this mean for him? He wanted so much to take her in his arms right there and kiss her soundly. But he'd need to bide his time on that. Wait until she wasn't in so much pain. And wait until a time when his mother wasn't snoring right beside them.

And he needed to sort through the questions still spinning in his mind. To wait until he knew exactly what his intentions were.

They arrived at the O'Hennessey place soon enough, but Cathleen declined to go in with him. Her color had grown paler than when he'd first pulled her up the cliff. He had to get her to town soon.

O'Hennessey agreed readily enough to go gather the horses and cow from the homestead and keep them at his place until Reuben could come back for them. It helped that Reuben offered another cow from the herd the man was already caring for. At this rate, they'd not own any stock by the time summer rolled around. But he needed to do this for Cathleen.

"'Preciate the pain powder." Reuben shook the man's hand as he prepared to leave. "You'll let the chickens out in the yard, too?"

"If'n that's what you want. Hope ya have some left when ya get back." The man sent a sluice of tobacco juice over Reuben's shoulder to land just past the stoop.

"Thanks again." With a nod, he headed back to the sleigh.

Cathleen took the powder willingly, not even asking questions about what it contained. A sure sign she was hurting, yet she didn't complain more than a grunt as the sleigh shifted under his weight.

Soon enough, they were back on the trail again. As the miles fell behind them, he could feel Cathleen's breathing grow steady. Maybe she finally had a bit of relief.

But the silence left him too long with his thoughts, and the scenes on the side of the cliff began to replay in his mind. The sheer terror when he'd first looked over the edge and made out Cathleen's still body so far below. How many times through the ordeal they'd come so close to death. Him. Cathleen. Mum. It was a wonder they'd all come out of it alive, with nothing worse than a broken arm.

No, it was more than a wonder. It was a miracle.

That feeling of utter helplessness fell over him again, the one that had overwhelmed him when he'd been down below with Cathleen and Mum had ventured so close to the cliff edge. He'd never meant a prayer more than that desperate plea.

And God had answered.

In the past, he might have said they'd gotten themselves out of that pinch. But too much had happened over the last few hours for him to discount God's hand in it all.

Cathleen surviving her fall. And landing on that tiny ledge instead of crashing to the rocks below.

The strength of the ledge to hold them both up.

Mum listening to Cathleen and obeying her direction.

Even Cathleen's ability to connect with his mother was a gift from God. He could see that now.

And since the three of them had come out of the situation alive, he could acknowledge the best part of all. Cathleen had come back to them. After he'd given her up—even told her to leave.

She'd come back. And that was a gift only a loving God could have granted.

There on the road, with the reins in his hands and a sleeping woman leaning against each of his shoulders, he finally opened his heart.

Thank you, Lord.

CHAPTER 26

"*Y*ou did what?"

Cathleen's hackles rose at the accusation in Bryan's voice as she stood at his door. She gritted her teeth against the response that itched to come out. "It's a simple break, Bryan. I just need it splinted."

"And she needs something for the pain," Reuben said. "And she was unconscious when I found her, so you probably want to check her head, too."

She sent a glare up to the man standing behind her. Honestly, Reuben was getting almost as protective as her brothers.

He touched the small of her back, and the contact eased her ire the tiniest bit. It felt good to have him there, sharing his strength.

Bryan motioned as he turned to go inside. "Come in. Let's get you doctored."

~

*R*euben jumped to his feet as Cathleen's brother finally stepped through the doorway from the kitchen he'd been using as an examination room.

Bryan motioned him back down into the chair, but his muscles itched to move. Even after the long, intense day they'd had, it didn't feel right to be away from Cathleen. None of this felt right.

"How's she doing?"

The doctor plopped into the overstuffed chair closest to the fire. "Not bad considering. A bump on her head, but her memory doesn't seem to have suffered. There seems to be a minor break in her upper arm, but I expect it'll heal quickly." The tiniest hint of amusement played at the corners of the man's mouth. "Must be that animal skin coat she was wearing softened the blow some."

One more mercy from God.

Reuben scrubbed a hand through his hair and sank back in his chair. What a day.

Bryan straightened and rose to his feet. "We have a bit to talk about, but it'll wait until daylight. I'm going to get some sleep. Did the ladies get you and your mother settled?"

Reuben let his hand drop to his lap and looked at the man. "Yes, Mum's staying at your sister-in-law's. Thought it might be best if I bed down in the corner there, since your brother's out of town."

A line creased Bryan's forehead. "You're welcome to a cot in the clinic, or I imagine Marcus and Lilly have an empty bed."

Reuben was too exhausted to even raise his head, so he let it flop against the chair as he shook it. "I want to stay close. Probably sleep better on the floor anyway." He'd not been in a bed for so long, his body wouldn't know what to do with it.

The doctor shrugged. "Suit yourself. I'm gonna get some shuteye." But before he disappeared through one of the doorways, he turned back to level a gaze on Reuben. "Tomorrow, we talk."

~

*B*ut the next morning, Doc Bryan was called away before he'd eaten his second bite of boiled oats. An expectant mother finally reached her time, Reuben gathered.

It was good to see Cathleen up and moving, even if her color still looked a little pale. But with the coddling her sisters-in-law gave her, she had no choice but to recover quickly. Which was good.

Still, between them and the time she spent with his mum, he barely found a spare second alone with her until late in the afternoon.

"How do you feel?" He leaned forward in the parlor chair as Cathleen rocked Bryan's little daughter with her good arm.

It might have been his imagination in the dim room, but it looked like a flush crept into her cheeks. At least it was a bit of color.

"Better. Bryan said it looks to be a minor break. With this knitbone tea Miriam's been feeding me, I shouldn't need to wear the splint more than a week."

He raised his brows at her. "Your brother said that?"

She dropped her gaze to the baby. "Well. Close enough."

She was going to be a handful, this one. But he was more than ready to take on the challenge. If she'd have him.

Reuben sank back in his chair. He'd have to wait for the right time to ask. Had to give her time to heal first. Even if he went stir crazy from hanging around this town that long.

~

*R*euben breathed a sigh of relief when Bryan finally dragged himself in for a late dinner. Although the weary slump to his shoulders meant even if they did have a chance to talk, the man's mood may not be especially genial. Still. It was time to make his intentions clear. To wipe away that distrust that tainted the man's gaze any time he looked at Reuben.

Cathleen had already left to walk the few blocks to Miriam's house to put Mum to bed. He would have escorted her and helped, but with Bryan finally home, it seemed best to stick around.

His patience was finally rewarded when Bryan clunked his coffee cup on the table and pushed up to his feet. "Well, Scott. You mind stepping outside with me for a minute?"

Reuben followed him outside, and they'd made it off the porch and down the quiet street before the other man finally spoke.

"My sister seems to feel some kind of obligation to you and your mother."

The words struck like a punch to his gut. Not that he hadn't thought the same thing at one time, but he'd come to hope it might be more than that. *Lord, do I have it wrong here?*

Bryan was waiting for his response, so he cleared his throat and tried to form an honest answer. "Your sister's special. No doubt about that." His mouth had gone dry, making it harder to force this next bit out. "I'm not sure if it's just obligation she feels, or if maybe there's something more. I'd like your permission to ask her."

The man gave him a sideways look, but with only a sliver of moon out and no house lights nearby, Reuben couldn't decipher his expression.

"You have reason to believe she might feel more?" Definitely reserve in that tone. But maybe not outright suspicion. Bryan seemed to have a smart head on his shoulders. Willing to consider all sides before passing judgement.

"A slim hope. But if she says no, I'll respect her answer and walk away."

They walked in silence for more long moments, and Reuben could almost hear the other man's pondering. He tried to relax into the quiet, enjoy the solitude. But a ball of nerves still tumbled in his gut.

"What Cathy wants isn't always what's good for her."

Reuben glanced over at him. "I know she can do a lot better than a mountain trapper. That's why I told her to go in the first place." How much should he say? How could he even put it into words? His mind scrambled for the best way to state his feelings, but nothing would come.

So he stopped right there in the road and turned to face the man. "I love your sister. Didn't think there was a way she could be happy tied to someone like me. Didn't think God would give me the chance. But now I wonder if maybe He has, and I'm not willing to let that slip away without at least trying."

Bryan regarded him for a long moment, his features still shadowed. At long last, he spoke. "I guess you better ask her then."

~

*T*he euphoria in Reuben's chest simmered over the next few days, as he watched for the right chance to talk with Cathleen. But people were always around—babies and neighbors and after-hours patients from the clinic. He couldn't seem to find even two minutes alone with her.

It didn't help that she moved over to Miriam's house to better care for his mum. He'd tried to stay close and be helpful where he could, and maybe get a chance to join her on one of her evening walks, but he couldn't seem to get his timing right.

Three days after his conversation with Bryan, they were all eating dinner at Bryan and Claire's home—for once, everyone together.

It was nice to have Cathleen positioned beside him, and the shy glances she'd been sending throughout the meal told him it was high time they talked. Tonight.

But when Cathleen was the first to rise from the table and start carrying used dishes with her good hand to the wash bucket, he bit back a groan. She always had to be doing something. Was he going to have to cause a scene just to get her away for a moment?

Miriam shot him a look, then stood and joined Cathleen at the sink. "Cathy, you cooked the meal. Take the night off for once and let us clean up. Go take your walk before it gets too cold out." And with a nonchalance that seemed a little too forced. "Maybe Reuben would like to stretch his legs, too."

Warmth crept hot to his ears, but he pushed his chair back and stood. They couldn't get out of there soon enough, as far as he was concerned.

Cathleen made some small protest, but when she glanced at him, the words died mid-sentence. She dried her hand on a cloth, one corner of her mouth pulling in the hint of a smile as she held his gaze. Did the woman know what he had planned? Or maybe she just needed fresh air like he did.

At the front door, he held her coat while she slipped her uninjured arm into the sleeve. He pulled the other side over her shoulder to cocoon the sling.

"I still love this fur, Reuben. It's perfect." Her words came out soft, a little shy maybe, but the room was too dark to see her expression.

"Your brother said he thinks it might've saved your arm from a worse break." He donned his own fur. "Gave you a softer landing."

She slipped her hand into the pocket as they stepped outside. He pulled the door closed behind them. A fresh layer of snow had fallen the night before, which had settled into slush and mud on the street. He kept them to the edge, trying to take the worst of the muck. Every day in this place made him crave the quiet of the mountain even more.

A sigh drifted from Cathleen as she settled into the stroll. He glanced over, trying to see whether it signaled good thoughts or bad. Her face was turned up to the sky, which made her pale skin almost glow in the scant bit of moonlight. Just like an angel. He wanted so badly to touch her, to pull her close. But for now, he kept his hands pressed into his coat pockets.

"Your mum doesn't seem to be adapting well to her new surroundings." Her voice held a tinge of worry.

"Is she any better now that you're staying in the same house?"

Cathleen's lips pinched. "A little. But we need to get her back home soon."

Home. Did she think of the mountain cabin as her home too? Even if she did, would she be willing to travel with him to his winter camp? Later, of course, after Mum was settled. For now, he could find enough trapping around the homestead to keep them going for a year or so. And either way, he'd do what he needed to for Cathleen to be happy.

He ran his tongue over his suddenly dry lips. If only she'd have him. And now was his chance to find out.

"Cathy, I don't want you to come back with us as Mum's nurse." The words flew out in a burst, not sounding at all like he'd planned.

She stopped mid-step, her whole body going still, but she didn't turn to look at him. When she picked up the stroll again, tension radiated from her.

"I mean, I don't want you to be just her nurse." He was making a muck of this. "I mean…"

He stopped and turned to face her, and she finally did the same. Although her gaze hovered somewhere around his throat, nowhere near his eyes. This was probably his last chance to get it right. He fought the urge to scrub a hand over his face.

"What I'm trying to say is, I'd like you to consider becoming my wife." Her face turned up to his then, and he rushed on. "I know I'm not anything like a proper husband for you. Not what you deserve. You're pretty, and kind, and"—he motioned down the length of her —"well, you take my breath away. You bring out the best in me. Make me want to be more. And the special thing is, when I'm with you, I feel like I actually can.

"I know you deserve someone who can give you all the fine things you had in Boston. More, even. I don't know that I can do that, Cathy, but I'll sure try. But the one thing I know I can give you, the thing you already have, is my love."

And that was it. He'd rambled on for so long, he wasn't quite sure what he'd said. But he'd gotten that last bit out, and that was really what she needed to know. Now it was time to wait.

Something glittered in her eyes. Tears? The moon wasn't bright enough for him to make out her expression. She didn't speak for the longest moment, then when she opened her mouth, she inhaled a little quiver. Was she crying? That couldn't be good.

"Reuben, I wasn't sure you'd ever say that."

She paused, which gave his mind too long to race through what that could possibly mean.

She sniffed, then spoke again. "I don't want fine things. I left Boston for a reason. It's not the things that matter, it's the people." She slipped her good hand up to his chest, and for the first time, he dared to hope. "I've never been happier than these weeks I've spent in the mountains with you and your mum. With you."

She shifted an inch closer, and his hands came up to her waist.

Another sniff, but this time he was pretty sure he heard a smile with it. "I love you, too, Reuben Scott. There's nothing I'd like more than to be your wife."

The words sank over him slowly, but with a power that almost brought him to his knees. She'd said yes? But did she really know what she was agreeing to?

He raised a hand to brush back a wisp of hair the breeze blew across her cheek. "Are you sure? I don't know if I can be everything you need, even though I'll try my hardest. I don't even know if we can stay at the homestead. I'm not good at working the land like my pa was. We may need to travel to where the trapping is better." He inhaled a breath. "Or, if you'd rather move back to town, I'll find a way to support us."

Her hand slid up from his chest, and a cold finger touched his lips, silencing him. "I don't want to move back to town. The homestead is perfect, or wherever we need to go." A soft smile touched her mouth. "I'd like to see more of the mountains. You need to use the gifts God gave you, and there's nothing more I want than to be by your side." She paused for breath as a twinkle found her eye. "That will be adventure enough, I think."

With those words echoing through his mind, he slipped both hands up to her jaw, letting his fingers slide into the softness of her hair.

Just before his mouth touched hers, he gave voice to the response flooding his heart. "Did I tell you how much I love you?"

CHAPTER 27

$\mathcal{R}$euben stepped into Miriam's kitchen the next morning, trying only slightly to suppress the smile that tugged at his mouth. Too much still whirled through his mind from the night before, but the part he was sure of was the fact that he was utterly happy.

The room was set-up much like the kitchen in Claire and Bryan's home, with a dry sink and cook stove on the left and a large rectangular table in the center. Cathleen sat at the table with his mum, and they both looked up at him when he entered. Cathleen sent him one of those smiles that lit her face, and he probably answered it with some kind of silly grin.

He slipped into a chair beside her and leaned over the table. "And what do you ladies have planned for today?"

Cathleen gave him a sideways glance, then looked at his mum and spoke loud enough for her to hear. "We were getting ready to go for a walk this morning, since the sun's out."

Reuben couldn't help slipping his hand up to the back of Cathleen's chair and letting his thumb stroke her shoulder. "Mum, did Cathy tell you the good news?"

Cathleen sat up straight, almost knocking his hand off her chair as she turned a raised brow on him. His thumb shifted into circles over the tense muscles at the back of her neck.

She relaxed into him, and he took that as a sign that he could continue. Honestly, this news was too good to keep quiet for long, especially from Mum.

Mum was fiddling with a cloth on the table, not paying mind to either of them.

He leaned around Cathy to take one of his mother's wrinkled hands in his. "Mum, guess what?"

She looked up then, her cloudy blue eyes studying him. "What is it, son?"

For once she knew it was him? He swallowed down the burn in his throat. "Cathleen finally agreed to marry me." He nodded toward Cathy, so his mother would know who he meant, even if she didn't remember the name.

Mum looked from him to Cathleen, then back to him. "That's right good, son. I'm proud of ya." The little squeeze of her fingers in his almost loosened the burn of tears that sprang to his eyes. She was proud of him? He couldn't remember ever hearing those words. And now...in this moment...

One tear did slip through his defenses, and he wasn't even ashamed when Cathleen saw it as she turned one of those smiles on him.

God, You are, indeed, good.

~

*I*t seemed surreal, that Cathleen finally stood in the church, across from Reuben Scott, pledging her life to him. How many times had she prayed for this? And now, the look Reuben sent her proved that God had answered beyond what she'd allowed herself to hope.

She offered her own smile as they turned to face Reverend Marcus, and Reuben's fingers threaded through hers in a strong grip.

"Dearly beloved, we are gathered here in the sight of God and you all."

Cathleen did her best to soak in every word the reverend spoke as he began the ceremony and prayed to bless their union. But when he asked "Who gives this woman to be married to this man?" that familiar prick burned the back of her eyes.

"Her family does." Bryan's strong voice carried through the church, and Cathleen turned to look at him. He sent her a wink before he sat down again next to Claire.

Reuben's thumb stroked the top of her hand, giving it a gentle squeeze, telegraphing his care. He'd asked if she wanted to delay the wedding until her mother and Alex were here. Somehow he'd known without her telling him that it would be hard without Dad.

But she'd said no. Of course she didn't want to delay. They could celebrate again when Mum and Alex arrived. But even with all she was gaining, there was still the tiny pang of loss that held a place in her heart. Dad would have loved Reuben. Would have been proud of the fine man who stood beside her.

Reuben shifted, pulling her attention back to the minister. It was a good thing, too, because they'd come to the part of the ceremony she'd looked forward to the most.

"Reuben Joseph Scott, do you take Cathleen Suzanne Donaghue to be your wedded wife, to live together in marriage? Do you promise to love her, comfort her, honor and keep her for better or worse, for richer or poorer, in sickness and health, and forsaking all others, be faithful only to her, for as long as you both shall live?"

For as long as you both shall live. May it be a hundred years more.

"I do." Reuben's deep voice spoke a caress over her as his gaze found hers.

She could barely hold back the tears again as the minister spoke her vows and she made her own promise. Yet, these were happy tears, and the joy overwhelming her chest wouldn't be contained.

Once again, Reuben's thumb stroked a gentle path over the back of her hand. A smile played at the corners of his eyes.

When the pastor finally gave him leave, Reuben lowered his mouth to hers for a gentle touch, so sweet, yet full of the promise to come.

And then the crowd of friends descended on them.

It was almost two hours later before the wedding breakfast was over and the two of them were able to sneak off toward Claire and Bryan's house. It was a good thing they'd opted for a Saturday morning wedding with only a few friends instead of a ceremony after Sunday services when the entire congregation would have been there. Of course, with her brothers being the only doctors in town, a *few friends* really was most of the congregation.

"Are you sure you don't want to wait a night before we head back up to the cabin? We could stay in a real hotel if you'd like."

Cathleen glanced at him as they walked, the thought of the upcoming night stealing a bit of her courage. "I'm sure. We've been in Butte almost two weeks now. It's time to go home."

Home. Finally, the place she really belonged.

"How's your arm holding up with all this activity?"

She tried not to wince as the question brought to mind the pain she'd successfully pushed out of her awareness. "Just fine. I'm not even sure it was a break, just a sprain probably."

Reuben's deep chuckle resonated beside her. "Bryan's still not happy you cut off the splint so soon."

"I didn't need it." At least she didn't need it encumbering all her movements.

"You'll put your sling back on now that the ceremony's over?"

She gave Reuben a sideways glance, intending it to be something like a glare. But she couldn't do anything except smile today. "Yes, husband."

~

*R*euben had never seen such a welcoming sight as the little homestead cabin when it came into view between the trees. They were home.

He reined the horses to a stop in front of the porch, then set the brake and settled the reins. Cathleen stretched in the seat beside him.

He eased his mother up from where she slept on his other shoulder. She'd seemed especially disoriented during the excitement after the wedding and had slept most of the trip up the mountain. It would be good to have her back in familiar surroundings. Maybe she could even regain the progress she'd made before.

"We're home, Mum." He spoke the words gently as his mother looked around them. Her stiff gray hair stood up in tufts where she'd rested against him, adding to her confused look.

What had he been thinking to allow their wedding night with his mother in tow? He leaned close to Cathleen. "I'm sorry to spend our first night like this."

She searched his gaze, a line furrowing across her forehead. "I'm not. There's no place I'd rather be than here, and it's her home, too." A mischievous sparkle lit her eyes, and it looked like she was about to say something more, but instead her lips pressed together.

He raised his brows. "And?" She wasn't getting off that easily.

A pretty pink crept into her cheeks. "And...she'll have her room. We'll have ours."

That brought on a belly laugh he couldn't hold back. "I'm going to enjoy being married to you, Mrs. Scott."

~

*C*athleen kept busy over the next few hours until dusk overtook them. While Reuben unloaded the sleigh, she put together a quick supper of fried ham and potatoes. Mrs. Scott—Mum, she was starting to think of her—already seemed to be relaxing in her familiar surroundings.

Over their simple meal, the older woman started to nod off several times. At the second occurrence, Cathleen slid Rueben a glance. "I suppose she's worn out."

She stood and moved around to help her new mother-in-law

toward the bed chamber. "Let me get her settled, and I'll be back to clean up."

After donning a nightdress, Mrs. Scott sank into the bedsheets with a relieved look and patted Cathleen's hand. "Thank you, dearie. I'm glad you're here."

Cathleen pressed a kiss to her forehead. "I am, too."

When she stepped back into the kitchen, Reuben stood over the bucket of wash water, sleeves rolled to his elbows. What a sight he made there, with his broad shoulders and towering presence, cleaning dirty dishes. A man strong in every sense of the word, yet gentle and thoughtful beyond what she would have imagined.

She stepped forward, keeping her tread light as she slipped up behind him and wrapped her arms around his waist. He straightened, then turned to face her, pulling her to his chest.

Thank you, Lord.

Her heart repeated the words over and over as she sank into the warmth of her husband, this man she'd come to trust and love more than she ever could have imagined.

EPILOGUE

*C*athleen reined in Tashunka beside Reuben's horse, and stared out at the view before them. A valley stretched out below, still unmarred by snow, unlike the peaks rising in every direction around it. The sheer majesty of the scene tightened her chest, and she drew in a chilly breath.

"It's beautiful, Reuben." She pulled her gaze from the picture before them long enough to glance his way.

He watched her, one corner of his mouth tipped, and a glimmer of pride touching his eyes. "You like it?"

More than she could put into words. But with Reuben she didn't have to, he seemed to understand her without the need to speak every thought. She met his gaze and nodded.

He reached across the distance between their horses and took her hand. The buckskin gloves he'd made her, with their detailed beadwork around the wrists, were pliable enough she could feel the brush of his thumb across the back of her hand. Just one of the many ways he made her feel protected. Loved.

She tried to show some of her gratitude in a smile, then allowed her gaze to be drawn back to the majestic sight before them.

After long moments soaking in the beauty, she broke the silence. "I'm glad my mother offered to stay with your mum so we could take a real wedding trip."

A soft chuckle drifted from him. "I still can't believe you want to spend it in my old winter cabin."

She gave him a look. "I want to see what your life was really like as Reuben Scott, trapper extraordinaire."

That chuckle again. "Darlin', it wasn't nearly as exciting as life these days."

A smile tickled her mouth. Yes, he'd long since set aside that impassive look that covered his thoughts. And every day it seemed there was more in him to love. His wit, his strength, his integrity, the depth of his wisdom. The intensity with which he loved those he cared about. His undivided trust in God's faithfulness.

She met his gaze again. "Do you miss it?"

He raised his brows. "Miss what?"

Her chest tightened as she thought about what she was asking. "Do you miss your life as a trapper? Independent, without all the rest of us holding you back."

His eyes shadowed for a second, then cleared. Did he regret marrying an outsider? She'd be willing to take up his old life with him, but they still had his mother to consider. And so many things would have to change.

His thumb stroked her hand again, and his eyes softened. "How could I miss that? What I thought was good before was just a shadow of our life now." A glimmer intensified his blue eyes. "I love our life, Cathy. I never thought I'd find my perfect match. Never thought God loved me enough to give me this gift. To give me you."

He raised her hand to his lips and kissed it, his gaze never wavering from hers.

She couldn't have spoken if she wanted to, but the joy in her chest spilled out in a single tear that trickled down her cheek. God had blessed them indeed. She never would have imagined He'd use the call of these untamed mountains to finally bring her home.

Did you enjoy Reuben and Cathleen's story? I hope so!
Would you take a quick minute to leave a review?
It doesn't have to be long. Just a sentence or two telling what you liked about the story!

∾

And would you like to receive a **free short story about a special moment in Gideon and Leah's happily-ever after?**
Get the free short story and sign-up for insider email updates by tapping here.

And here's a peek at the next book in the series, *This Treacherous Journey:*

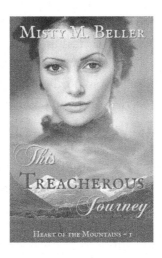

AUGUST, 1851
ROCKY MOUNTAINS, MONTANA TERRITORY

Simeon Grant glanced at his wife as another moan slipped from her lips.

Nora clutched her swollen belly, bent over from the pain. She'd turned in the saddle so she almost rode sideways. It must've hurt too much to straddle the horse.

Should he stop and set-up camp here? Or press on until they reached shelter? Surely it couldn't be much farther to the smoke he'd seen curling up through a break in the trees. *Lord, let it be a home, and let there be a woman there who can help us.*

His wife straightened in the saddle and offered him a weak smile. "That pain is gone."

He tried to offer an encouraging smile. Nora was always so strong, always taking on the burdens for those around her. If only he could take this burden from her now. He had to get help soon— for both her and the wee one inside.

He glanced around, a scent touching his nostrils. Wood smoke.

Thank you, Lord. "I think we're not far now." He glanced at his wife. "Do you think you can make it a few minutes longer?"

She gave a weak nod, which turned to a grimace as she pressed her eyes shut and curled into another pain in her midsection.

How had he let this happen? He'd brought the love of his life into this mountain wilderness to chase *his* dream. She'd never once dashed his enthusiasm, just willingly sold off their meager home, loaded what possessions they now carried on the pack horses, and headed out to settle the wild Montana territory.

Never had he imagined Nora might be with child so soon after their marriage. Never had he thought the journey would take so long. And now the remote, unsettled freedom of these mountains that had drawn him was the very thing that jeopardized his wife's life.

But even with the length of their journey, wasn't it still too soon for Nora's time? They'd only be married eight months. Not that he doubted her faithfulness. No, the thought struck a deeper fear in him. Would coming early put the baby at risk? And Nora, too? If only he knew how to stop this.

He would give everything he had to find a doctor right now.

Ellen Scott paused at the porch steps, one hand on the rail and the other balancing a pail of milk. Listening.

She could have sworn she'd heard the nicker of a horse. Not one of their animals, she was sure of it. Quinn would be out in the hayfield for a few more hours yet, which meant it was her job to protect the homestead.

After rushing up the stairs, she pulled the latch-string and pushed through the cabin door. She grabbed the rifle hanging beside the threshold, swung the milk bucket onto the table, and strode to the window in the sitting area. Once again, she sent up a prayer of thanks that Quinn had had the foresight to bring the window glass with them when they'd settled here.

After checking the cartridge in the rifle, she peered through the window again. All she could do now was watch and wait.

She hadn't always been this suspicious. Had almost been as social as the next person back in Virginia. There were times she missed the regular human interaction they'd given up when they'd settled the homestead in these beautiful mountains. But here they didn't have neighbors for miles. The Indians they'd taken to trading with were friendly, mostly from the Apsaalooke bands. However, for every pleasant Indian, there were five more that would rather chase them off. She had no choice but to be cautious.

A horse appeared through the trees. Three more trailed it. Two figures sat atop the front animals. A man, tall and broad on the lead horse, then someone hunched low on the paint mare. Supplies loaded down the horses behind.

The wide, round brim of the fellow's hat bespoke a white man. Which was a good sign but didn't always mean safety.

But it was the pale blue material worn by the other figure that made Ellen's heart leap.

A woman? Glory be. She hadn't seen a female yet this year.

She stepped outside, lowering the rifle so it hung easily from her right hand, yet still at the ready should she need to aim and fire. These people would know her man wasn't around from the sheer fact she would greet them instead of Quinn.

If there was a woman along, surely they meant no harm.

As the couple approached, the posture of the lady ducked lower, cradling something in front of her. She sat sideways in the saddle too, sort of like the women back east rode sidesaddle—but different.

The man led his group right up to the porch and removed his hat. "My wife needs help. Can she come inside?"

Well, that was sure getting to the point. Ellen took a closer look at the woman's face, saw the way it pinched from pain, her damp hair clinging to her face. Then Ellen's eyes trailed down to what the woman cradled. Her very rounded stomach. *Dear, Lord.*

It was the woman's time. *Help me, Father.*

"Bring her inside." Ellen spun on her heel and headed back

through the open doorway. She dumped a bucket of clean water in the pot on the stove, stoked the fire, and then strode toward her bedroom. It would be nice to put the woman in the spare room, but it still didn't have a bed.

They'd planned to put a crib in there when the time came, but God hadn't seen fit to bless them with children yet. Not for three years now, but she hadn't stopped praying every day for the gift. So that meant this strange woman would give birth in the large bed Quinn had built for the two of them.

By the time Ellen had a spot on the bed prepared, the man was half-guiding, half-carrying his wife into the room.

"Lay her here."

After the woman eased down, Ellen helped position pillows behind her back to prop her some. "How far along are you, honey?"

The woman looked to be between labor pains, exhausted and white as new snow. "I think somewhere between seven and eight months." She gritted her teeth as another pain hit.

Ellen glanced at the overlarge bulge under the blue flannel. She had to be further along than that. Without asking, Ellen pressed her hands against it, feeling the strength of the contraction. Tight as a drum skin.

"Well, dearie, this baby's comin' whether you're ready or not."

Simeon paced the small bed chamber.

Nora's screams tore his insides apart. How much longer could this go on? How much more could she endure?

"Bring another cool cloth." Mrs. Scott barked at him from her position beside the bed.

Simeon spun on his heel to face her, then as her request sank in, he turned back to the basin to obey. After wringing out the towel, he approached the bed and knelt by Nora's head where he would be out of the midwife's way.

Nora's eyes found his, exhaustion clouding their depths as her lids drooped to half-mast.

With the cloth, he stroked away the beads of sweat marring her face. So beautiful. Yet her skin was so pale it looked almost translucent, and her lips blazed a bright red. Was she feverish?

He pressed his palm to her forehead, but at the touch, her face contorted.

"Another one. Raise up and push, dearie."

Nora's eyes squeezed tight as she curled her chin into her chest. Red flooded her face from her efforts. Or maybe from the pain. He didn't know, but if he could have taken it all on himself, he would have already done it.

Her hand fumbled with the covers, and he slipped his big fingers around hers. She clutched with more strength than he would have thought possible from her little body. Then another piercing half-moan, half-cry escaped her.

"Here. He's almost come." The midwife's voice raised a notch in her excitement. "Just one more push."

But Nora sank against the pillow. "I can't."

"We'll wait for another pain," the woman said. "Rest a minute."

Simeon wanted so badly to peek. To catch a glimpse of their precious new life. But he couldn't quite bring himself to look. Instead, he stroked Nora's hair and rubbed his thumb across the top of her hand. "You're doing splendid, love. It's almost over."

She didn't crack an eyelid, just kept sucking in deep breaths. But a corner of her mouth lifted just a fraction.

Then another pain hit.

As she curled into herself, the midwife kept up a steady stream of instructions.

"You've got to push harder this time, honey. He has to come out."

Was the child a boy, then? He didn't have time to stop and think before Nora loosed another awful scream.

Then a different cry filled the room. A baby.

Mrs. Scott held up a tiny person, and Simeon couldn't take his eyes from the writhing little body.

"It's a boy." She placed the child on a blanket, then wrapped him up tight. She started to hand him to Nora, but then a frown touched the older woman's face.

Simeon's gaze slipped to his wife. Nora was still curled up in that ball, as if she hadn't already delivered the baby. Her face was mottled red and white.

Mrs. Scott shoved the swaddled baby toward him instead. "Hold the lad."

Simeon almost dropped the bundle, but scrambled to gather the child and the blankets to himself. Only the little face peeked out at him from the covers. A tiny face, not even as big as his palm. A hint of white residue covered the features, but didn't diminish the awe that surged through Simeon's chest.

The babe's face pinched as he let out another lusty cry.

A different scream filled the air at the same time. Nora.

Simeon glanced at his wife. She still curled in around herself. In pain. No...agony. If he didn't have the child in his arms, he would have dropped to his knees by her side again. Surely there was something they could do to relieve her pain. His gaze slid to the midwife, back to her original post and working hard at something.

Fear sluiced through him. The pains should be gone now. Right? "What's wrong?"

"Looks like another one's coming." The midwife spoke in a clipped tone, obviously intent on her work.

The words struck like a blow, and he swayed a bit from the impact. Another baby? His gaze found Nora again. She rested against the covers now, in between pains.

Clutching the baby carefully to his chest, he lowered himself to his knees beside the bed. "We have a son, love. He's beautiful. And another on the way."

One of her eyelids cracked open, and Simeon tried to hold the babe so she could see him.

But another pain took her then, and he pulled back to give her space. He shuffled the baby into his left arm so he could hold Nora's hand again with his right. If it helped in the least, he could do that for her.

The pains kept coming. Over and over.

The baby took up crying too, especially as Nora's screams echoed through the bed chamber. Simeon paced with the child, snuggling it close and bouncing it gently—anything to soothe.

Yet nothing he did seemed to help. Every muscle in his body was drawn tighter than a violin string. What was taking so long?

A noise from the other room caught his attention for a moment. Then a male voice called, "Hello?"

"Quinn. Bring me the extra quilts from the trunk." Mrs. Scott barked the words, and if he wasn't mistaken, there was a note of panic in her tone. Did that mean something was going wrong? Surely not. She seemed so competent. And she'd helped deliver this beautiful baby boy already.

A man appeared in the doorway, middle-aged, maybe a few years older than Mrs. Scott. He paused to take in the scene, then stepped forward and laid a load of blankets on the bed. "What else can I do?"

The man's surprise at finding strangers in his bedroom seemed to have passed rather quickly.

"More warm water. Not too hot. Then bring a cup of goat's milk and a spoon."

Nora was in the midst of another pain, and Simeon stepped back to her side. The labors seemed so close together now, barely giving her time to catch her breath in between. Her face didn't turn as red now when she pushed, more like a flushed pink. It couldn't mean the pain had lessened, because her screams surely hadn't. Was she losing strength?

Lord, please help her. Fill her. Strengthen her. He sent up the request for the thousandth time. God would intervene. Nora was His child. He had to.

223

When Mr. Scott—he assumed that's who Quinn was—came back into the room, his wife barked another order.

"Drip a few drops of milk into the babe's mouth."

Simeon supposed that instruction was meant for him. There was one straight-back chair in the room, and he settled into it as Mr. Scott brought the supplies over. The man nodded a quick greeting to him, then held the cup while Simeon took the spoon.

It wasn't hard to get the babe's mouth open, because he let out another lusty cry. The four drops of milk seemed to stop him short though, and he scrunched his lips together as he worked to swallow the liquid.

"The next one's coming."

Mrs. Scott's announcement forced all thought from Simeon's mind as his pulse gathered speed. He leaned forward to get a better look at Nora. Exhaustion flooded every part of her body.

"Push, darlin'. You've got to push harder or the babe will never come." Exasperation touched Mrs. Scott's voice.

When Nora sank back against the pillow, Mrs. Scott looked over at her husband, standing in front of Simeon. "Quinn, take the baby. I need the husband here to help her."

Simeon handed over his precious bundle, and his legs barely supported him as he rose to his feet.

But when he knelt beside Nora, true fear slipped into his chest. She looked one shade darker than death. *Lord, you have to help her. Please.*

They worked together. Simeon wrapped an arm around her shoulders and helped her curl into the pushes.

After what had to be a quarter hour of agonizing effort, Mrs. Scott finally glanced up at him. A weary smile touched her face. "It's a girl."

Lightness filled Simeon's vision, and he had to blink to bring the woman's face back into focus. A boy *and* a girl?

He pressed a kiss to Nora's damp forehead. "You did it, love. A boy and a girl."

Nora murmured something he couldn't understand as she sank into the pillow.

He took the second bundle from Mrs. Scott and stared down into another tiny face. A smile started in his chest and spread up to his mouth. So beautiful. Just like her mother. "She looks like you, Nora."

He glanced up at his wife, but what he saw poured dread into his chest.

She was perfectly still, eyes shut. "Nora?"

Her lips moved then, the slightest parting to allow air through. But it only lessened his fear a fraction.

"Nora?" He touched her hand. Cooler than it should be.

He looked to Mrs. Scott, but the woman was focused intently on whatever she was doing at Nora's feet. "What's wrong?" The panic in his voice was nothing compared to what clawed in his chest.

"She's losing blood."

Sheer terror iced through him. "Nora." He turned back to his wife, stroked a hand across her forehead and down her temple, smoothing back the hair from her face. Her lifeless expression never changed

"Nora, you can't leave me. Please." He leaned closer, watching for any response. Nothing, except the faint parting of her lips. At least she was still breathing.

"Nora, please." Tears blurred his vision, slipping down his face. "God, help her." His voice cracked on the words as every part of his heart poured into them. "You can't take her."

His love. Nora. She couldn't leave him.

Nora's lips parted a little more this time, like she wanted to speak. He leaned even closer, not daring to breathe.

"My...love." She whispered the words with the faintest breath.

Those same words flooded his own heart, too.

Something in his chest cracked until he could barely draw breath through the tears. "I love you, too."

And there, with the baby in his arms, he leaned over his wife...and wept.

❧

Simeon woke in darkness, his knees pressed into a hard wood floor and a pain crimping his neck. He was slumped over the side of a bed, his right arm draped over his wife. He glanced at her face, and a wave of grief pressed down on him.

He touched her cheek. Surely it had all been a terrible dream. She was only sleeping. But the skin there was eerily cold. He cradled his hand around that precious cheek, the one he'd stroked so many times during their short marriage.

How could she possibly be gone? How could God snuff out her beautiful life at such a young age? Only nineteen at her birthday last month. Yet there'd never been a woman so loving and strong and full of life. Never anyone like Nora. No wonder God wanted her for heaven.

As the tears came again, he laid his head against her cold hand and gave in to them.

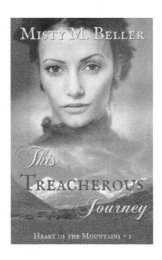

Get THIS TREACHEROUS JOURNEY at your favorite retailer.

ABOUT THE AUTHOR

 **Misty M. Beller** is a *USA Today* bestselling author of romantic mountain stories, set on the 1800s frontier and woven with the truth of God's love.

Raised on a farm and surrounded by family, Misty developed her love for horses, history, and adventure. These days, her husband and children provide fresh adventure every day, keeping her both grounded and crazy.

Misty's passion is to create inspiring Christian fiction infused with the grandeur of the mountains, writing historical romance that displays God's abundant love through the twists and turns in the lives of her characters.

Sharing her stories with readers is a dream come true for Misty. She writes from her country home in South Carolina and escapes to the mountains any chance she gets.

Connect with Misty at www.MistyMBeller.com

ALSO BY MISTY M. BELLER

Call of the Rockies

Freedom in the Mountain Wind

Hope in the Mountain River

Light in the Mountain Sky

Courage in the Mountain Wilderness

Faith in the Mountain Valley

Honor in the Mountain Refuge

Peace in the Mountain Haven

Calm in the Mountain Storm

Brides of Laurent

A Warrior's Heart

A Healer's Promise

A Daughter's Courage

Hearts of Montana

Hope's Highest Mountain

Love's Mountain Quest

Faith's Mountain Home

Texas Rancher Trilogy

The Rancher Takes a Cook

The Ranger Takes a Bride

The Rancher Takes a Cowgirl

Wyoming Mountain Tales

A Pony Express Romance

A Rocky Mountain Romance

A Sweetwater River Romance

A Mountain Christmas Romance

The Mountain Series

The Lady and the Mountain Man

The Lady and the Mountain Doctor

The Lady and the Mountain Fire

The Lady and the Mountain Promise

The Lady and the Mountain Call

This Treacherous Journey

This Wilderness Journey

This Freedom Journey (novella)

This Courageous Journey

This Homeward Journey

This Daring Journey

This Healing Journey

Made in United States
North Haven, CT
13 April 2022

18223067R00134